HIPAA
Hysteria

Nonfiction HIPAA works written by Jonathan P. Tomes
and published by Veterans Press:

The Compliance Guide to HIPAA and the DHHS Regulations,
4th ed. 2010.

HIPAA Documents Resource Center CD, 4th ed. 2010.

Electronic Health Records: A Practical Compliance Guide,
2d ed. 2010.

Medical Records Retention Guide, 3d ed. forthcoming.

Basic HIPAA Training Video with Workbook, 2d ed. 2010.

HIPAA
Hysteria

A Novel By

Jonathan P. Tomes

This novel is a work of fiction. Any resemblance of any character to any person living or dead is purely coincidental.

Cover design: Jonathan P. Tomes, based on the painting "The Scream," by Edvard Munch in 1893 in Norway, now in the public domain in the United States.
Print/bind: Network Business Products, Inc., Grandview, MO.
Editing & internal design: Alice M. McCart.

Published by
Veterans Press, Inc.
7111 W. 98th Terrace, Suite 140
Overland Park, KS 66212
Phone 913.341.8783
Fax 913.385.7997
Email hipaa@veteranspress.com
Website www.veteranspress.com

Printed in the United States of America

First Edition

First Printing

19 18 17 16 15 14 13 12 11 10   10 9 8 7 6 5 4 3 2 1

ISBN 1-880483-23-8   ISBN 978-1-880483-23-7

Dedication

To all of my HIPAA seminar attendees and consulting clients.

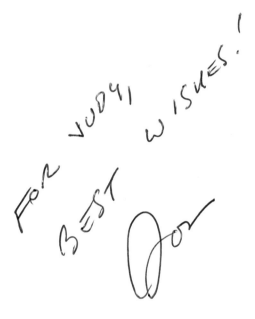

Acknowledgments

I appreciate the contributions and support of many people who helped make it possible for me to write this novel. First, again, thanks to all of my HIPAA seminar attendees and consulting clients. Second, thanks to the people who read the manuscript and offered comments and suggestions: Karen Sunderland, HIPAA Privacy Analyst, Saint Raphael Healthcare System, New Haven, CT; Kathy Buder, General Manager, The Pouch Place, Inc., Knoxville, TN; and my wife, attorney Kenda Tomes, Partner, Stinson, Morrison, Hecker, Kansas City, MO. I also want to thank my workout buddy, Kevin Joel Kelly, author of the book *Letting the Lotus Bloom* and founder of the Lotus School of Flower Arranging, for patiently listening to my ideas for various chapters and offering constructive criticism. Third, many writers often thank their families for their patience and understanding while the author is preoccupied writing a book. I, of course, again thank my wife and our daughter, Aree Tomes, but I would also like to extend that thanks to my law partner, Richard D. Dvorak, and to our office staff, office manager Sherry Page and paralegals Patricia Gildehaus and Jolene Stewart. Fourth, I also thank my editor of the past 25 years, attorney Alice M. McCart.

Prologue

A Brief HIPAA History

The federal government enacted laws protecting privacy long before the Health Insurance Portability and Accountability Act of 1996 ("HIPAA"). In 1965, the U.S. House of Representatives created a Special Subcommittee on the Invasion of Privacy. In 1973, the predecessor to the Department of Health and Human Services, the Department of Health, Education, and Welfare, issued "The Code of Fair Information Practice Principles," which established the first formal federal rule governing information privacy. This rule formed the basis for the federal Privacy Act of 1974, which regulates the government's use of personal information. The Privacy Act limits the disclosure of personally identifiable information, allows consumers access to information that the federal government maintains about them, requires federal agencies to specify the purposes for collecting personal information, and provides civil and criminal penalties for misuse of information.

Regarding electronic billing, a group of health care providers and payers met in 1975 to discuss creation of a standard hospital claim form. The group, the National Uniform Billing Committee, worked until 1982 to reach consensus on what became known as the UB-82 claim: the industry's first standard claim. This first standard claim ultimately led to HIPAA's standard transactions and code sets requirement.

In the early 1990s, the first Bush Administration called a group of health care industry leaders together to discuss how health care administrative costs could be reduced. This group concluded that reducing costs could be done best by increasing the use of electronic data interchange ("EDI") within the industry. This advisory group later organized as the Workgroup for Electronic Data Interchange ("WEDI"). WEDI conducted a number of studies to determine how to accomplish this goal and eventually recommended that Congress enact federal legislation requiring the adoption of a consistent set of standards that could be used across all states. Many of WEDI's recommendations were included in the Clinton Health Plan, which failed to pass, and similar provisions were included in other draft legislation.

In 1996, Congress enacted HIPAA, which President Clinton signed into law on August 21, 1996. Congress intended the law to save health care costs by so-called "administrative simplification" —that is, by standardizing the claims process by adoption of standard transactions and code sets for electronic billing. HIPAA did not require so-called "covered entities,"[1] those entities that had to comply with HIPAA, to bill electronically, but the thought was that the payers would ultimately require providers to submit claims and other documents used in the claims process electronically because of the administrative efficiencies. HIPAA required DHHS to adopt the standards for these electronic submissions. Realizing that patients would be concerned about the confidentiality of their data floating around cyberspace, HIPAA called on Congress to enact a medical privacy statute and asked the Secretary of Health and Human Services to provide Congress recommendations for protecting the confidentiality of health care information. Congress further recognized the importance of such standards by providing the Secretary authority to promulgate regulations on health care privacy in the event that lawmakers were unable to act within the allotted three years. DHHS also had to adopt standards for claims

---

[1] Covered entities initially consisted of health plans, health care clearinghouses, and health care providers that submitted one or more of the standard transactions (essentially reimbursement transactions) in electronic format. Subsequently, Congress added Medicare prescription drug sponsors to the list of covered entities.

attachments, for unique identifying numbers for individuals, health employees, and providers, and for authentication of electronic signatures.

Next, in 1997, a presidential advisory commission, the Advisory Commission on Consumer Protection and Quality in the Health Care Industry, recognized the need for patient privacy protection in its recommendations for a Consumer Bill of Rights and Responsibilities. That same year, Congress enacted the Balanced Budget Act (Public Law 105-34), which added language to the Social Security Act (18 U.S.C. 1852), which required Medicare to establish safeguards for the privacy of individually identifiable patient information. Around that same time, the Congress enacted a provision of the U.S. Code to provide for confidentiality of medical records in Veterans Administration cases involving drug abuse, alcoholism or alcohol abuse, HIV infection, and sickle cell anemia (38 U.S.C. 7332).

The first draft HIPAA rule that DHHS promulgated was the draft security rule in August 1998, setting standards for the security of electronic individually identifiable health information. Dr. William Braithwaite wrote the security rule, using the British Security Model as its basis.

After consulting with industry experts, DHHS adopted the ASC ANSI X12N standards version 4010 for all transactions with the sole exception of pharmacy claims. DHHS selected the widely used standards maintained by the National Council for Prescription Drug Programs ("NCPDP") as the HIPAA standard for pharmacy claims. Consequently, DHHS issued the Standards for Electronic Transactions on August 17, 2000. The initial compliance date was February 26, 2003. Because only a small percentage of covered entities could meet this deadline, however, Congress extended it to April 14, 2003, for those covered entities who filed a request for an extension along with a compliance plan for making the latter deadline. Apparently, DHHS did not have to approve the contents of the compliance plan. Rather, the covered entity just had to file it.

In compliance with the congressional mandate to provide recommendations for protecting confidentiality, DHHS submitted recommendations to Congress on the Privacy Standards on September 11, 1997. When Congress failed to pass such legislation before the three-year deadline had passed, DHHS issued a draft privacy regulation on November 3, 1999, and a final regulation on December 28, 2000. April 14, 2003, was the compliance date for covered entities other than small health plans, which had an extra year to comply.

Thereafter, on February 20, 2003, DHHS finally published the final security rule, almost five years after publication of the draft rule. Its compliance date was April 21, 2005.

This piecemeal adoption of the HIPAA requirements caused much confusion and increased the costs of compliance. For example, the Privacy Rule, which went into effect two years before the Security Rule, required "appropriate safeguards" for all individually identifiable health information maintained in a system of records (protected health information or "PHI"). Yet the Security Rule, which governed electronic PHI ("EPHI"), came out in final form only less than two months before the Privacy Rule compliance date—hardly giving covered entities time to adjust to the changes from the draft to the final security rule.

Congress and DHHS estimated that HIPAA compliance would cost $3.2 billion for the first year and $17.6 billion for the first ten years. Industry experts, however, estimated the cost to be between $25 and $43 billion for the first five years, and that estimated cost didn't include the implementation inefficiencies inherent in the piecemeal adoption of the regulations. Nor should cost be limited to money spent on compliance. How much time has been spent training personnel on HIPAA? What clinical inefficiencies have resulted from so-called "HIPAA anxiety disorder," a situation in which a health care worker refuses to give out information out of fear of going to HIPAA jail? And HIPAA compliance has human costs, too . . . .

1

Margaret Nicks practically skipped up the long sidewalk leading up to Kansas City Memorial Hospital. She was so excited. Today, June 3, 2002, was her first day on the job as a brand new RHIT. Registered Health Information Technician. She had just graduated from the University of Washington with a bachelor's degree in Health Information Management followed by a master's in Health Administration and had qualified for her RHIT from the American Health Information Management Association, known to all medical records types by its acronym, AHIMA. An RHIT was an essential credential to get a job in a hospital's Health Information Management Department. Those who weren't in the know might call it by the old-fashioned term, Medical Records Department. But she knew that the newer name was more accurate because her job would be so much more than just maintaining old paper medical records.

Medical records had fascinated Margaret since she had landed a summer job after her junior year in high school at a doctor's office in her home town of Belton, Missouri, which was practically a suburb of Kansas City. The doctor was retiring and had to do something with 30 years of medical records. The Health Department had told him to contact patients at their last known address and to run newspaper announcements to see whether they wanted their records. Those that were not wanted and were more than 20 years old could be destroyed. The physician had to make arrangements for another physician to maintain the newer records. So Margaret's job was to go through the records and find the patient's last address, record the date of the last treatment, and segregate those in which the last treatment had occurred more than 20 years ago. Apparently, the doctor, an elderly physician from the Philippines who had somehow managed to get licensed in Missouri and to open a family practice, didn't believe in throwing anything away because the small office was overflowing with boxes of records. His wife, who was the office manager, receptionist, and everything else, told Margaret that she couldn't talk about anything that she saw in the records outside of the office and, after that, pretty much left her alone.

Although the job seemed daunting, Margaret found herself fascinated by the medical histories of the patients. Fortunately, the physician had good handwriting and didn't use too many abbreviations. Many that he did use weren't hard to figure out. "Imp." was almost certainly "impression." An "L" in a circle had to represent the left arm, leg, ear, and so forth. She already knew that Rx stood for prescription. So she could figure out most of the entries.

Perhaps with some doctor's charts, she could have figured out a format and quickly found the administrative data, such as the address and the last treatment date on either the top or the bottom page of the clinical section of the chart, for example. But if Dr. Alambat had a format, Margaret couldn't figure it out. So she had to leaf through much of each chart to find what she needed, often stopping to read some particularly interesting patient history or progress note. Who would have thought that Mrs. Olson down the street had been diagnosed with borderline personality disorder? Although Dr. Alambat was a family practitioner, not a psychiatrist or psychologist, he had referred Mrs. Olson for a psych eval and filed the report of the evaluation in her chart. So Margaret, out of curiosity as to what the heck borderline personality disorder was, found a book in the doctor's library called the Diagnostic and Statistical Manual of the American Psychiatric Association, 4th Edition, known as the DSM-IV, and found that this mental problem involved frantic efforts to reject others so that they would respond by clinging to the person with the disorder. Now that she had read the diagnostic criteria, she could understand why Mrs.

Olson acted the way that she did and could even feel some sympathy for her even though she had seldom been nice to Margaret.

Even though she understood that she could not breach patient confidentiality, just knowing these intimate details of the health and lives of members of the community gave Margaret a feeling of power. The feeling was one that she didn't get at home with her dictatorial mother, who controlled every aspect of her life, such as what elective classes she could take, what activities she could participate in—no you can't run cross-country, women can't sweat—and certainly whom she could and could not date. "You can't go out with Brad. He's beneath your social standing and just wants to get in your panties!" What high school boy doesn't want to get into any halfway presentable girl's panties? Margaret had thought, wistfully thinking that a grope or two might have been more fun than the dreary conversations that she had on dates with the nerds that her mother had approved of. Yeah, they might end up Bill Gates the Second and be the richest man in the world, but in the meantime . . . .

So Margaret loved her summer job. And she loved it even more when she found her mother's chart. Her mother had also had Dr. Alambat refer her for psychological counseling—to a licensed clinical social worker who had diagnosed her with depression and something called 301.81 Narcissistic Personality Disorder. From her memories of Greek mythology, which her freshman history teacher had been enamored of, Margaret believed that Narcissus was some Greek guy who somehow fell in love with himself or at least with how he looked. Sounded like her mother so far. When she looked this disorder up in the DSM-IV, the diagnostic criteria fit her mother to a "T." Margaret had always resented how her mother always framed every issue in terms of how it would make her look, not whether it would make Margaret happy, or better educated, or whatever. Now, at least she knew why.

When summer vacation ended, Margaret went back to school with the intention of working with medical records. The doctor's wife had told her that hospitals had formal medical records departments with a director and other employees to ensure that medical records were accurate and available when needed and to respond to requests for copies of patient records. An internet search found a number of colleges offering degrees in health information management, and Margaret finally knew what she wanted to take in college. She was so excited that she even brought her grades up from A's and B's to all A's for her senior year so that she would have a better chance of getting into such a program. And not only did the University of Washington have such a program, but also it was a long way from Belton, Missouri, and her domineering mother.

So here she was after four years of undergraduate and two years of master's study at the University of Washington, with two degrees and a certificate, ready to start work. Many schools offered two-year programs, but her mother had insisted that an associate degree was not good enough for a Nicks. It was hard enough to convince her that health information management was a prestigious enough career for a Nicks, so fighting to get only an associate degree was a nonstarter. But the master's degree somewhat pacified her mother.

Margaret looked at the Kansas City Memorial Hospital directory and saw that the HIM Department was in the basement. This location was not surprising. Even though, in her opinion, health information was absolutely essential to taking proper care of patients, it hardly had the status of a clinical department. But she didn't care about any lack of status regarding location because she knew how important the HIM Department was.

When she came to the door of the department, she stopped and took a deep breath. Her heart was racing with excitement, and she wanted to look like a calm, cool professional to make a good first impression.

Margaret didn't really know it, but she would have made a very good impression. She had always considered herself a little bit plain—somewhat colt-like and gangly—but any lack of attractiveness in high school was more a function of her mother not letting her wear any make-up except for a little not-too-dark-lipstick on special occasions and the very conservative hair-dos and clothes that her mother imposed on her than any lack of attractive features. With not being allowed to wear her hair in anything but the most conservative cut and only minimal makeup, she was hardly the sex kitten of her high school class. But the stylist that her mother had do Margaret's hair had told her, "Honey, if your mother would let me, I could make you look like a fox!" But there had been no chance to find out.

And in college, she had been too busy studying and working part-time to help pay for school to worry much about her appearance. Her infrequent dates were just going to the basketball games or to a free student concert and didn't require her to dress up. But for her first day on the job, she thought that she looked pretty darn good: a new outfit, a new hair style, tasteful jewelry, a leather briefcase, and a designer handbag. The hair stylist had done a great job setting off her oval face. Her mother had always made her wear bangs, which the stylist said did nothing but cover up her best features. "Let your face show, girl! Don't hide it behind bangs," he had said. "Let's put on a little rinse that will highlight the blonde in your hair." Her mother had always said that she was a honey blonde. She didn't know whether she could really call herself a blonde or not or that she even wanted to. What she did know was that every summer the sun bleached her hair to where she almost was a blonde. But otherwise, she was a light-colored brunette. Nor was she sure that being a blonde was all that helpful in trying to be a professional in a health care organization. She'd rather be thought of as a smart brunette than a dumb blonde.

Her lightweight white ribbed turtleneck sweater was set off nicely by her new summer weight gray skirt and navy blazer that made her slender 5' 6" frame look a little taller. Yes, she looked like a very attractive young career woman as she drew another deep breath and pushed the door open.

"Welcome," a grandmotherly looking woman said, smiling. "You must be Margaret. Welcome to the HIM Department. I'm Emily."

Margaret knew that Emily was her new boss. Margaret, being way out in Washington, had interviewed for the job telephonically and had not actually seen Emily before. But she certainly knew who Emily was. Emily was the goddess of AHIMA—the past president. She was widely renowned in the medical records—oops, HIM—circles as the last authority on health information issues. So Margaret was thrilled at getting to learn the business from the goddess of AHIMA. Her first impression was that Emily was going to be just fine to work for. Emily was only about 5' 2" tall with a warm smile and gray hair pulled into a bun. She looks like Mrs. Santa Claus, Margaret thought, taking Emily's outstretched hand and shaking it firmly.

The next few hours were a blur. Margaret met the other workers in the HIM Department, was shown to her desk, and was taken to personnel to fill out a zillion forms. Then, she went to the security office to be photographed for a badge—all hospital employees wore badges. Then, she had to watch training videos covering all sorts of subjects from what to do in a disaster to hospital policy on sexual harassment. But she didn't mind this minutia. It was her first day as an employee in a real hospital HIM Department, and she was actually getting paid. And the other employees of the HIM Department seemed nice, particularly Pam, the second-in-command until Margaret had displaced her. But she didn't seem to mind at all. She couldn't have been more welcoming. Pam wasn't her real name. It was just what everyone called her because Pam was Thai and her name was totally unpronounceable to a non-Thai. Phak-Phimonphan. Margaret had met some Thai Army officers and their families when her father was in the Army and had to escort them around to witness training and found them to be a delightful people. So she was happy when Pam said that they would have to go out to dinner after Margaret got settled. She suspected that she had found a friend.

Finally, all of the in-processing was done, and Margaret returned to the HIM Department. Emily waved her into her office and gestured for her new employee to sit down. "I've got a few things to go over with you before we take the tour of the hospital,"

Emily said, smiling. "First, since we hired you, we lost our most experienced employee after me. And none of the other HIM employees have an RHIT and a master's degree, no less. So you are going to be second-in-command. I talked to Pam about it, and she's happy not to be in charge when I'm out at an AHIMA annual meeting or the like. No more money for you at first, but in six months, we'll review your compensation and bump it up if you are doing well—as I'm sure you will. Second, I'm putting you in charge of responding to subpoenas for medical records. I've been doing it myself because none of the other employees seems to get it right, and we spend way more time hassling with the lawyers than we should. I want you to develop a step-by-step procedure for handling subpoenas, court orders, and other legal requests for health information."

"Be happy to." Dealing with lawyers and subpoenas was hardly the fun part of managing health information, but Margaret knew that it was one of the more important aspects of any medical records operation. She had taken a course called "Medical-Legal Aspects of Health Information," as part of her college curriculum and was quite certain of the importance of medical records in litigation. They were important in malpractice cases, personal injury cases, criminal cases, family law cases, disability cases, and the like. The records had to be complete and accurate but never disclosed without proper legal authority. Her instructor, a nurse with a law degree, had told the class horror stories of HIM personnel who had been fired and even sued for giving lawyers copies of medical records without proper authorization.

The instructor had not been very complimentary about lawyers who tried to get medical records. As a general rule, she said, they thought that all they had to do was sign a subpoena and the hospital would roll over and play dead and deliver the records.

Finally, the day was over, and Margaret walked the half mile to her apartment. She loved her apartment. It was close to the hospital and on the fringes of Kansas City's Country Club Plaza, the upscale shopping district that was actually the first shopping center in the world designed to accommodate shoppers arriving by automobile. First opened in 1923, it reflected classic European-Moorish influences, especially those of Seville, Spain, with intricate tiled decorations and many upscale shops and restaurants. And more importantly, having her own apartment on the Plaza meant that she wasn't living at home with her mother in Belton. Her mother had pressured her to live at home—to save money—but really to control her daughter. But Margaret had brilliantly come up with the theory that she couldn't live that far away from the hospital. It would have been more than a half hour drive in the best of conditions. No, she had to be able to get to the hospital in ten minutes if there were a medical records emergency. That excuse was pretty much just that, an excuse, but her mother didn't know any better and gave in.

So Margaret went to bed happy after her first day on the job. She retired early, so that she would be fresh for her second day. As she fell asleep, she thought, a good job, a good boss, close, but not too close, to my mother, and a neat apartment just off the Plaza. How could things be better? Now, I just want to meet a nice guy.

2

Having gone to bed so early, Margaret was up well before the alarm clock rang. After she had gone through her morning routine, she pondered what to wear. She had only the one blazer, but thought that she could wear it again with a different skirt and a blouse instead of the turtleneck. I've got to get a few more business outfits, she concluded. After all, if I'm going to be the second-in-command (her father was a retired Army officer so she often used military terminology), I've got to look the part. She was still thinking about the best place to shop for business attire— Brooks Brothers on the Plaza was out of her price range—as she left her apartment for the short walk to the hospital.

As she entered the hospital, the security guard stopped her. She had forgotten to wear her newly issued badge. She took it out of the pocket of her blazer—glad that she had decided to wear her one blazer again today—and clipped it on. The guard peered at it and said, "Yes, Ms. Nicks. I have a message that you are supposed to go see the Chief Financial Officer as soon as you get in. His office is just down that corridor," pointing to his left—the executive suites. Margaret asked why, but the guard only shrugged and again pointed to the corridor.

Margaret knew that health information management departments often fell under the supervision of a hospital's financial manager, along with patient accounts, risk management, and the like. Maybe as her boss Emily's boss, he just wanted to welcome her.

There was no one at the secretary's desk outside the CFO's office, so Margaret knocked on the open door, stuck her head in, and said, "You wanted to see me, Sir? I'm Margaret Nicks."

The occupant of the large, well-furnished office, turned around in his swivel chair—he had been working on some kind of spreadsheet on his computer—and waved her in. "Welcome to Memorial. Glad you joined us. Have a seat."

Margaret took a quick look around as she settled into one of the two chairs facing the desk. She saw a framed certificate behind the desk that told her that Ken Mahan was a Certified Healthcare Financial Professional (CHFP) by HFMA—an acronym that she later learned stood for Healthcare Financial Management Association. Mr. Mahan was a tall, bespectacled man with a stern face that brightened considerably when he smiled.

"I'd love to chitchat with you," he said. "But we have a problem."

This ominous announcement caused a frisson of fear in the hospital's newest employee. Was she going to be fired already? No, she hadn't been on the job long enough to have done anything wrong.

Mr. Mahan sighed and said, "Your director, Emily, had a stroke last night. We got all over it, and she is going to recover, but it is going to take months of rehab. So the upshot is that you are now the acting director. None of the others in the department has a degree in HIM or an RHIT. So you're it. I'm going to get you a little more money, but in the meantime, you're in charge. I know that it won't be easy, but I know that you can do it. If you need anything—extra training, professional seminars, other resources— let me know. We will box up the personal items in Emily's office, and it's yours for the duration."

Margaret sat there stunned. Her long-term goal was to be an HIM director, but not yet. And not this way. Poor Emily.

Mahan continued, "And there's more bad news. You're familiar with HIPAA, right?"

"Yes, we had an introduction to it in our medical records confidentiality class at school. The Department of Health and

Human Services hadn't published any of the final regulations yet, so the instruction was pretty vague."

"Well, you are going to have to get all over it now because you are also the head of the HIPAA Steering Committee, and you have only ten months to get the hospital compliant. Emily had been scheduled to attend a HIPAA seminar given by Cross Country Education this Friday, June 7. We've switched it so that you can attend. The speaker appears very knowledgeable. He's even spoken for my professional organization, HFMA, at its Annual National Institute. Here's your enrollment information. Go learn all that you can. Meet with me next week, and let's go over what we've got to do. The doctors are going to be very hostile towards yet another compliance requirement, but we've got to do it. Any questions?"

"No, Sir."

"Ok. My door is always open if you need help. See you next week."

"Thank you, Sir."

Her head spinning, Margaret got up and walked out into the corridor. She leaned against the wall, shook her head, and tried to gather herself before walking downstairs to what was now her department.

3

Margaret got out of her car in the parking lot of the Marriott Kansas City Airport, the site of the HIPAA seminar. A sign just inside the door said that the HIPAA seminar was in Salon A on the lobby level. Once she had found Salon A, she was stopped by an elderly woman seated at a table outside the room. "Here for HIPAA?" she asked.

"Yes."

"Ok. Your name?"

"Margaret Nicks."

The registration assistant found Margaret on the list of attendees, checked her off, and handed her a sign-in sheet, saying that it was to ensure professional education credit. Margaret filled it out because she needed 12 hours of continuing education annually to keep her RHIT credential from AHIMA. The assistant handed her a course book and said, "You're all set, dear. Coffee and rolls are in the back of the room. Sit anywhere you like."

Margaret dropped her course book and notebook at a vacant seat at the first row table. She always liked to sit up front where she could hear well and see the screen if there was a slide show or PowerPoint presentation. Here, a PowerPoint slide was already up with the screen showing "How to Comply with HIPAA and the DHHS Regulations—Administrative Simplification Not! by John Thomas."

After having gotten coffee and a roll, she started leafing through the course book, which had the slides reproduced followed by text. She started reading the speaker's bio to see whether Mr. Mahan was right—that the speaker knew something about HIPAA.

The speaker was a lawyer—not a good sign. Margaret remembered how boring the lawyer was who taught her legal issues in health information course in college. The information was interesting, but the lawyer was so dry. She droned on in a monotone until Margaret's eyes glazed over. But today's speaker's list of publications gave her some hope: *Electronic Health Records—a Practical Compliance Guide* and similar titles looked as if they were practical guides and not just a bunch of legalese. And he was a retired Army officer, a plus in Margaret's mind because her father was a veteran. And more importantly, he had to know something about HIPAA. He had written *The Compliance Guide to HIPAA and the DHHS Regulations, The Physician's Guide to HIPAA Compliance,* and *the HIPAA Business Associate Guide.* Finally, the bio noted that he had done HIPAA consulting for federal, state, and county agencies and for hospitals, physician practices, and other health care entities.

The room slowly filled up with about 40 to 50 people, most of them women. They must be health information workers like me, Margaret thought. About five minutes before the 9 A.M. starting time, the instructor walked up to the front of the room. He was about six feet tall with brown hair and a graying mustache. He must be in his late 30s or early 40s, Margaret thought—and not bad looking for an older man.

And he's got a commanding voice, she mused, as he introduced himself and outlined what the seminar would cover. He said that he wanted to give them HIPAA Anxiety Disorder and then cure it by showing them how to get into compliance.

One of the attendees—a bearded, gray-haired, pony-tailed man dressed in blue jeans and a corduroy sports coat with suede elbow patches, for heaven's sake—asked, apparently in jest but maybe he was challenging the instructor, what the diagnostic criteria for HIPAA Anxiety Disorder were.

The instructor said, "Good question. You must be a psychologist." The questioner nodded, somewhat smugly, Margaret thought.

"Well, as you know, Doctor, the DSM-IV—the Diagnostic and Statistical Manual of the American Psychiatric Association, 4th Edition, for those of you who are not familiar with the acronym— does not yet have an entry for HIPAA Anxiety Disorder. But although I'm obviously not a mental health clinician, I've formulated my own set of diagnostic criteria, as follows:

"If, when someone asks you whether you work with health information, you always answer by saying, 'I invoke my privilege against self-incrimination,' that's a diagnostic criterion." Everyone laughed, even the psychologist.

"If you have attended more than five HIPAA seminars to date—"

"Oh no!" one of the attendees shrieked, "I've attended six— this one will be my seventh. Do I have HIPAA Anxiety Disorder? I'm certainly worrying about how in the world we are going to get compliant by the compliance date."

"You don't necessarily have it. Like the other disorders in the DSM-IV, you have to have more than one diagnostic criterion to be so diagnosed. Let me ask you a couple of questions, Ma'am. Do you make your patients wear a disguise and assume a cover identity when coming in for an appointment?"

"No." The woman actually looked relieved as the others in the room laughed.

"Finally, do you assign all of your data users 128-character passwords using a combination of the Thai, Cyrillic, and Sanskrit alphabets?"

To more laughter, the woman started to get into it. "No, but maybe I should!"

"We'll answer that question as we go through the day, but the good news is that you meet only one diagnostic criterion, so you don't have the disorder—as yet! But all of you may have it by the time you hear the penalties for not being HIPAA compliant!"

Then, he started talking about the sensitive nature of health information. No shit, Sherlock, Margaret thought, every health information professional knows that.

First, the instructor talked down the bullets on his PowerPoint slide about how known parties, such as employers, insurers, your children's school personnel, and so forth, could use health information in a foreseeable adverse manner—not to promote an employee or maybe even to fire the employee or to deny insurance coverage, or the word gets out at school and your child is harassed. He proved his point by recounting some tales about those situations, including a management employee that he had represented whose employer had fired him when he learned that he had been hospitalized with a manic episode of bipolar disorder. He concluded by saying, "Yes, you are probably thinking that he's protected by the Americans with Disabilities Act, and you would be right in legal theory, but having done a fair amount of employment law, I can guarantee you that you are better off with a good job than a good lawsuit. Yes, I got him some compensation, but he would have preferred not to have lost his job."

Ok, everybody knows about cases like that, Margaret thought, but she became more interested at the second bullet on the PowerPoint, "That an unknown party will obtain and use health information in an unforeseeable adverse manner."

"That sounds paranoid, doesn't it," Mr. Thomas asked, "Did anybody see that old Mel Gibson movie 'Conspiracy Theory'? Where everyone was out to get him?"

Several of the attendees nodded their heads.

"Well, you know, it doesn't sound as paranoid to me as it used to in these days of the USA PATRIOT Act. The official title of the USA PATRIOT Act is 'Uniting and Strengthening America by Providing Appropriate Tools Required to Intercept and Obstruct Terrorism.' Would anyone fall over in a dead faint if tomorrow's newspaper headline read, 'Government program to mine electronic health records for data on the war on terror unveiled?' I sure wouldn't."

Then, he said that in his opinion the real reason that the government enacted HIPAA wasn't as stated—to save the industry money by doing away with the inefficiencies of using 2,000 plus paper claims forms and having everyone bill the same way with the standard transactions and code sets. Supposedly, after recovering the $4 billion in implementation costs, which turned out to be $24 billion, demonstrating how good the government is at estimating health care costs, the industry would save money down the road.

"Do you want to know the real reason? So that they can audit you more easily. Think how much easier it is for an agent of the OIG—the Office of the Inspector General—the friendly folks who audit for Medicare fraud, to run a computer program against standardized electronic claims than to have to pore over tens of thousands of paper claims to detect suspected upcoding—assigning a code that gets a higher reimbursement than the service actually performed."

Well, so far I don't know how good he is at HIPAA, but he sure seems to know the health care industry, and he's pretty good at scaring me, Margaret thought.

Then, the speaker turned to the last bullet on the PowerPoint slide, which said that inaccurate medical information could cause harm. He said that he had a confession to make and that the audience might want to make the sign of the cross and hiss at him—or if they weren't religious, just hiss at him—because he was a former medical malpractice attorney who used to sue them. Margaret didn't hiss, but some in the audience did, although apparently good-naturedly. He said that he had given it up when he started HIPAA consulting on the theory that they were unlikely to hire him as their consultant if he was suing them. "Good theory!" one woman in the audience called out from the back of the room.

Then, he recounted a case in which his client had lost 40 points of IQ because his provider had administered four times the dosage of Dilantin to control seizures as he should have received because of inaccurate information. "Yes," he said, "the nurse should have caught it. This much Dilantin? This can't be right. But the chain of events started with inaccurate information."

"I don't know about you, but I don't have 40 points to spare," he said to laughter, which increased when he said, "My ex-wife said that I didn't have four points to spare!"

The laughter broke the tension of thinking about how an illegible prescription or other inaccurate information could cause great harm to a patient. As she laughed, Margaret thought, ex-wife? So maybe he's still single? She looked and didn't see a ring. What are you doing, girl, she thought. You need to focus on HIPAA.

Then, John—he had said to call him John when one of the attendees prefaced a question with "Mr. Thomas" —talked about how these three concerns change when health information is automated. Providers collect more information, it's more sophisticated, there's more commercial use of the information, and perhaps most importantly, computers just let you do so much more with the data.

"I've got another confession to make," John said. "Before becoming a lawyer, I was in that contradiction of terms 'military intelligence.' And in that branch of the Army, I was trained in and served in Europe in HUMINT—human intelligence—recruiting and running human sources. Fascinating work, as you can imagine, and I'd still be doing it, but the Army decided that they didn't need human sources anymore because they had spy satellites and signals intercept. I had to find a new home, so I went to law school. I knew that it was a big mistake to do away with HUMINT, but the Army wasn't about to listen to some dumb captain. A spy satellite isn't all that helpful for a cave in Tora Bora.

"Anyway, I bring this topic up because suppose a big drug company finds out about my strange past and hires me to infiltrate your hospital or physician practice to get health information that they can use to direct market a new drug. And let's say that I'm good enough to come up with a cover identity and false documentation, like I'm from CMS doing an audit. Now, I know it would be difficult. You'd be suspicious. But I've even got it backstopped. I've bribed someone in CMS to backstop me—to confirm that I'm for real when you call for verification. So let's just say that I can pull it off.

"Look at the chore I've got if you're still paper. I've got to figure out the format. Is it chronological or is it SOAP?"

Wow, Margaret thought. A lawyer who knows medical records formats!

He continued, "Then I've got to go through thousands, maybe tens of thousands of charts. I've got to locate the data, I've got to record the data, and I've got to carry it out of there.

"But what if you have an EHR and you're networked? Now, I don't need a cover identity. I don't need to take the risk of coming to your facility, where I could be identified if you learned that it was a breach. I just hire this young lady here." He pointed at Margaret. She felt a flash of excitement. She didn't know whether she was afraid he was going to use her as an example or was complimented that he had picked her for his example. That's what happens when you sit up front, she concluded ruefully. Calm down, she thought to herself. It doesn't mean anything.

"She just happens to be the best hacker east of the Rocky Mountains. See, she isn't even denying it!"

A blush from Margaret. Laughter from the audience.

"And she hacks into your system and writes a program that extracts just the fields that I need in nanoseconds."

He pulled a memory stick out of his pocket and held it up. "And she gives it to me on this, formatted by zip code to facilitate my direct mail campaign. And even if she can't hack in remotely, it's a lot easier to come up with a cover identity as a technical rep from the vendor there to put a patch in than one as an auditor from the OIG. And how hard is it to smuggle this out of your facility?" he asked, holding up the memory stick. He walked down the isle between the rows of tables holding up the memory stick so that all could see it. "Yes, computers just let us do so much more with the data. By the way, would someone explain to me how this device can possibly hold five gigabytes?

"So that brings up the question of whether computers increase the risks of breach of confidentiality or data integrity? Well, perhaps because I'm a lawyer, I can make an argument either way. Anyone ever lose a paper record—it gets signed out to an outpatient clinic and doesn't make it back to the HIM Department?"

Most of the seminar attendees either nodded their heads or raised their hands. One woman blurted out that she was lucky if they got signed out so she knew where to look.

"Well, when you automate, that chart can be pulled up on the screen in the outpatient clinic but still remains in the server in the HIM Department or the IT Department. See, that's why I'm good at HIPAA. Twenty years in the Army. I can do acronyms."

As the audience laughed, Margaret thought, Ok, he entered the Army at 18 or more years old, so add 20, he's got to be over 40 because he's been out a while to have done all this HIPAA consulting. Too old for me! But he looks mid-30s. Oh, come on. You're here to learn HIPAA, not to find a husband.

"But computers certainly add risks, like our best hacker here." Margaret could feel herself blush as he pointed her out again. "You know, I do a lot of study of breaches of confidentiality around the country, and I am firmly convinced that the real risk isn't pieces of paper and it isn't bits and bytes. You know what the real risk is? People—loose lips.

"Did any of you hear about mother/daughter day in the hospital in Jacksonville, Florida? This one was really cute. Mother works in patient accounts. She brings teenage daughter to mother/daughter day, doesn't give her any kind of confidentiality briefing, and after about five minutes ignores her. Predictably, teenage daughter is quickly bored out of her skull. So to amuse herself, she starts rummaging around the department and stumbles across the billing documents for HIV tests. So she amuses herself by calling up the patients who tested HIV negative and telling them that they had tested positive. One woman gets such a call, hangs up the phone, goes to her bathroom, undresses, draws a hot bath, gets in, and slits her wrists. Fortunately, she didn't know what she was doing and cut this way." He made a cutting motion, drawing his hand as if he was holding a knife across his wrist. "Not this way." Another cutting motion, but this time down the length of the forearm. "So the veins retracted and they were able to save her. But she'd have a pretty good lawsuit."

The seminar attendees definitely reacted to this story. Some gasped. One woman covered her eyes and laid her head down on the table. Some shook their heads.

"By the way," the seminar presenter continued, "I do like my seminars to be valuable to people. Have you heard the concept 'value added'—something more than what was advertised?"

Most of the attendees nodded and a few answered that they had.

"Well, see, you're not just learning about HIPAA—you're also learning how to effectively cut your wrists." To laughter, he continued, "Hopefully, you won't feel a need to do so as the seminar goes on. But if you do, we have a psychologist in the room!" pointing at the bearded, pony-tailed man who had asked about the diagnostic criteria for HIPAA Anxiety Disorder. "He can counsel you so that you don't act on your suicidal ideations." This comment drew another round of laughter. And the psychologist got out his card case and held up his business card.

This guy's all right, Margaret thought. He's got a good sense of humor. Maybe this seminar won't be as boring as I thought.

The instructor got another horrified gasp as he recounted something that one of his seminar attendees had told him—that she, as the HIM Director, had had to fire a transcriptionist who saw one of her friends in a group of about a dozen people at a party. The transcriptionist ran up to the group saying, "What a coincidence! I didn't know you were going to be at this party. I was just working on your chart today. Has your genital herpes cleared up?" The instructor pointed out that the patient was less than thrilled at this particular disclosure—at a party. Put a little crimp in the patient's social acceptability. And firing was the only appropriate employee discipline because you couldn't legally shoot her.

Margaret was horrified when she found herself blurting out, "Couldn't it be justifiable homicide?" Why was she drawing attention to herself?

"Good point," John laughed along with many of the other seminar attendees.

"But think about it," he went on. "Did it matter whether the billing documents for the HIV tests were paper or electronic? Did it matter whether the transcriptionist was typing on an old manual typewriter or an EHR? The breach was oral and caused by the person, not the media."

"But Congress thought that computers really increased the risk, so we have HIPAA."

That comment concluded his introduction to what HIPAA required. So-called covered entities had to implement reasonable and appropriate security measures to ensure integrity and confidentiality of individually identifiable health information, known as protected health information or PHI. Then, he discussed the penalties for failure to comply with HIPAA, starting with the criminal sanctions. What he called the "biggie" was if one knowingly and improperly accessed or disclosed PHI with the intent of personal gain, commercial advantage, or malicious harm. A conviction for the biggie could result in ten years' imprisonment and a $250,000 fine. He also discussed civil penalties for noncriminal violations, such as failure to conduct the required risk analysis.

After having given some of the attendees, including Margaret, some HIPAA anxiety, he turned to avoiding liability by getting into the subject of compliance. He spent the rest of the morning session explaining the Security Rule. It was pretty vague. It said, for example, that covered entities had to have a sanction policy, but didn't specify what it should say. It said that they had to have a method of authentication to ensure that they could tell who made an entry in an electronic health record or EHR but didn't say whether it could be a unique user ID and a password, or a retinal scan, or a thumbprint reader. Apparently, each covered entity had to figure it out on its own.

One tall, heavyset woman broke in just as he was finishing up, saying, "Wouldn't it just be so much simpler if they just told us what to do?"

"Yes, but you wouldn't like that either. They would have to set the bar so high—enough security to protect the data of a celebrity mental health practice—that would require you to do way more than you need for your non-celebrity podiatry clinic. The way that they did it allows you to select reasonable, cost-effective security measures rather than having some DHHS bureaucrat decide what security measures you need."

After lunch, he turned to the Privacy Rule. The Security Rule applies to security measures for EPHI—electronic protected health information—whereas, the Privacy Rule specifies permissible uses and disclosures for all health information regardless of form or format. His seminar had shown the Security Rule to be vague, but the Privacy Rule was so complicated and detailed. Margaret listened intently but wondered how she could ever successfully be in charge of HIPAA compliance if HIPAA and the DHHS regulations were this complicated.

Finally, he talked them through a risk analysis. It was a six-step process. First, get a good team together—clinicians, technical types, health information types, human resources types, financial types, and the dreaded attorney. If you didn't have all of those people, get as many as possible involved because you had to look at all the risks—clinical, technical, legal, and so forth. Second, identify assets. What data does the covered entity have to protect? To the extent that the covered entity is automated, that data resides in a system, and you must identify all of the components of the system to protect the data therein. Then, identify risks. Then, quantify the risks—analyze how likely they are to occur and how harmful it will be if they do occur. Then, select reasonable, cost-effective security measures by balancing the cost of the security measures against the cost of the harm that would occur if the security measures were not implemented. Finally, test and revise the system as things change.

He made it sound easy, but Margaret thought that getting all of any risk analysis team from her hospital to agree on anything would be daunting at best. The doctors certainly weren't about to listen to some wet-behind-the-ears acting director of the HIM Department. In a sudden flash, Margaret realized that she needed a HIPAA consultant—like John.

After the seminar was over, she stalled filling out the critique sheet that all attendees were to complete till everyone else had left. John was packing up his computer and projector. So Margaret went up to him and asked, "How much do you charge to get a hospital HIPAA compliant?"

John was fairly tired at this point. The third all-day seminar in three days with a couple hours of travel time between seminar cities. His first thought was to blow her off because she looked too young to have any clout to hire him as a HIPAA consultant. But she was kind of cute, so he decided to spend a few moments talking to her before rushing to the airport to get home to Chicago. "That's really hard to answer without knowing a lot more. My usual rate is $3,000 per day, although sometimes I back off that figure a little if it is an interesting consultation or in a great city. Sometimes, I can complete a small operation in a couple of days. I've had big clients that have taken months. Some big governmental covered entities, such as the Alabama Department of Mental Health and Mental Retardation, took more than a year. But instead of hiring me for the whole compliance effort, why not do it in stages? Hire me to do a gap analysis to figure out where you are already HIPAA compliant, where you're not, and how we could bridge the gaps. Then, we will know exactly what you need to get in compliance, and I can price the rest of the work accurately."

"That sounds good. How much for a gap analysis?"

"I price it two ways. Way one, I come onsite and do it, with the help of the HIPAA Steering Committee. Way two, I give you a questionnaire to fill out and then analyze it and give you a written report and an onsite briefing or a telephone conference if you don't want to spend the funds to bring me onsite for the whole analysis. Way one, I would do for $4,000 plus airfare from Chicago and two days' hotel and meals. Way two, is $1,500 for the report and phone conference or $2,500 for the onsite report, again plus travel expenses. If you want to send me an email, I can put a proposal in writing for you."

Margaret had serious doubts that she could pry any money out of Mr. Mahan, but also seriously doubted that she could get the hospital HIPAA compliant on her own, even though the seminar had taught her what she had to do. But she agreed, saying that she would email him as soon as she got to work the next day.

John also had serious doubts that he would ever hear from her. But he had always had the philosophy that, if you threw enough pieces of paper up against the wall, some of them would stick. She seemed earnest enough, and maybe she could convince the powers that be.

As she drove back down I-29 away from the Marriott and back home to her apartment on the Plaza, Margaret was already formulating how to approach Mr. Mahan to get approval to hire John as the hospital's HIPAA consultant.

4

Margaret drew a deep breath, held it for a minute, and then let it out to prepare herself for her meeting with Mr. Mahan. She had to convince him to let her hire Mr. Thomas as the hospital's HIPAA consultant. She was wearing a brand new Brooks Brothers suit that she had bought from the upscale shop on the Plaza. She had thought that she had better look professional if she was going to convince Mr. Mahan to spend hospital funds to get HIPAA compliant. Thank God, the store was having a big sale. After all, she was the HIM Director. Well, the acting director.

The secretary picked up the phone, apparently connected with Mr. Mahan, and told Margaret that she could go in. Margaret drew another deep breath, got up, and walked to the door. She stood there uncertain whether to enter or not. But Mr. Mahan looked up from a stack of papers, smiled, and waved her in. "Have a seat. How was the HIPAA seminar?"

"It was excellent, Sir. But it was also pretty scary because I learned how much we've got to do in order to be compliant and how severe the penalties for noncompliance can be."

"Why don't you give me a rundown?"

"Yes, Sir, but I took the liberty of putting it into a short report." She handed him the two-page summary that she had written the night before. It had cut into her beauty sleep, but she was nervous enough about the meeting that it had ended up helping her get to sleep to put the report in writing. Besides, she had remembered that her father had always said that he had to do a trip report for his commanding officer whenever he returned from a TDY (temporary duty) trip for training or a conference or any other kind of meeting when he was in the Army.

Mr. Mahan read the report, frowning occasionally, which did nothing to reduce Margaret's anxiety. Finally, he said, tersely, "Ok."

"Do you have any questions?"

"Yes, but first, I must say that your report confirms my general opinion from a breakout session at HFMA's ANI that we've got to comply with this mess."

"Thank you, Sir." Margaret knew that HFMA's ANI was the Healthcare Financial Management Association's annual convention, although she had no clue what ANI stood for. As she remembered from her first visit to his office, Mr. Mahan's certificate as an HFMA Certified Healthcare Financial Professional was prominently displayed right behind his desk. It confirmed her belief that, because he was a financial type, she had to make her pitch in terms of cost-effectiveness.

"Ok, enough with the 'sir.' I've never been in the military. You're a department director, even though you are just the acting director for now, so you can call me 'Ken,' unless we are in a meeting with higher ups, in which case I'm 'Mr. Mahan.'"

Margaret almost had to bite her tongue to avoid saying "Yes, Sir,"—would she ever outgrow having a military retiree for a father? But she recovered quickly enough and managed to answer, "Ok. Ken it is. What are your questions?"

"I get it that we've got to do it, but as you doubtless know, we don't have a lot of excess funds in the budget—we didn't really budget for HIPAA compliance."

"I know. And it might seem counterintuitive, but I'm convinced that the most cost-effective way to get compliant is to bring in an outside consultant—preferably Mr. Thomas, who gave the seminar and who had a ton of examples of how he had saved his clients money by implementing cost-effective security measures.

"He said that a lot of consultants make HIPAA security compliance a lot worse than it needs to be to justify their consulting fees. He, on the other hand, says that his business model is to justify his fees by saving his clients money. He told a story about a hospital that another consultant had told that they needed to spend $25,000 to rewire the hospital so as to be able to move the computers so that patients and others could not see what was on the screens. Instead, he had them paint a red line far enough away from the screens so that no one could read the data on the screen and then put up signs that no one could cross the red line and approach the workstation without permission. The data user was instructed not to let anyone cross the line and approach the workstation unless they were authorized to see what was on the screen, such as another member of the hospital workforce, or the data user had the screen turned off or a screen saver up. He said that, for the price of a can of red paint, some turpentine to clean the brush, and a couple of pieces of poster board, they fixed that problem and saved about $24,990 of the $25,000 that the other consultant would have had them spend. This—"

"Yes, I know he's good," Ken cut in. "HFMA has had him speak on HIPAA compliance, and it reviewed his compliance products and found them to be cost-effective. But I'm not sure that we have enough money in the budget to pay him $20K or so."

"Yes, I told him that we might not be able to afford him, and he suggested that we hire him to do a gap analysis—to find out where we are already compliant, where we are not compliant, and how we could bridge the gap. He said that he could do a two-day onsite gap analysis for $4,000 and that he could then price actually getting us complaint. We would know what we could do ourselves and what we might want his help on. I think that such a plan would be really cost effective." There, she'd worked cost-effectiveness into the discussion several times.

"What about his expenses?"

"He said that he has another consulting job in the area, so his airfare is already paid for, and he'll just need two days' meals, lodging, and rental car. He said that the Marriott down the street would be fine."

"Well, I would have to go through the CEO to the board to get approval $20,000 or more, but I can approve a $4,000 plus expenses expenditure. So get me a written proposal and a draft contract that I can run by the CEO, and we'll make this happen."

"Yes, Sir—I mean Ken!" Margaret gushed, thrilled at how easy it had been to get John aboard as the hospital's HIPAA consultant, even in this limited role. She knew that, once he had completed the gap analysis, he would sell himself to help with getting the hospital HIPAA compliant. But she wondered, as she left Ken's office, whether she was thrilled at getting help with her enormous responsibility of getting the hospital HIPAA compliant or at getting to work with John. She also wondered just how hard the hospital's CEO would be to convince because she had not met him yet and did not know how he was going to be to work with.

Back in her office, she emailed John the good news. He responded with a written proposal with a scope of work and a sample contract. Wasting no time, she promptly forwarded it to Mr. Mahan and finally exhaled the deep breath that she felt as if she had been holding for hours. She had gotten it done and had set her plan in motion. Whew.

5

Offices of EMR Legal, John's consulting firm, Monadnock
Building, 53 W. Jackson Boulevard, Downtown Chicago

John was scrolling down his email in the office suite that he
leased in the famous old landmark Monadnock Building. He loved
the old-style building with its somewhat retro offices with oak, not
plastic, crown molding; oak molding around the huge windows,
and solid oak door with frosted glass window with his name
stenciled on it. The 1893 building was arguably the world's first
skyscraper and definitely the tallest building with masonry load-
bearing walls. The walls on the first floor were much, much thicker
than the walls on the 16th floor.

Even though the building had great old-fashioned charm,
John's office had all the modern amenities. He belonged to several
listservs devoted to health information and communicated with
most of his clients and seminar attendees by email, so he had
dozens, if not hundreds, of emails on any particular day. One
listserv that he belonged to was titled "HIPAA Hopping," which
most of the HIPAA experts, real or supposed, subscribed to in
order to keep abreast of all the latest HIPAA developments and to
pick the brains of the real HIPAA experts when they had a tough
question. John had never asked a question of the listserv, nor had
he answered anyone else's. Maybe that made him a leech or some
kind of jerk or what his editor's boss at the American Health
Lawyers Association had affectionately termed a lurker, but he saw
no reason to provide his in-depth knowledge of HIPAA to people
who were too lazy to even attempt to figure it out for themselves

and who would steal his HIPAA clients in a heartbeat if they had half a chance. And his position on the matter wasn't total paranoia on his part because he had had several clients stolen from him by less qualified experts.

There were two aspects to John's belief that he should not answer these other so-called experts' questions on the listserv. One, he was the expert—he had paid his dues and learned the health information business from the bottom up, unlike other so-called experts who just read the HIPAA statute and the Department of Health and Human Services regulations implementing HIPAA and who wrote, spoke, and consulted on HIPAA compliance with no practical knowledge of health information whatsoever. They didn't even know the difference between an RHIT and an RHIA. The former, a Registered Health Information Technician, was a credential from AHIMA, the American Health Information Management Association—the association of the medical records professionals, now more properly the health information management professionals, for those who had certain training and expertise in health information management. The RHIA credential was the higher credential, reserved for the Registered Health Information Administrators, those who administered the HIM (Health Information Management) departments in their hospitals or other facilities, supervising the RHITs and others in their HIM Department, which credential required even more training and experience. John would have been willing to bet that 95 percent of the lawyers that tried to pass themselves off as HIPAA experts—if, indeed, there were any of them besides him—didn't know the difference between these two essential health information management credentials. But he hadn't just learned the law. No, he had also learned the business—the practical side of health information management.

But there was a downside to this situation. John dealt with the HIM professionals. Many, if not all, of the other lawyer HIPAA consultants dealt with the hospital or other health care facility's general counsel or outside counsel—lawyer to lawyer. And this situation had cost John many opportunities to get lucrative consulting contracts. He would impress a director of HIM at a hospital, who would then bring him on board to train the hospital staff and do a gap analysis. After he had performed those services, the HIM Department and even the medical staff would recommend that the facility hire him as their HIPAA consultant. But the hospital administrator would say that his college frat brother was a partner in the local hot-shit law firm and had a Harvard degree and maybe he should be the hospital's consultant. And John would lose the consulting contract to a lawyer that knew nothing or next-to-nothing about HIPAA, but was a frat brother of the facility administrator and had a Harvard law degree.

For example, in one case, he had given a presentation to the doctors of a large medical practice in North Carolina, won them over—which, by the way, had not been easy—and had the HIPAA steering committee, the doctors, and the practice CEO all recommend to the chairman of the governing board that they hire him only to have that functionary say, "First, let me see whether my college roommate's law firm can do this." Apparently, they had said that they could, although in reality, they couldn't because they were clueless. John would have bet his HIPAA earnings for the year that he could have done it way more cost-effectively than a law firm in which the lawyers didn't know HIPAA from a hippo or an RHIT from a REIT—a real estate investment trust. But that knowledge wasn't a total sop for losing a large contract under which he could have helped his client comply with this complicated federal law in a cost-effective manner.

But there was enough HIPAA business out there that he didn't lose a lot of sleep over the missed consulting opportunities. Ok, so they hired their local bud lawyer, but they then spent two or three times the money that they would have if they had hired John. First, their local lawyer was more expensive because he would bill them for all his ramp-up time to learn HIPAA—something that John already had under his belt and didn't have to bill his clients for. Second, they didn't really understand HIPAA and would make their clients implement way more expensive security measures than HIPAA required. They would, for example, make their clients reconfigure their waiting rooms so that no one could hear the receptionist calling a patient by name rather than just putting up a sign stating, "If you don't want us to call you by name, tell us, and we will make other arrangements." Some went so far as to make their HIPAA clients buy restaurant flasher-beepers—what they give customers to tell them when their tables were ready—to give to patients in the waiting room. John had always thought that doing so indicated that the provider had not done a risk analysis—an assessment of whether the risk of the patients dying when the flasher/beepers went off and startled them so much that they had a heart attack was worse than the minimal risk inherent in calling a patient by name in the waiting room—a risk that was significant only if they were celebrities or mental health clients, or the like.

John had received such a restaurant flasher/beeper when he was a podiatry patient. To be frank, he could not have cared less if everybody in the waiting room or, indeed, everybody in the country, had known that he was there to have the podiatrist perform orthopedic lithotripsy. He wasn't going to lose any business for having a heel spur. It wasn't like having AIDS or borderline personality disorder or a cocaine addiction. In fact, he could even put a macho spin on it. He hadn't taken good care of his feet. Army Airborne. Jumping out of perfectly good airplanes when you land as hard with the chute as if you had jumped off a one-story building. And 13 marathons, several triathlons, and dozens of other, shorter, road races, had not been good for his feet. Not to mention close to 20 years of Army full-court basketball and racquetball. No, he hadn't been good to his feet. But it was hardly something that he had to be ashamed of. But no one was going to fire him or refuse to hire him because he had a heel spur. In fact, they might hire him on the theory that his foot hurt too much to go play golf and that he would actually work on their case. So he could not have cared less if the podiatry doctor's receptionist had called out, "Mr. John P. Thomas, attorney, the podiatrist is ready to perform orthopedic lithotripsy to help with the pain of your heel spur."

But they hadn't done a good risk analysis of the risks inherent in their security measures. Sometimes, the security measure can be riskier than the breach that would occur without the security measure. For example, an automatic log-off of the electronic health record ("EHR") in the emergency department after five minutes of nonactivity if the emergency department physician had better things to do than turn away from saving the patient's life to hit a key to restart the five-minute timer would be riskier than any possible breach of confidentiality inherent in the ambulance personnel, the nurses, or the family members seeing what was on the screen. John might have been wrong, but as a former malpractice attorney and patient himself, he thought that the risk of being given a contraindicated drug—perhaps Mannitol to control brain swelling when it conflicted with his blood pressure medication—was a far greater risk than the risk of a breach of confidentiality of that particular health information. He would hardly lose any clients if they learned that he had been administered that drug after a traffic accident.

Overreactions to HIPAA were caused by clueless consultants who wanted to justify their fees by making HIPAA way worse than it was. Perhaps, the worst one that John had learned of was the consultant that would show up at a hospital with an architect in tow, announcing that he was there to redesign the building to get it HIPAA compliant. John actually thought that this maneuver was fraud. No, he knew that it was fraud.

Ah, an email from Margaret Nicks in Kansas City. Perhaps, she had gotten approval for him to do a gap analysis. Not only did John want the business, but also he was attracted to the energetic young woman. Not that he would do anything about it, but it was nice to work with someone personable rather than some old grouch.

John had an inviolate rule that he had made up on the spot once: he didn't get involved with his legal clients. He was once representing a woman facing a federal government employee disciplinary hearing in Washington, DC. John would never have dated her, even though she was both smart and attractive. She had told him that she had adopted three special needs children. John's marriage had died on the rocks of one special needs child, a profoundly brain-damaged in utero child. Far from being a saint, he would rather blow his brains out than go through that again. So special needs times three was a nonstarter even if the woman were a "10."

The evening before the hearing, John had said, "Let's meet in the hotel lobby, find a quiet corner, and go over your testimony for tomorrow."

The client had responded, "The lobby would be too public and noisy, so let's do it in my room."

And John had stupidly agreed. John was not unintelligent. He had graduated first in his law school class and had out-thought almost every attorney that he had gone up against in a legal dispute. But when it came to women, he was stupid. He hadn't always been stupid in that regard, but getting divorced after more than a decade of marriage had cast him adrift on the seas of dating woefully unprepared. He had learned about his cluelessness while still serving in the Army and running into an old friend. The friend had invited John, who was by himself for the first time in over a decade, to every one of his unit's functions. And an attractive female officer was there, Major Marcie.

John had just had his first book published, which apparently, although he didn't realize it, had made him attractive as being a published author. So Major Marcie bought a copy and had him autograph it. He vaguely noticed that she always seemed to be in the group that he was hanging with at these parties, but didn't attach any significance to it. He didn't even attach any significance to her purchasing another copy of his book.

Nor did he attach any significance to her calling him in his BOQ (Bachelor Officer Quarters) and saying that she had to come over and pick up another signed copy for her brother's birthday. When she arrived and did not seem in any particular hurry to leave, he had fairly brusquely rushed her out the door. His about to be ex-wife was supposed to call to negotiate some of the property division, and he didn't want to piss her off by having her hear a female's voice in the background. So he had gotten rid of Major Marcie as quickly as possible.

Five minutes after he had completed the discussion with his legally separated wife, the phone rang. He would never forget the conversation.

"Hello."

"Hello. It's Marcie. Are you stupid or what?"

Not having the faintest clue what she was talking about, John answered, "I guess I'm stupid."

"I've been throwing myself at you for a week. Are you going to come over to my BOQ and fuck me blind or what?"

The first option seemed preferable to the ill-defined "or what," so John had finally clued in and gone to her BOQ. It turned out to be worth being called stupid for.

But this experience, enlightening as it was, didn't wise John up enough to decline to go to his client's hotel room to go over her testimony. He did wise up, however, when she excused herself to "freshen up" and returned in her birthday suit, calling him her "white knight" and her "savior."

So he quickly responded, "Jean, I have an inviolate rule (which he had just made up) that I never get involved with a client during a case. If I do, I lose my objectivity and cannot adequately represent my client." And it wasn't too long before state bars began implementing professional responsibility rules prohibiting sexual relations with clients.

Fortunately, the client bought this theory, excused herself, and returned fully dressed. They concentrated on her testimony and ended up with a very good result. Rather than a discharge for misconduct, he had obtained for her a temporary letter of reprimand that would be removed from her records after two years. She subsequently even got promoted because the letter of reprimand was no longer in her file.

So there was no way that John was going to get involved with Margaret. Not that there was necessarily any consultant/client ethical prohibition against doing so, but he was an attorney, and an attorney/client prohibition on sexual relations certainly existed. He didn't think that it was worth casual sex to have to litigate whether he had been acting as a pure consultant or as an attorney if his relationship with a HIPAA client blew up and the woman complained to the Illinois Attorney Registration and Disciplinary Commission that her lawyer/consultant/whatever-he-was had engaged in an inappropriate sexual relationship with his client. But he still felt as if she would be good to work with, to say nothing of to look at.

So he emailed her back:

From: John Thomas [john@emrconsultants.com] Sent Mon 6/10/02
To: Margaret Nicks [MNicks@KCMemHosp.org]
CC:
Subject: HIPAA Consulting
Attachment: ◉ Consulting Contract doc.

Great news! Here is a contract for your review and signature by someone with authority to bind the hospital. When you return it, I will send you a list of what to have ready for me to review to start the gap analysis process. Look forward to working with you! John

CONFIDENTIALITY NOTICE: This message, including any attachments, contains information from EMR Legal that is confidential and privileged. The information is intended solely for the use of the addressee(s). If you are not an addressee, your disclosure, copying, distribution, or use of the contents of this message is prohibited. If this message has been sent to you in error, please notify the sender by return email and then delete this entire message. Thank you for your cooperation.

So pretty soon, he had a signed contract and sent Margaret another email:

From: John Thomas [john@emrconsultants.com] Sent Mon 6/17/02
To: Margaret Nicks [MNicks@KCMemHosp.org]
CC:
Subject: HIPAA Consulting
Attachment:

Thanks for the prompt response on the contract. Here is what you need to get together for my review once I arrive on site:

1. All insurance policies (malpractice, errors and omissions, general liability, property and casualty, etc.).
2. A list of all entities with which you exchange information, including what information, in what format, and the purpose of the exchange.
3. Any policies and procedures relating to security, such as a physical security policy, an email policy, an internet use policy, and so forth.
4. Any disaster or emergency plans.
5. Training records relating to health information, if any.
6. Copy of any confidentiality pledges for workforce members.
7. Any policies relating to workforce discipline, such as an employee handbook, a sanction policy, and so forth.
8. Retention and/or destruction policies, if any.

Having these things standing by will avoid wasting time looking for them when I arrive onsite. Let me know what days work for you next month. Thanks. John

CONFIDENTIALITY NOTICE: This message, including any attachments, contains information from EMR Legal that is confidential and privileged. The information is

intended solely for the use of the addressee(s). If you are not an addressee, your disclosure, copying, distribution, or use of the contents of this message is prohibited. If this message has been sent to you in error, please notify the sender by return email and then delete this entire message. Thank you for your cooperation.

So now, the ball was in her court. And John turned his attention to the dozens of other HIPAA clients that he was working with.

6

Health Information Management Department
Kansas City Memorial Hospital

What a hassle! Margaret did not think that assembling the list
of things that John had asked for in his email would be so difficult.
Some departments saw no particular reason to do anything for an
Acting Director of Health Information Management, if indeed they
would do anything for the real director with any enthusiasm.
Margaret had learned in school that the HIM Department was
always somewhat beyond the pale or below the salt or whatever
saying indicated that one was not one of the elite. She felt that this
perception on the part of the other departments of a hospital was
wrong—they couldn't function without accurate and available
health information—but that's the way it was. No board-certified
fellow of some fancy-schmancy medical society clinical
department chief was going to view any nonmedical department
head as anything but a low-level pest. They might date an
attractive nurse or even marry one, but treat them as an equal in the
hospital? No way. Margaret had always remembered the story that
her aunt, now a nurse, then a student nurse, had told her about
how, when she was on her surgical rotation, so that she could see
whether she wanted to be a surgical nurse, the surgeon had told her
to get her tits out of his way when she had leaned over to observe
the procedure. Hardly politically correct, but was a student nurse
going to report the Chief of Surgery for sexual harassment and still
expect to graduate? And because she was much more endowed in

that area than Margaret, she had to admit that her tits were in the way.

The financial data and the contracts that Mr. Thomas wanted weren't difficult to get. Mr. Mahan had provided that information very expeditiously. After all, as an accountant, he had all that stuff organized. But the data that Margaret needed from the clinical departments was another matter.

The worst hassle that Margaret faced was the request for the list of entities with which the hospital exchanged health information. And HIPAA defined health information broadly to include not only clinical data, but also financial, demographic, and lifestyle information. About the best response (and some weren't printable) that Margaret got when asking a clinical department for a list of whom they shared their individually identifiable health information with was, "We'll get to it when we can."

And when some departments did eventually provide her an answer, it was often so vague as to be worthless: "We send encounter information electronically to various health plans." What information? What health plans?

So Margaret dreaded the arrival of Mr. Thomas, even though she had desperately wanted his help. She was afraid that she had blown it by not having gathered all of the information that he had wanted. But when he showed up for the onsite gap analysis and she told him how few of his questions she had answers for, he just laughed and said, "You did better than most. You have to drag this data out of the clinical departments. The gods—I mean the doctors—don't want to be bothered by these compliance issues, and I can't totally blame them—so we just have to be slick to get the data."

Over the next couple of days, Margaret watched with a degree of awe at how Mr. Thomas—she couldn't quite bring herself to call him John out of fear that who knew what such informality might lead to—worked the worker bees to provide the information that their supervisors were too busy to provide. He usually framed it to make them believe that they were saving their bosses from HIPAA jail by giving him the information that he needed to get them compliant. Margaret, as the acting director, had gone to other department directors and struck out. John, the exceptionally well qualified lawyer/consultant, who was clearly on the same intellectual level as the clinical department heads, worked the worker bees and got the information that Margaret hadn't been able to get. Well, maybe she could have if she had been bright enough to butter up the worker bees, but she was too concerned about her tenuous status as the Acting Director and didn't want to lessen whatever status that she had by not acting like a director and talking director to director. But John didn't care about his status or lack thereof. He knew that the worker bees knew more about what was really going on than the doctors. So he schmoozed the worker bees and got the information that he needed and that would be far more likely to be helpful. He was able to do so because he had learned the practical side of the business. He was probably the only lawyer who knew the difference between Margaret's health information credential, RHIT (Registered Health Information Technician), and an RHIA (Registered Health Information Administrator, the higher credential) (formerly ART and RRA, respectively). He was also probably the only health lawyer who knew the difference between the chronological and the SOAP formats for the medical record. So this knowledge of the practical side of health information impressed the health information worker bees enough that they were willing to help him out, especially because he didn't lord his doctorate (Juris Doctor) over them like their medical doctor bosses did. So Margaret took away from this observation that she couldn't go to a fellow department director, say the Director of the Emergency Department, and get anywhere. She had to go to the worker bees who wanted to protect their director from these compliance issues and any potential liability for noncompliance and who would often be flattered that a director, even a nonclinician director, wanted their help. She wondered why they hadn't taught her this stuff in her health information management program at college.

Perhaps, the one speed bump on the process was the IT Department. The director, who was on the HIPAA Steering

Committee, viewed HIPAA as a lot of work that he didn't particularly want to be bothered with and had communicated that feeling to his staff. And he would be key to dealing with all of the technical security measures that HIPAA would require. But they didn't seem to want to share their technical knowledge with the non-computer literate—apparently anyone who didn't work for the IT department or who didn't think in binary. And even though John was a HIPAA guru, he had admitted to Margaret that he was a little weak on its technical aspects, although Margaret wasn't sure that his apparent weakness in that area wasn't a ploy to get the IT types buttered up to help him. But his alleged lack of in-depth IT knowledge was why he had techie types on his consulting team. Like Charles. John had said that he didn't understand a word that Charles said about computer systems, but he apparently communicated well with the IT types and that all of the consulting that he had done to date had gone well insofar as dealing with the technical aspects. But he couldn't bring Charles onsite for a gap analysis. Not at what the hospital was paying for it.

But John didn't give up. He asked around and found that the IT Director, James McManus, loved barbeque. And one could find 'que in KC. So John went online (he was at least that computer literate) and read the reviews of the barbeque restaurants in KC. And although reviewers' opinions differed significantly, Fiorella's Jack Stack Barbecue appeared a safe choice. So John had gone out there by himself to check it out. After all, he had to eat anyway, and the hospital was paying his consulting fee plus expenses. Their burnt ends were great, as were their barbecued beans. So he asked James whether he would be willing to join him at Jack Stack so he could pick his brain about the hospital's system. The plan worked like a charm. A couple of Jack Daniels on the rocks, some burnt ends and sides, all on John's AMEX card, and James was now John's best bud. And the resistance to divulging IT Department data to John magically evaporated in the uncharacteristically cool July evening breeze.

Once they had the information—the data that they had to protect; the media that it resided on; and, where they were automated, the components of the system—it was time to review who should be on the HIPAA Steering Committee. Margaret had the list from the first (disastrous) meeting that she had presided over, but basically didn't remember much about any of the committee members—just that they looked at her as if she were some total doofus, a military term that she had learned from her father, a synonym for dud. He had often commented, as they watched Gomer Pyle reruns together, that Gomer had portrayed a doofus perfectly.

But John had her go to Human Resources and to the departments that the committee members came from and get their personnel records and CVs so that she and John could evaluate which members were going to be good on the committee and which should be replaced.

Late in the afternoon, they met in the director's office. Margaret couldn't yet bring herself to call it her office, perhaps in the futile hope that the real director would magically recover from her stroke and take back over but leaving Margaret in charge of getting the hospital HIPAA compliant so that she could keep working with John. Even though he hadn't shown any sign of interest in her other than as a colleague, she enjoyed working with him.

They pored over the HIPAA Steering Committee list.

Doctor Benvenista from Podiatry. A sixty-year-old doctor who had been on staff for 20 years. John had told Margaret that they had to check with his worker bees, but typically, older doctors wanted nothing to do with automation or new technologies. They were often hide-bound and set in their ways. They needed to find a young, tech-savvy, doctor who could get into the security of health information, particularly electronic health information.

So they interviewed Doctor B's staff and learned that he had the worst bedside manner of any doctor on the staff. They told John and Margaret that a patient had recently complained about Doctor B. The patient had showed up for an office appointment. The doctor said, in a fairly angry tone, "So what's wrong with you?" The patient answered, "I've got a right metatarsal neuroma."

The patient just happened to be a malpractice attorney who had some clue about medicine. A malpractice attorney had to learn the medicine to be able to win a malpractice case if, for no other reason, to be able to effectively cross-examine the medical expert witnesses. So it didn't take a rocket scientist to do a web search on pain in the ball of the foot and discover metatarsal neuroma—a swollen nerve going into the toes.

"Well, we'll just see about that, doctor!" he said angrily, pissed that the patient had presumed to self-diagnose.

So after having completed the diagnostic imaging, the doctor returned, did not look at the patient, and muttered you've got a right metatarsal neuroma." The patient told the hospital ombudsman that he wanted to say, "No shit, Sherlock," but he knew that the doctor was going to inject steroids into this swollen nerve with a thick needle and poke it around to get the steroids well injected and didn't want to piss him off.

Well, according to the complaint, he might as well have pissed the good doctor off, because it couldn't have been any more painful. The patient recounted that he had had kidney stones and poking the thick needle around the inflamed nerve was way more painful. He hadn't known it during the procedure, but his reaction to the pain was a common side effect. His feet had started sweating like Niagara Falls. So the podiatrist said, "Do your feet always sweat like this? Have you ever heard of Odor Eaters?

The patient, not only a lawyer but also a retired Marine who was a devotee of mixed martial arts, had told the ombudsman that this insensitive question had made him want to form two spear hands, slap them forcefully onto the doctor's ears, thereby deafening him, slide his hands back behind the doctors head, and pull his head onto the patient's knee, thereby driving the doctor's mastoid bone into his brain, killing him instantly. But he had thought that such an attack would, with his luck, break the thick needle off in the neuroma, so he had better cool it.

So finally, the podiatrist finished and said, "Well, doctor, that's it. If this doesn't work, we will have to cut."

The patient said that the chance that he would let this doctor operate on his foot was about equivalent to his agreeing to a sex change operation without anesthesia. But he simply said, "You know, doctor, it is doctor. But it's Juris Doctor not Medical Doctor," thinking that any doctor with a clue would think, "Juris Doctor, must be a lawyer who would love to suc me in a heartbeat," and ease off. But no . . . .

The doctor started writing up the procedure and saw that the patient had TRICARE Prime military retiree insurance and did stop with the "doctor" insult, but started calling him "corporal."

"It's colonel, not corporal, *doctor.*"

It didn't faze the podiatrist, who simply said, "Whatever," and waved the patient out of the room.

After John and Margaret had heard this story, they knew that they had to replace Doctor B on the HIPAA Steering Committee if they wanted to get anywhere. So they asked a number of worker bees which physician was the most tech-savvy one on the staff. And the clear winner was Doctor Jimmy Frame, the second-in-command of the Emergency Department. He was always campaigning for the adoption of an electronic medical record which, of course, the old fogies, like Doctor B, resisted strenuously. And as John pointed out, the HIPAA Steering Committee had to analyze the clinical risks, and an Emergency Department doctor was far better qualified to assess all risks than a podiatrist. An ER doctor had to deal with the full range of medical issues, from heart attacks, to problem pregnancies, to trauma, to strokes, to infectious diseases. A podiatrist might be great on foot problems, but might know less than nothing about when to administer Mannitol to reduce brain swelling in a closed-head injury Emergency Department patient. No, Jimmy was light-years better qualified than Doctor B and was going to be light-years easier to work with. And as one of the few doctors on staff that Margaret had met, she thought that he was a hunk (although she didn't share that particular thought with John).

The representative of the nursing staff was Nurse Patty Ratchet. John had burst out laughing when he saw her name on the list. "Nurse Ratchet? The same last name as the nurse in *One Flew over the Cuckoo's Nest.* How does she survive that name in a hospital?"

"She got past her name by being perhaps the most respected nurse at the hospital. She really knows her stuff. The patients love her. And she always goes out of her way to help other staff members. If anything, she's the antithesis of Nurse Ratchet."

"Ok, we keep her. Who's next?"

"Our outside legal counsel. Stanley Deutsch. He works for Badami, Lower, Huffman, & Deutsch, one of the larger firms in the city."

"What does he know about HIPAA?"

"Next to nothing. He's probably read it but hasn't a clue as to the practical aspects of HIPAA compliance. I talked to Mr. Mahan, who said that he may be fine at negotiating physician contracts so that they don't violate the Anti-Kickback Act, but that he's not a litigator and doesn't understand health information."

"Ok, we dump him. I'll handle the legal risks. Who's next?"

"Well," Margaret said, mischievously, "there's this Margaret who is the chair of the HIPAA Steering Committee."

"Is she worth anything?"

"Well, she's pretty new. But she was sharp enough to hire you!"

"Ok," John said, smiling, "She stays."

Margaret had a little frisson of excitement at this decision but ignored it and moved on. "Thanks, I think. We have James McManus, as the Director of IT. He made me nervous, but you seem to have won him over, so I'm ok with him. No one knows the technical issues better than he does."

"What about the risk manager, Jerri Sinclair?"

"She's cool. She just wants to reduce risks. So she will be very helpful in reducing HIPAA risks. And she may be the one non-MD that the doctors listen to because they don't want their names in the National Practitioner Data Bank as having committed malpractice or be indicted for Medicare fraud or even be hassled for a HIPAA violation."

"Ok, she stays. Who's next?"

"Sherry Page from patient accounts. Ken Mahan might know more, but he is my boss, and I don't think it would work for him to be a member of the committee that I chair. And from everything that I have heard, Sherry really knows her shit—oops, excuse me—because my father is retired military, I sometimes lapse into his language."

John laughed, "Having spent 20 years in the military before retiring, I've heard far worse. Don't worry about it. Sherry stays. Who's left?"

"Jan Wray, Human Resources Director. She's ok. I dealt with her a lot during my hiring process. She knows the HR process up and down. She will be a big help with the human risks and what personnel security measures we can implement without violating employment contracts or some HR rule."

"Again, sounds good."

"So we are done?"

"Almost. What about QA?"

Margaret frowned, "Why would we need quality assurance?"

"Well, remember that HIPAA is just about as much about data integrity as confidentiality: that is, that the data is available and that it is accurate. Remember at the Cross Country seminar where we met when I said that HIPAA is just as much concerned with data integrity as with confidentiality? So the QA expert probably has a clue about how accurate and available health information leads to quality health care or, put another way, avoids bad patient outcomes that may result in malpractice claims."

This time, Margaret laughed, "Ok, I give, O HIPAA guru. The QA person works for the risk manager, but we can add her to the committee. In my limited time here, she seems both knowledgeable and reasonable. Unless our checking with the worker bees brings up something indicating that she would not be helpful, she's in. Now, in your seminar, you talked about having a technical rep from the vendor on the team. Do we need one?"

"No, the Director of IT can handle the technical security risks. So with these changes, we are set. But let's recap to make sure that we've got this figured out."

So they went down the list again and found it good enough to stick with. Margaret agreed to get the modified list to the hospital administrator for approval. They would have the team together when the gap analysis was done and it was time to move on to the risk analysis.

"So let's go over the gap analysis," John said. "See whether you agree with each conclusion. You have a formal security program and policy, but it is not specific to health information, correct?"

Margaret nodded, "Yes, it's more take the patient out in a wheelchair on discharge and have a guard go through the parking lot every half hour than anything about health information, although I never really understood the take the patient out in a wheelchair business. Aren't they cured at that point, at least most of the time?"

"That's to prevent slip and fall liability. So the first gap that we have is no health information security policy. I'll have a draft from one of my templates for the next meeting of the HIPAA Steering Committee."

"Shouldn't we wait until we have completed the risk analysis before we draft it?"

"Some might do it that way, but I like to at least get a draft done first. It sets the strategic direction for the risk analysis. And we've got the key positions appointed. You're the Privacy Officer, and James McManus is the Security Officer, and the patient ombudsman is the complaint official."

"Why do we have to have a Security Officer at this point? We don't have the final Security Rule yet, and once we get it, we will have time to appoint a Security Officer then."

"You are correct, but the Privacy Rule requires us to have safeguards in place for all health information even though it doesn't spell out any safeguards the way that the Security Rule does for electronic data. But remember I said at the seminar that we would use the principles of the Security Rule as the best guidance we have for protecting paper records and oral communications. And not only is having a Security Officer required by the Security Rule, but also it just makes sense to have one. And I'm willing to bet that the final Security Rule won't change much from the draft."

"Ok, again, I give," Margaret laughed, throwing up her hands in mock surrender. "As long as it isn't me. I'm nervous enough about being the Privacy Officer.

"As well you should be," John responded, "especially with such a flaky HIPAA consultant. I'll probably end up having to bail you out of HIPAA jail!"

7

Medical Staff Meeting Minutes
July 15, 2002
Conference Room

Opening Remarks—Dr. David Goldstein

Dr. Goldstein called the meeting to order at 5:30 P.M. Copies of the minutes of the last meeting and the agenda for this meeting were posted on the intranet and were available as hard copies for review. He thanked everyone present for coming.

Approval of the Minutes—Dr. Goldstein

Dr. Goldstein asked for a motion to approve the minutes of the previous meeting. Dr. Thomas Handy moved, and Dr. Abdul Tarique seconded. The attendees unanimously voted to approve the minutes as written. Copies will be available at the Chief of the Medical Staff's office for review.

Physician Recruiting—Dr. An Kwan Pak, Chair, Credentialing Committee

Efforts to recruit physicians have been moderately successful. Barriers to recruitment include all the restrictions on recruiting in the federal fraud and abuse laws. Dr. Pak is working with outside counsel to devise compensation packages that do not violate the Medicare fraud and other laws governing physician compensation. Outside counsel, Mr. Stanley Deutsch, gave a briefing on the Baptist Hospital Medicare fraud trial of the hospital administrator who got a four-and-a-half-year jail sentence for hiring two physicians in a case in which the government proved that a part of their compensation was an illegal kickback to induce referrals to the hospital in violation of the federal Anti-Kickback statute. He recounted that the scary thing about the conviction was that two well-qualified health lawyers had opined that the compensation package did not violate the anti-kickback rules. So how did the administrator have the requisite criminal intent to violate the law after he had been told that his compensation package was legal? This briefing engendered a heated discussion by members of the medical staff as to how they were supposed to practice medicine with all these incomprehensible rules.

Dr. Pak asked for a motion to approve the appointment of Dr. Chopra to the medical staff in the Urology Department with admitting and operating privileges as set forth in the unanimous recommendation of the Credentialing Committee. Dr. Handy again so moved, and Dr. Devon Benvenista seconded. The attendees unanimously voted to approve the appointment.

Budget Issues—Mr. Ken Mahan, Chief Financial Officer

Mr. Mahan reported that the hospital was on track with the budget even with added physician compensation and large increases in employee health insurance. The major concern going forward was with capacity issues. Insurance companies were getting stricter as to the length of a hospital stay that they would pay for. He suggested that the medical staff consider how to document the need for additional days before discharge so as to avoid losing the revenue by a premature discharge of a patient.

Miscellaneous—Dr. Benvenista

Dr. Benvenista complained about the so-called HIPAA consultant and the Acting Director of Health Information Management. He objected to their bothering his staff to provide them information as to whom the Podiatry Department shared health information with. He noted that his staff had enough to do to support him so that he could practice medicine without having to get involved with issues like HIPAA.

Mr. Mahan responded that HIPAA had tremendous criminal and civil liability for noncompliance and that his observation was that it was far better to have the HIM Director and the hospital's consultant get them compliant than to have the clinicians worry about it. He pointed out that Dr. Benvenista was being replaced by Dr. Frame on the HIPAA Steering Committee. This information seemed to mollify Dr. Benenvista, who continued to grumble, but agreed to put up with it if he didn't have to do anything. Mr. Mahan said he couldn't promise absolutely no involvement, but that Dr. Benvenista was off the HIPAA Steering Committee.

Dr. Frame suggested that the consultant should brief the medical staff on how HIPAA would impact their practices. Mr. Mahan agreed to set up such a session. Some physicians objected to wasting their time at such a session until Mr. Mahan said that he was convinced that he could get continuing medical education credit for the session and that he would provide a free lunch buffet.

Following these concessions, the medical staff agreed to the training.

The meeting was adjourned at 7:15 P.M.

/s/

Dr. David Goldstein
Chief of Staff

8

MEMO TO: Margaret Nicks
FROM: John Thomas, EMR Legal, Inc.
DATE: July 31, 2002
RE: Gap Analysis Report

  Enclosed please find the Gap Analysis Report that I completed for your hospital this month (with your excellent help!). Please get with Mr. Mahan and any others (such as members of the HIPAA Steering Committee) and let me know when you want to schedule a telephone conference to go over the report and answer any questions.

Gap Analysis Report
Kansas City Memorial Hospital
By John P. Thomas, EMR Legal, Inc.

1. Neither your malpractice insurance policy nor your general liability insurance policy nor your errors and omissions insurance policy for your high-level officers clearly covers a lawsuit based on a HIPAA violation. Although a breach of confidentiality lawsuit because of a violation of the Privacy Rule is arguably covered by your malpractice policy as being based on negligence, you should get an opinion from your malpractice carrier as to whether such a case is covered by the policy and, if not, obtain such coverage from your carrier.

2. Your Sanction Policy is not specific enough to violations involving health information to qualify as the sanction policy required by both the Security Rule and the Privacy Rule. The HIPAA sanction policy is a statement of progressive discipline, such as verbal warning, written reprimand, suspension of access privileges, suspension from employment, termination of employment, and, in an appropriate case, referral to law enforcement or to professional licensure and disciplinary authorities. You need to amend the hospital's existing sanction policy to be more specific as to health information breaches or adopt a separate policy for health information security breaches. I have enclosed such a sample policy for your review.

3. The most important requirement that you have not accomplished is to perform a written risk analysis. Not only is such an analysis a required implementation specification under the Security Rule, but also it is how you know whether all of your security measures are compliant or not. If you implement a security measure without a formal written risk analysis, you are just guessing. And guessing will not impress the Office of Civil Rights if they are investigating a breach based on an inadequate risk analysis. And with the Security Rule's documentation requirement, if you don't have a written risk analysis, you haven't done one. I can lead the HIPAA Steering Committee through a risk analysis or provide you tools to do it yourself.

4. Your Physical Security Plan does not satisfy the Security Rule's requirement for such a plan, which should be called a Health Information Physical Security Plan. Your plan, which quite properly requires staff to take patients out in a wheelchair upon discharge to prevent slip and fall liability is not specific to health information, such as who locks the door to the IT Department. The Health Information Security Plan is

important to your security compliance because it sets the strategic direction for your security measures. I enclose such a draft plan for your consideration. You should not, however, finalize any plans, procedures, or policies until you have completed your risk analysis so that you will know whether the document is sufficient.

5. Your Clearance Procedure likely satisfies the HIPAA requirements if you document it better. Remember that we are talking about clearance to access individually identifiable health information or protected health information ("PHI"), which is not necessarily synonymous with employment screening. Although I agree that what the Credentialing Committee of the Medical Staff does to screen a physician before giving him or her admitting or operating privileges is more than sufficient to give the physician chart access, you need to specify in your Clearance Procedure that the credentialing process is also the HIPAA policy on clearance to give access. Parenthetically, wouldn't it be fairly stupid to have a separate clearance procedure for access to health information? Do you want to tell a doctor that he is cleared to operate, but not to see the chart?

6. You need to do a risk analysis of whether the screening that you do for other members of the workforce before engaging them is sufficient to give them access. It usually will be, but you need to have written documentation that you have determined that it was sufficient. For example, is the screening that you do before hiring a nurse sufficient to give her access? It probably is, unless you terminated two nurses in the past year for using patient information to commit identity theft. If that were the case, then your employment clearance procedure was probably insufficient to give them access. I enclose a sample clearance procedure for your consideration.

7.   You do not have a Report/Response Procedure for breaches of health information. The Report Procedure should specify what breaches must be reported, to whom, and whether any particular form, format, or contents of the report are necessary. The Response Procedure specifies what happens when the responsible official receives the report, such as who investigates, who gets the report of investigation, who takes remedial action, and who takes disciplinary action, if appropriate. I enclose a sample Report/Response Procedure for your consideration.

Margaret read through the entire Gap Analysis Report. This report is golden, she thought—the specific guidance as to what she had to do to get the hospital compliant and, more importantly, the ammunition that she needed to get approval to hire John to take the hospital through the risk analysis and the adoption of the security measures necessary to achieve compliance. And she thought, somewhat sheepishly, the information that she needed to get to work with him some more.

9

P.F. Chang's China Bistro
The Country Club Plaza
Kansas City, Missouri

Margaret waited patiently under the large sculpture of a horse
outside the P.F Chang's restaurant on the east end of the Plaza for
Pam to arrive. They were to meet for lunch. The horse was
supposed to be a replica of some horse sculpture buried in some
tomb or the other by some Ming or other dynasty emperor who
was buried with effigies of his soldiers and their steeds in terra
cotta or some other substance that Margaret could barely
remember from high school history classes and had little interest in
other than that she thought the horse looked neat. And she loved
Chinese food.

Pam was a little late, but Margaret didn't mind. She loved
people watching on the Plaza. She had never paid much attention
to fashion, but now that she was "management" as the Acting HIM
Director, she thought that she needed to upgrade her look, and
watching the well-dressed women shopping on the Plaza gave her
some good ideas as to what was both fashionable and professional
looking. And what wasn't.

Look at that woman, she thought. I love her pants suit. But her
shoes don't match her Coach purse, which has too many different
colors and fabrics—as if she has to show off that she's got enough
money to afford a Coach purse rather than wear an understated one
that would match her shoes and suit, like a Dooney and Bourke

bag. And she's got too much gaudy jewelry, as if she has to show her money off that way, too.

Margaret's fashion reverie came to a halt when she heard Pam call out, "Here I am. Sorry I'm late."

As they hugged, Margaret responded, "No problem. They have lots of empty tables."

As they settled in with their menus, Margaret thought how lucky she was to have Pam for a friend. Pam could have been offended that Margaret had been made acting director over her. Yes, Margaret had the RHIT credential, but Pam had worked there for three years. But Pam had been nothing but supportive—cluing Margaret in as to the strengths and weaknesses of the other HIM Department employees and as to what she had to watch out for from the medical and administrative department directors. And she seemed endlessly willing to listen to Margaret talk about the hassles of trying to avoid her domineering mother when she was working so close to her childhood home, where her mother still lived. Maybe because Pam's family was half a world away and her only contact with them was infrequent international phone calls—infrequent because of the cost—she seemed to view Margaret as a substitute sister, which Margaret didn't mind at all. At least, it made Pam willing to listen to Margaret bitch about her mother.

Margaret decided to splurge. "Let's have some pan-fried dumplings! I know they have a zillion calories, but I've survived two months as the Acting Director—with your help."

"Sounds good to me." As an Asian, Pam could deal with almost any Asian meal. Well, maybe not thousand year eggs or kimchee—the spicy Korean fermented cabbage. But almost anything else.

So they ordered dumplings to share. And Pam ordered Kung Pao chicken because she loved spicy Hunan style food. Margaret's food wasn't quite so spicy because she had grown up with her mother thinking that black pepper was too spicy. But she was slowly learning to like some spice and found that she liked Mongolian beef with its slightly spicy Hoisin sauce and green onions.

"So what's going on with your HIPAA compliance effort?" Pam opened the conversation.

"Well, with John doing a great job prying the necessary information out of the departments, we got a great gap analysis done. And we have a telephone conference scheduled next week with the HIPAA Steering Committee to determine how to proceed. But Mr. Mahan has already said that he would support hiring John to do a risk analysis and take us the rest of the way into compliance."

"That's great. It must really take the pressure off of you to have a real expert consultant."

"Yeah, it does. It's hard enough to function as the acting director without having to get the hospital HIPAA compliant, too."

Pam smiled—somewhat snidely, Margaret thought—and said, "And I'm sure you don't want to keep working with John."

Margaret's response was somewhat weakened by her blush. "Come on, Pam, he's kind of cool, but the last thing that I'm interested in is a relationship, particularly with a consultant in a case in which, if I screw up at all—I didn't mean that (blushing more furiously)—if I mess up, the department directors who are hostile to HIPAA compliance will use that relationship as a conflict of interest to derail my compliance efforts."

"Ok, whatever," Pam said, clearly not buying it.

Margaret protested too much. "He's really neat, Pam, but my first and really only priority is to do a good job as acting director. I'm not going to mess that up by coming on to our HIPAA consultant."

Pam was not convinced, but didn't want to offend her new friend and boss. So she changed the subject. Pam shared the hospital gossip. How Doctor Graham was having a torrid affair with the head nurse on the oncology ward when his wife was a patient there, suffering from breast cancer. How a patient services representative was rumored to have accessed the chart of Larry Holmes, the Kansas City Chiefs pro football halfback, to see whether he would play the next game so she would know whom to bet on.

Margaret was horrified by the latter information. Even though the Privacy Rule compliance date was still months off, so it wasn't a Privacy Rule violation yet, it was still a huge breach of confidentiality, she thought. I've got to report this. "Why didn't you tell me about this before, Pam? This incident is a serious breach."

"Sorry. I didn't think it was a big deal. This stuff goes on all the time."

Margaret digested this tidbit while picking at her Mongolian beef. She was starting to realize that implementing security measures and HIPAA documentation, such as Notice of Privacy Practices, authorization forms, and policies, might be the easy part of HIPAA compliance. The real problem was going to be in changing the culture so that everyone understood that they could no longer play fast and loose with patient information just because they were a heath care worker and the subject of the information was a mere patient. John had warned her about this situation several times, but it hadn't really sunk in until now. If Pam, who worked in the Health Information Management Department, didn't think that such improper access was a big deal, how could she convince management and the medical staff?

So Margaret changed the subject. She wanted to think about this quandary before quite possibly alienating her best friend at the hospital by coming on too strong about the cavalier attitude that Pam—as a health information management professional, for God's sake—had about such breaches of confidentiality.

So they talked about what movies that they wanted to see, whether they should go shopping over the weekend, and whether Pam should come over Friday night to watch TV and eat pizza. And then they went back to work.

But Margaret didn't sleep very well that night. How was she going to change the hospital's culture from one that didn't value patient confidentiality to one that did? She hadn't figured out the answer as she got up to go to work the next morning. So she emailed John:

From: Margaret Nicks [MNicks@KCMemHosp.org] Sent Fri 8/2/02
To: John Thomas [john@emrconsultants.com]
CC:
Subject: HIPAA Consulting
Attachment:

I just learned about some breaches of patient confidentiality that no one at the hospital seems to take seriously. I'm afraid that, even if we do a great job of risk analysis and of implementing security measures, without having a culture of confidentiality, our work will go for naught. Help! Margaret.

CONFIDENTIALITY NOTICE: This message, including any attachments, contains information from Kansas City Memorial Hospital that is confidential and privileged. The information is intended solely for the use of the addressee(s). If you are not an addressee, your disclosure, copying, distribution, or use of the contents of this message is prohibited. If this message has been sent to you in error, please notify the sender by return email and then delete this entire message. Thank you for your cooperation.

An hour later, she had an answer:

From: John Thomas [john@emrconsultants.com] Sent Fri 8/2/02
To: MNicks@KCMemHosp.org
CC:
Subject: HIPAA Consulting
Attachment:

Not to worry. If you remember, I warned you of this attitude. I'll just scare the snot of the powers that be at the hospital and instill in them a culture of confidentiality. In other words, if you breach confidentiality, you are going straight to HIPAA jail! John

CONFIDENTIALITY NOTICE: This message, including any attachments, contains information from EMR Legal that is confidential and privileged. The information is intended solely for the use of the addressee(s). If you are not an addressee, your disclosure, copying, distribution, or use of the contents of this message is prohibited. If this message has been sent to you in error, please notify the sender by return email and then delete this entire message. Thank you for your cooperation.

After this reply, Margaret slept fine the next night—except for waking up feeling guilty for having had a romantic dream about going on a vacation to Hawaii with John after John had made the hospital HIPAA compliant and the compliance date had passed.

10

Doctors' Lounge, Kansas City Memorial Hospital

John walked up to the podium to begin the medical staff's HIPAA briefing. "Good morning, doctors. As some of you know, I'm John Thomas, the hospital's HIPAA consultant. Let's get it out of the way now. I'm a lawyer, so go ahead and boo me."

The vast majority of the doctors hissed or booed. One made the sign of the cross and hissed as if John were a demon who had to be exorcised. Doctors tend not to like lawyers, viewing them about as favorably as IRS auditors. Plaintiff malpractice attorneys sued them, resulting in a lot of hassle even if the defendant doctor successfully defended the case. Their malpractice premiums went up, and they had to spend hours, if not days, in depositions and other preparation. Even the defense malpractice lawyers were not loved because they seldom made the case magically go away before the doctors had to be deposed. And the hospital's counsel always seemed to come up with some new compliance issue to make them take time away from the practice of medicine (or the golf course). No, lawyers were almost universally loathed by the medical staff. So John wanted to try to lessen their hostility right up front so that some chance would exist that they would listen to him.

"Thank you for that warm welcome." This comment elicited some laughter. "The good news is that the hospital has gotten approval for this HIPAA briefing to count towards your continuing medical education requirements. And after we have finished, the hospital will provide a free lunch."

Now the doctors were, if not happy about having to listen to a lawyer talk about the dreaded HIPAA, at least not openly hostile.

Margaret, who was sitting in the back so that she would know what John told the medical staff, smiled. *He told me that he was going to win them over, and he is,* she thought.

So John started his PowerPoint presentation. He didn't simply reprise his Cross Country seminar. He had only an hour as opposed to the whole day of his commercial seminars. And he wanted to make it specific to his target audience. So rather than scaring the snot out of his audience right off the bat, he tried to reduce their anti-HIPAA hysteria by showing them that they could be HIPAA compliant without its adversely affecting their practice of medicine.

"I'm sure that all of you have heard HIPAA horror stories, such as you can't call out a patient's name in the waiting room, you can't place a chart in the box outside the doctor's office, and you have to get a signed consent before calling a specialist to get his or her input on a case."

One elderly doctor, whose name tag identified him as Doctor Silverman, angrily blurted out, "Yes, and I'm so sick of all these governmental regulations impeding my ability to care for my patients."

Shades of Doctor Benvenista, Margaret thought.

"Well, I can't help you with other government overregulation," John answered, "such as the complexities of coding to avoid Medicare fraud or whether you can accept lunch from a drug rep without violating the anti-kickback laws." John was hoping to get them at least a little on his side by letting them know that he understood the other compliance issues that drove them crazy. After all, in Kansas City, they were well aware of the Baptist Hospital Medicare fraud trial in which several doctors and the CEO had received prison terms for illegal kickbacks—consulting salaries to the doctors for running the hospital's geriatric clinic— salaries that the jury found were more than fair compensation for services rendered and, thus, in part were an illegal kickback to induce the doctors to refer their nursing home residents to the hospital for acute care. One of the doctors had even driven his car into a concrete abutment at high speed the day before he was to report to federal prison. Sounded like suicide to them. No, Kansas City doctors knew about Medicare fraud and how easy it was to screw up the almost incomprehensive billing or anti-kickback rules.

John continued, "But I can help you with HIPAA. None of those rumors is necessarily true. Let me pick on you, Doctor Silverman. Do you have any celebrity patients? Members of the Kansas City Chiefs, for example, where it is particularly sensitive if they have a heel spur that may prevent them from playing?"

"No."

"So what is the risk, if any, of calling patients by name in the waiting room? Probably none unless, again, they are celebrities who don't want the others in the waiting room to know that they are, say, celebrities or mental health or substance abuse clients.

"And what have they been talking about in the waiting room? The deforestation of the Brazilian rain forest? The red-shift of the galaxies as they recede from each other in intergalactic space? Or the difference between a quark or a pi-meson in subatomic theory? No, they've been talking about their health problems."

To laughter, John continued, "And isn't there a risk in not calling a patient by his or her full name? Misidentification? So one of your physician assistants performs the wrong procedure on the patient. Believe it or not, HIPAA does not require you to do anything clinically stupid.

"So notwithstanding what some clueless HIPAA consultants may have put out, HIPAA does not prohibit calling a patient by name in the waiting room. Now, you are going to use some common sense, and if Britney Spears is your patient, you are going to smuggle her into your office avoiding the waiting room. So you analyze whether a risk exists in your particular practice and, if so, what a reasonable, cost-effective method to handle it would be. Why not put a sign up at the reception desk, 'If you don't want us to call you by name, tell us?'"

"But I just had a complaint from a patient that I called her by name," a doctor in the back of the room announced. "She said it was a HIPAA violation!"

"Well, as I said, it wasn't a violation. Your answer would be, 'did you request alternate communications—that we not call you by name? If you had, we would have honored it. Do you want to make such a request now?' You know, HIPAA puts a large part of the burden of protecting patient information on the patient. The hospital provides each patient its notice of privacy practices. That notice tells the patient of his or her right to request restriction of how that patient's data is used, of his or her right to request correction, and of his or her right to alternate communications, among other rights. But the patient has to make the request. You or your staff members do not have to be psychic—this patient is the one in a hundred that might object to being called by name. I don't think that it is being psychic to realize that you need to smuggle Britney in—avoiding the waiting room.

"And the HIPAA Privacy Rule permits you to call another clinician and discuss a case without any signed consent or authorization. The Privacy Rule authorizes covered entities to share PHI without consent for purposes of treatment, payment, or health care operations. Health care operations are such things as quality assurance and peer review. Actually, a good argument exists that HIPAA lessens patient privacy because of this provision. You are no longer required to get patient consent before using or disclosing the patient's data for those purposes—known as TPO—treatment, payment, and health care operations, unless some other state or federal law requires a signed consent, such as 42 C.F.R. Part 2 does for substance abuse treatment information."

"Do you have an example of a HIPAA hassle involving this misconception?" a severe looking female physician asked.

"I have a real horror story. An ambulance brings a patient to the emergency room, unconscious, unresponsive, and unaccompanied by any family members. A card in his wallet reveals the identity of his family practice physician. The Emergency Department physician calls up the practice to find out what conditions he may have and what meds he's on. The practice manager refuses to provide the information without a signed consent from the patient. The ED physician asks to speak with the family practice physician. He sticks by his office manager and instructs the ED doc to get a court order. By this time, 15 wasted minutes have gone by, and the patient is deteriorating. So the ER Doc does the best that he can with limited information and fortunately manages to stabilize the patient until they are able to track down a family member and get substituted consent."

After the doctors had quieted down—gasps, groans, and even some amazed laughter—John continued, "Now, how D-U-M dumb is that? How much more critical need for treatment can you get than an unconscious, unresponsive patient in the Emergency Department?

"And think about this theory. HIPAA compliance can cut down on malpractice liability." This comment got the doctors' attention. He continued, "Most everyone thinks of HIPAA in terms of confidentiality. But it is just as concerned with data integrity—the data is there when you need it, and it is accurate. Think about how many malpractice cases involve inaccurate data. To the extent that we fix that situation with HIPAA, it will help you avoid malpractice liability."

After a few more examples of how HIPAA was not a barrier to the effective practice of medicine, Margaret concluded that John had effectively won over the vast majority of the doctors. But he apparently had not won over the hospital's lawyer.

"Yes," John said, pointing at the only member of the audience who wasn't wearing a white coat but was waving his hand as if he had the world's most crucial question. The questioner was a tall, gray-haired gentleman who was wearing what appeared to John's semitrained eye as an Armani suit.

"I'm Stanley Deutsch, the hospital's outside legal counsel, and I think this attempt of yours to scare the snot out of the doctors here is b.s.

"Simply stated, the HIPAA criminal provisions apply only to covered entities. And none of the members of the medical staff are covered entities. Yes, they are employees of covered entities, and yes, they could be covered entities if they were independent practitioners who billed electronically. But they aren't. They are employees of covered entities. So HIPAA doesn't apply to them personally, and they cannot commit a HIPAA crime."

Margaret, who was still sitting in the back of the room, blanched at this flagrant attack on her—well, the hospital's— HIPAA consultant. How was he going to instill a culture of confidentiality in light of this attack?

Asshole, John thought. Undoubtedly some Harvard Law School graduate that doesn't have the first clue about trying a real criminal case. But John was polite as he skewered the jerk. "That analysis is very sophisticated, counsel. But let me ask you a question. How many criminal cases have you tried—either as prosecutor or defense counsel?"

"Well, none, but I can read a statute."

"Well, Sir, I've tried hundreds of criminal cases. And if you can read a statute, you should read 18 United States Code Section 2, which punishes 'as a principal' anyone who 'willfully causes an act to be done which if directly performed by him or another would be an offense against the United States.' By this interpretation, an employee who commits what would be a HIPAA criminal act if committed by a covered entity is himself or herself criminally liable.

"And even without 18 U.S.C. § 2, an employee of a covered entity could be liable as a coconspirator, as an aider and abettor, or as an accessory after the fact. So I think that I'm quite properly, as you put it, scaring the snot out of the doctors if they play fast and loose with health information. And I haven't even gotten to the HIPAA civil and criminal penalties yet."

Margaret couldn't help smiling at Mr. Deutsch's apparent discomfort at this response by her consultant. And the doctors appeared not to mind Mr. Deutsch's being put in his place. "Well, I'm not convinced," Deutsch said, "but I'll read the statute that you cited."

John didn't want to totally alienate hospital counsel, so he attempted to mollify him. "I will tell you this much. If I represented an employee who was charged with a criminal HIPAA violation, I would certainly move to dismiss the charge if they hadn't specifically pled 18 U.S.C. § 2 for the reason that you stated."

Mr. Deutsch smiled, apparently feeling somewhat vindicated.

"And thank you, Mr. Deutsch, for the lead-in to my next topic—the HIPAA criminal and civil penalties."

Now that John had won over the majority of the physicians, he did scare the snot out of them. Not by threatening them directly, but by pointing out the effect on their practice of medicine if their support staff or the hospital itself suffered these penalties. "For example," he said, "if the Department of Health and Human Services fines the hospital $1.5 million for a HIPAA violation, what does that do to your attendance at medical conferences or your ability to add to your support staff?"

Margaret thought that John was smart not to threaten the doctors with going to HIPAA jail themselves but by talking about their staff facing such punishment, thereby only implying that the doctors faced it, too. Although he had even told them that he knew that they would never commit a criminal HIPAA violation (even though both of them knew that a doctor could do so), he made them aware that a big civil penalty would adversely affect their ability to get continuing medical education boondoggles, because without their support of the HIPAA compliance effort, their staffs could face those penalties. And having a member of their office staff convicted of a HIPAA crime would not reflect favorably on their practice. Margaret happily noted that many of the doctors were nodding in agreement as John made this point.

John concluded by detailing what the HIPAA Steering Committee was going to do in order to get the hospital compliant—without serious interference with the doctors' practices. Margaret could tell that the doctors liked this approach. But she blushed when he pointed her out and asked her to stand up as leading the compliance effort as the Chair of the HIPAA

Steering Committee, the Acting Director of Health Information Management, and the Privacy Officer. He continued, "So the next thing is to perform a risk analysis. We may need a little input from your staffs, but we will keep it as minimal as possible."

"What's a risk analysis for HIPAA purposes?" a Middle Eastern looking doctor asked.

"It is the process of identifying risks to health information, quantifying them—how likely are they to occur and how harmful will it be if they do occur—then selecting reasonable and appropriate security measures to guard against the risks by balancing the cost of the security measures against the cost of the harm that would result if the security measures were not implemented.

"And cost doesn't just mean money. It includes such things as training time, making the clinician or workforce inefficient, irritating patients, and the like. For example, automatic log-off after a predetermined period of time is more secure than a manual log-off or a password protected screen saver. But how stupid would an automatic log-off be for an electronic health record in the Emergency Department? Might not the Emergency Department physician have better things to do than to remember, 'Oh, I've got to touch a key every five minutes so that I don't have to log back on and call up the chart?' Isn't the real harm there the lack of immediate access to critical health information so that, for example, the ER doc knows what meds the patient is on so that he doesn't give a contraindicated drug? So in that case, the cost of automatic log-off would include possible adverse patient outcomes. No, the security measures that I will recommend will make practical and clinical sense, as well as financial sense."

Again, Margaret noted that the doctors seemed pleased with John's approach. A number of them nodded, and a few actually smiled.

John ended his talk, "That's it, doctors, unless there are more questions. I'll stick around while you eat in case any of you have a question that you didn't want to ask in front of everybody. Thanks for your attention and the warm initial reception!" The doctors laughed, and a few even applauded. As the caterers brought the food in, Margaret was pleased to see a number of doctors clustered around John in what appeared to be a friendly discussion. And several of the otherwise usually snotty doctors nodded at her as they walked past. One even said, "Good work! Keep it up! Looks like you hired the right consultant."

Margaret floated back to the HIM Department. John was right. He had won the doctors over, at least most of them. But as she walked into the department, she sobered up. They would have to watch Mr. Deutsch. He could be trouble.

11

Risk Analysis Meeting of the HIPAA Steering Committee
Conference Room A

Margaret came through the door and smiled at the eight others seated around the oval table in the spacious, well-appointed conference room. The medical staff and occasionally the governing board met here, and the hospital wasn't about to make them feel as if they were meeting in a second-class room. "Thanks for coming."

"It's not like we had any choice," Jimmy Frame pointed out, but good-naturedly. A few hours talking about risks to health information was certainly going to be less stressful than his duties in the Emergency Department. Jimmy was 5'10" tall, with dark hair, and what the nurses said were bedroom eyes. They were so blue that they were almost purple. Jimmy had cut quite a swath through the nurses. The word was that he was like Hawkeye Pierce on M.A.S.H., except that he seemed to always score whereas Hawkeye usually seemed to strike out. But Jimmy was one hell of a good Emergency Department physician, and he treated his support staff well.

Sitting next to Doctor Frame was Nurse Patty Ratchet, who might be stuck with that name, but she certainly didn't look like the character in *One Flew over the Cuckoo's Nest*. She was petite, blonde, and cuddly looking. Perhaps the only physical characteristic that she shared with the movie character was steely eyes that seemed to say, "I may look petite and demure, but don't mess with me or my patients."

Going around the table, Jerri Sinclair was next. Jerri was a tall, attractive woman with prematurely gray hair. She wore a no-nonsense suit with no jewelry except for small gold studs for earrings. Although she looked very no-nonsense and focused, she had a great sense of humor and was a welcome addition to almost any hospital committee or meeting.

Jerri's office mate, the hospital's Quality Assurance Officer, sat to Jerri's right. Mary Cady was an attractive, middle-aged blonde dressed in slacks and a blazer. She had a stack of paper charts in front of her that she was going through to assess the quality and appropriateness of care. Having just come from an Infection Control Committee meeting and with another meeting to review the hospital's stroke protocol with a committee of the medical staff following the risk analysis meeting, she took any time that she could find to accomplish her chart review.

Sherry Page, a former Marine Corps gunnery sergeant, ran patient accounts with an iron hand. She was medium height with short brown hair styled as if she still had to face Marine inspections. Almost no makeup and only a wedding ring for jewelry. She looked as if she could report for Marine duty in a minute. She was always friendly and polite, but you didn't want to cross her.

Even though John had somewhat won over Mr. McManus, the IT Director, he didn't look thrilled at being at the meeting. John had told Margaret that IT types typically were resistant to HIPAA on the theory, not without some justification, that HIPAA was going to cause them a lot of extra work. John knew that this scenario was unlikely, at least when he was the consultant, because he expected the risk analysis to confirm that they were handling the vast majority of the risks properly now. What hospital doesn't back up its electronic health records? But a lot of HIPAA consultants felt that they had to justify their consulting fees by making HIPAA way worse than it was and felt that they had to require a lot of changes to their clients' technical security measures. But not John. He believed that he would get more clients in the long run by making HIPAA as user-friendly as possible and by selecting cost-effective security measures that made medical, financial, and practical sense.

James looked like a stereotypical IT geek. He was sort of short and scrawny, with thick, black-framed glasses, wearing jeans with a non-color-coordinated shirt with all sorts of electronic devices hanging off his belt. Margaret knew what the cell phone in its holster was, but what were those other devices?

Jan Wray, the Human Resources Director, was to James's left. She was a tall woman, with long black hair framing her attractive face. She was always well dressed but not ostentatiously so.

Completing the clockwise rotation around the conference table was John. Margaret had expected him to sit at the head of the table, but got a warm fuzzy feeling that he was sitting to her right as if he were her right hand man. He's slick, she thought. He doesn't need to enhance his credibility by sitting at the head of the table, but knows that, as a newbie Acting Director, I need some help in that regard.

Margaret's nervousness at beginning the risk analysis process, which John had repeatedly stressed was the key to compliance, evaporated. John would get her through this ordeal.

"Ok, let's get started. Does anyone want to be the recorder?" When no one volunteered, she said, "Then, I'll do it. Our consultant, John, whom you've all met, will be facilitating the risk analysis, so I can play secretary. John has made it perfectly clear that, for HIPAA compliance, if it is not written, it's not. So we have to have a written risk analysis. Unless anyone has any preliminary questions of me, I'm going to turn the meeting over to John."

"Thank you, Margaret. And I'd also like to add my appreciation to that of our HIPAA Steering Committee Chair. Yes, as Doctor Frame pointed out, you may have had to be here, but you have all suppressed whatever irritation you have had at being stuck with this duty and participated whole-heartedly, and Margaret and I appreciate it.

"You will remember the training that we did on the risk analysis process. We have completed the first two parts—selecting the risk analysis team, us, and identifying the assets that we have to protect, including both the data and the components of the system that houses the data. Today, we are going to begin the process of finalizing the risk analysis except for the last step, testing the security measures and revising them as necessary because of changes in risks, technology, or your business operations. We obviously cannot do that last step until we have the initial security measures in place.

"What we are going to do today is to identify the risks, quantify them—how likely are they to occur and how harmful will they be if they do occur—and then select reasonable, cost-effective security measures by balancing the cost of the security measures against the cost of the harm that would occur if the security measure were not in place.

"Let's start with the first category on the inventory—paper charts. What are—"

"Wait a minute," Mr. McManus interrupted. "Why do we have to do a risk analysis of paper records? The Security Rule, which requires risk analysis, applies only to electronic PHI." As an IT puke, James was totally disinterested in any information that was not in electronic format and didn't want to waste time on such mundane things as paper charts.

"As I said in the risk analysis training, the Privacy Rule, which applies to all PHI regardless of form or format, requires appropriate safeguards for all PHI. You cannot select appropriate safeguards without conducting risk analysis. And isn't the harm of a lost paper chart about the same harm as a lost electronic one? So my risk analyses always include all PHI."

James grimaced before saying, "Ok, let's get on with it."

John continued, "Ok, I want you to turn off the left brain, which allegedly controls logical thinking, and turn on the right brain, which is the creative, intuitive part of the brain, and brainstorm risks to paper records. I don't want to hear any, 'That's stupid.' That kind of comment will chill other team members and keep them from tossing out potential risks and might make us miss one. After we have brainstormed all potential risks, we will turn the left brain back on and go back and evaluate them logically.

"So what are the risks to paper records? What do you think, Margaret? You're our medical records expert."

"Well, remembering your HIPAA training, availability, integrity, and breach of confidentiality."

"Good, let's take them one at a time. What are the risks of the paper medical record being unavailable?"

"That's easy," Jimmy Frame answered, "lack of information to make clinical decisions. And that could certainly result in poor patient outcomes and maybe even malpractice suits."

"Inability to bill? We don't have a record of the service," Sherry added. She's always thinking about reimbursement, several of the team members thought. Some of them even thought, thank God, she keeps the hospital afloat so that we don't have to think about reimbursement.

"Identity theft." Jerri, as a risk manager, was pretty good at knowing about risks.

"A lot of time spent trying to find them?" Margaret said. "Time that could be used more productively."

"All right. What about integrity?"

Doctor Frame stepped up. "The risks are pretty much the same—making clinical decisions on inaccurate information. Again could lead to a malpractice lawsuit."

"What about breach of confidentiality?

Terry spoke up, "We had to settle a small breach of confidentiality lawsuit a couple of years ago. Even though our insurance carrier defended it, we had to pay the deductible, which was six figures."

Sherry pointed out that bad publicity from such a breach could cause the loss of current or prospective patients.

"Anything else? John asked. "Ok, this part was fairly easy. Now let's quantify the risk. How likely is it to occur? How often does this happen? Margaret?"

"Well, I haven't been here all that long, but in the weeks that I've been here, we haven't lost a chart permanently. Usually, it gets signed out to some clinic and doesn't come back to the HIM Department. So we waste some time tracking it down."

"The wasting time aspect comes up later," John smiled as he said it, not wanting to embarrass Margaret.

"Ok. But I checked with people in the HIM Department, and they said that it has been years since they completely lost a paper chart."

"So the risk of permanent loss would appear to be low?"

"I think so," Margaret responded.

"Anyone disagree?" John looked around the table, and no one responded. "Apparently not." He smiled as he said this last part, remembering when he was a military judge and had to give the court members—military jurors—the opportunity to ask questions, a procedure that none of the lawyers liked because who knew what questions a member might ask. He always followed the question, "Are there any questions?" with an abrupt "Apparently not" about a second later, purposely not giving anyone a chance to inhale, much less think to ask a question. Once in a while, after he had said that string of words, a member would raise his or her hand and say, "Wait, I've got a question," but most of the time, the members didn't want to contradict the military judge up on the bench in his black robe.

John continued, "But would the risk of unavailability of the chart because it was temporarily misplaced or signed out but not timely returned be greater? Moderate probability or low probability?"

"I think moderate," Margaret answered. Again no one disagreed. Doctor Frame even supported Margaret by noting that once or twice a month the HIM Department couldn't immediately provide him the chart of a patient who had just been brought into the Emergency Department so that they could check what meds the patient was on to make sure that they wouldn't conflict with a drug commonly used for, say, stroke patients.

"What about the harm? Is the risk of a permanently lost or temporarily lost paper chart high or low? In other words, is the harm high or low?"

"I think it's high," Jimmy Frame pointed out. "As we talked about, it could result in a bad patient outcome and even a malpractice suit."

John looked at the risk manager and quality assurance officer. "Have we had those things occur here over the last five years? And if so, what harm, if any, resulted?"

Jerri looked at Mary. Mary looked at Jerri. Mary deferred to her boss. Jerri recounted the story of how a missing chart had resulted in a dialysis patient receiving a contraindicated blood thinner, which caused the patient to bleed so badly that the patient almost died. The patient brought a malpractice suit, which settled out of court in the high six figures, so the hospital was out the $100,000 deductible, and its malpractice premium probably went up. And the hospital lost a lot of time with the physicians and others being deposed. She also recounted two other cases in which the patient suffered a bad outcome that had not resulted in a lawsuit, but in which the hospital forgave the bill for the extra treatment necessary to fix the problem. They had not had an identity theft that they knew of and only the one minor breach of confidentiality lawsuit. But even with only the two lawsuits, everyone agreed that, although the probability of permanently losing a chart was low and of temporarily misplacing it was moderate, the risk was high. And they estimated that the cost was $40,000 a year, consisting of two $100,000 deductible payments spread over the past five years, plus another estimated $100,000 in fees for treating patients who suffered bad outcomes because of missing charts and time spent trying to track them down. John congratulated the team on determining the annual loss expectancy, the ALE, but cautioned that, if they had a really big malpractice event due to a missing chart, that ALE might even be low.

"So now that we have quantified the risk, we can start bouncing the costs of security measures against the ALE. Right brain on again! Let's brainstorm security measures."

"We could implement an electronic health record," Jimmy Frame volunteered. "Then the ED physician could call up the chart at the workstation, but the data would still reside the in the IT

Department or the HIM Department or wherever the server is located. And we would need an offsite backup, as well. Then, we could scan the paper charts in."

John didn't want to evaluate this idea yet. He wanted to brainstorm all of the solutions. So he asked for other ideas.

Jim McManus did not want all the work of implementing an EHR just yet—he knew that it was coming, but might be able to retire and not have to deal with it if the hospital would wait a few years. And he well remembered the hassle of implementing the HIPAA standard transactions and code sets. To him, a crosswalk was not where you crossed a street but rather the tedious chore of cross-walking—mapping the change from existing codes to the HIPAA codes so that they could continue to get reimbursed. He had had enough of HIPAA. So he suggested that they microfilm or microfiche the paper records.

Mary Cady suggested that they could develop a face sheet that would be kept separate from the paper chart that would have the diagnosis, treatment plan, medications, allergies, and the like on it so that the clinicians, who would obviously have to be involved in developing it, would have the critical data that they needed if the chart got lost.

Margaret, remembering a discussion in her health information class, suggested that they pretend to lose a record and then see how much of it they could reconstitute from patient account records, pharmacy records, shadow charts that the physicians were improperly keeping but that they would forgive if it let them reconstitute the chart, and the like.

Shadow charts were improper because if they varied from the official record, it could really harm the hospital's litigation position in a malpractice case.

Jerri mentioned a new product that had been on display in a booth at a risk management seminar that she had attended. It looked like a microwave. You put your paper chart inside and hit a button. Then, it zapped each page of the record with an invisible electronic microdot. Then, you put sensors on all the doors and all the staff's badges.

She went on, "So just think. If a chart gets signed out to Doctor Jimmy in the Emergency Department and doesn't come back to the HIM Department, you look at the computer, call him up and, when he says that he doesn't have it, say—reading off his badge— patient Thomas's chart is 12 inches away from you, and you've removed the latest lab report. How much fun would that be!"

Everyone laughed except Doctor Frame.

"Ok, anything else?" John knew that part of successful facilitation was to keep things moving, especially if they seemed about to disintegrate into frivolity. Again, "Apparently not.

"Now, we have to quantify the costs of the security measures. We probably cannot finish that process at this meeting. I know of a hospital about your size that just spent three quarters of a million dollars implementing an electronic health record but maybe we need some more data.

"Margaret, why don't you get with Mr. McManus and Sherry as the IT and financial types and price EHRs and microfilm/fiche. Mary, you suggested the separate face sheet, so why don't you and Doctor Frame see what it would take to develop one and any associated costs. Margaret, are you writing these tasks down?"

When she nodded, he continued, "Jerri, can you get us some information on that machine that you talked about? And Margaret, Doctor Frame, and I will see whether we can reconstitute a lost chart from patient accounts and so forth.

"Let's turn to lost electronic data. You don't have an EHR yet, so looking at our inventory, we are talking about our electronic billing data, physicians' dictations transmitted to our transcription service, and any data that clinicians or others have on laptops or other devices. Right?"

"The real problem is the laptops," Margaret said. "The billing information is sent encrypted, as are the dictations. Both use 128-bit encryption. And I know that we still have to do a risk analysis of those transmissions to confirm that this encryption is reasonable and appropriate, but the laptops are the problem."

"Right," John smiled at Margaret for setting up the discussion so well. "What is the probability of loss or theft of the approximately 100 laptops identified in the survey?"

Only Jerri answered, "I don't know for sure, but it has to be high. With 100 laptops floating in and out of the hospital, the risk of loss or theft has to be high."

"Ok, let's see whether we can substantiate that theory, which is what I'd call a 'gut feeling.' You don't want to use 'gut feeling' as your support for your conclusion in litigation or an audit by DHHS. My sources tell me that those audits will come from the Office of the Inspector General, OIG, of DHHS, the same friendly folks who audit for Medicare fraud. If I remember correctly, the hospital purchased the laptops five years ago. What I need someone to do is check with purchasing and find out how many replacements were purchased in which the reason on the purchase order is not 'crashed hard drive' but rather is 'lost or stolen.'"

"I work for the CFO," Sherry said. "I can do that."

"Also, Jerri can you report at the next meeting whether any litigation, investigation, or audit has occurred as a result of a missing laptop and what it cost the hospital?"

"Yes, that's easy."

After going through all of the other categories on the inventory, John concluded the meeting. They were able to quantify some of the risks on the spot. Others required more research. John verified that everyone understood the tasks that they had to perform before the next meeting. He concluded, "I don't know about you, but I think that we made good progress today. No, we didn't complete the risk analysis, but we completed a good hunk of it, and if everyone completes their tasks, we will be pretty close at the next session. I told you at the start that, except for the smallest, least sophisticated practices, which this size hospital is clearly not, we would run up against questions that we couldn't answer without further research. So don't be discouraged. We are making great progress. See you next week."

Margaret felt good about what had happened at the meeting. The team members did not seem pissed as they left, even though each of them had some tasks to perform. John, she thought, is good at stroking them so that they felt that they were doing well. Is that a required trait for a consultant? If so, he's good at it.

But she felt better when, after everyone else had left, he asked her, "Should we go to dinner?"

They had had lunch together in the hospital cafeteria a few times, but he had never asked her to join him in a meal outside the hospital. She didn't know whether this scenario counted as a date or not, but didn't waste any time accepting.

"Where do you want to go? It's on me. How about the Classic Cup?" John asked. He actually hated the Classic Cup, but his G2—intelligence—was that women loved it. John thought that it was too frou-frou, and the one time that he had gone there, he had had the worst hamburger of his life. It had blue cheese on the cheeseburger. The beef was great, everything was great, but the blue cheese ruined it. Even after scraping it off, he couldn't remove the taste. Ok, it may be wrong to condemn a restaurant based on its having put blue cheese on an otherwise great hamburger, but as a Scorpio, John never forgot. But he thought that Margaret would want to go there.

But Margaret intuitively knew that John didn't really want to go there, even though she really liked it. They had great salads and pasta. But she suggested, "No, let's go to Plaza III. They have great prime rib." She had quickly figured out that John was a carnivore. She was far from being a vegan—no meat, no milk, no eggs, no honey (bee spit), as one of her old college friends was. She was a chicken breast, salmon, shrimp type who could do without a steak for months. But she knew that John would enjoy Plaza III's beef more than anything served at the Classic Cup even though she had had a great steak there. And she could get a good salad.

"Great. Can I pick you up about seven?"

Again, Margaret wasted no time in agreeing and gave John her address. But she was conflicted about the short time before he would pick her up. She wouldn't really have time to change clothes and didn't know whether she had anything appropriate to change into anyway. And she wasn't sure that she should wear something softer than a business suit. She wasn't sure whether this dinner invitation was a date. And she was worried that, if he thought that she were coming on to him, it would ruin the consulting relationship.

"Good job today," John said. "See you at seven."

I'm so glad that I hired him, Margaret thought, as she gathered up her notes. I couldn't have done this alone. And dinner will be fun!

12

Margaret's apartment just off the Plaza

Margaret was almost asleep. After the very nice dinner with John at Plaza III, he had driven her home, gotten out of the car, and walked her to the door. For a moment, she thought that he was going to kiss her, but he just took both her hands in his and said, "Good job today, and I really enjoyed the dinner. I'll see you tomorrow."

"See you. Thanks for dinner. I enjoyed it, too."

Margaret unlocked the door to her one-bedroom apartment with its small living room, breakfast nook, kitchen, and bedroom, entered, and shut the door behind her. After setting her purse down and hanging up her coat, she carefully pulled back the curtain and looked out. John was still there, looking at her door. Just as she started to let the curtain fall back so that he wouldn't see her looking out, she saw him smile and then turn away and walk back to his car. She watched him drive off. Why had he stood there looking at her apartment? She couldn't read his mind, but it seemed as if he were reluctant to see her go.

So Margaret, while not sure that she regretted the lack of a good-night kiss, had a warm fuzzy feeling that she happily took to bed. As she undressed, she saw the message light on her phone flashing, but decided to ignore it. If the hospital needed her, they would call her on her cell. It was probably her mother—about the only one who called her on her apartment phone besides telemarketers. And the last thing that she wanted to do was talk to her mother. She just wanted to bask in the glow of a good day at work and a great dinner—whether it was a dinner date or not—and fall asleep thinking happy thoughts. Work was going well. She liked her staff. And even Mr. Mahan wasn't bad. After all, he'd let her hire John.

After putting on a plain Jane pink cotton flannel nightgown that her mother had gotten her last Christmas—complete with white eyelet edging—Margaret snuggled under the covers. She liked to fall asleep looking at the framed Edward Hopper reproductions on the wall. They always seemed so serene—the lighthouses and stately New England homes. But just as she was dozing off, the phone rang. The ring seemed even shriller than usual. It must be her mother.

"Margaret."

"Yes, Mother."

"Why didn't you return my call? You are obviously home."

"I just got home and thought you would be asleep. I didn't want to wake you." Ok. it was a lie, but a white lie.

"What are you doing out so late?"

Margaret considered another white lie, to tell her mother that she had to work late at the hospital. But she didn't trust her mother not to try to check her alibi out, so she told the truth. "I went to dinner with our HIPAA consultant."

"Until 10:30 at night? Who is this consultant?"

"He's a lawyer out of Chicago who is one of the national experts on complying with HIPAA. Remember I told you that, as the Acting Director of Health Information Management, I am responsible for getting the hospital compliant with the HIPAA security and privacy requirements."

"Yeah, yeah, but why did you have to go out with him? Is he married?"

Margaret wondered whether, if she told her mother that John was a retired Army officer, that tidbit would mollify her. More likely, it would just set her off along the lines of if he spent 20 years in the Army and retired, he must be too old for Margaret. But no. Nothing would mollify her mother except Margaret's abject surrender. But she tried to placate her mother anyway. "It wasn't a date, Mother. We had a long risk analysis meeting, and we just decided to get a bite to eat and talk about the next steps."

"Until 10:30 at night?"

"Yes, we had a lot to talk about."

"I'll just bet you did. But whatever. Why don't you invite him to dinner with your father and me?"

Margaret knew that this suggestion was nothing more than her mother's desire to check out this lawyer from Chicago, to find something wrong with him, and to give her ammunition to try to control Margaret's social life. But Margaret agreed, knowing that she had no intention of asking John to dinner at her mother's. They had a good working relationship, whether it ever ripened into something more or not, and she didn't want to blow it by exposing John to her domineering mother. She just knew that John wouldn't kiss her mother's butt enough to gain parental approval. And even though her father was also a veteran who liked servicemembers, he wasn't going to go against the real commander of their home.

As she crawled back under the covers, Margaret regretted having answered the phone and certainly regretted not having lied through her teeth, such as by saying that she was out with Pam or some other member of her (all female) staff. Now, her mother was going to tell her sisters that Margaret had something going with an older man, even though she didn't. And they would pester Margaret to death for details—details that they could report back to their mother. If Margaret didn't give them enough salacious details, they'd just make something up, anything to create a family feud. Her sisters reveled in getting each other in trouble with their mom. And they were much more concerned with being in her good graces than Margaret was, maybe because they were younger and had not escaped away to college for six years.

Much as she liked her job, Margaret wondered whether she should have taken a job on a coast—either coast. With Kansas City close to the center of the country, a coast was as far away as she could get from her mother. But what about Alaska or Hawaii?

Margaret finally dropped off, but it wasn't to pleasant dreams. She spent a restless night, tossing and turning, worrying about her mother's inability to stop trying to control her life.

13

Mr. Mahan's Office

Mr. Mahan welcomed the odd mix of hospital personnel that had been required to attend this late-afternoon meeting—a couple of doctors and nurses, support staff, and Margaret, the Acting Director of HIM. After raising his hands in what Margaret supposed was a welcoming gesture—apparently a hard thing to do for an accountant—he welcomed them to the meeting.

"As you know, the annual Hospital Hill Half Marathon is coming up this June. And we are again one of the corporate sponsors. Hospital Hill—we're a hospital on the route—so our involvement's a no-brainer. I'll take care of the sponsorship—funding, volunteers for the aid stations, medical personnel at the finish line for any problems, and so forth. But we also have to provide a team to run the half marathon. Margaret, your resume states that you were on your college's cross-country team and that you placed third in your conference cross-country meet. So you are the captain in charge of getting our team together, and although I don't necessarily expect the team to win, I do expect a decent showing. And the rest of you are here because you appear to be serious runners. So help Margaret out and sign up for the team! Anything to add, Margaret?"

Margaret wanted to sink into the sunset. She had enough problems trying to get the hospital HIPAA compliant without having to worry about being in charge of some loser hospital half-marathon team. And her relationship with the doctors was tenuous at best, without trying to coerce them into running in some, to use one of her father's military terms, doofus half-marathon. But she didn't think that she could let Mr. Mahan think that she wasn't a team player, so she simply responded, "Ok, let me get a handle on this thing, and I'll be in contact with all of you about how we can make this project a success."

Margaret was supposed to meet Pam to go shopping after work. So after she had checked back at the HIM Department to make sure that no crisis required her attention, she went to the front door of the hospital to meet Pam. Pam was already there.

"Come on, Margaret. Let's go spend some of that nice salary that they give you as the Acting Director!"

"I don't know. I'm kind of bummed out. My mother has been ragging on me, and now Mr. Mahan dumped the Hospital Hill Run on me."

As they walked down the circular walkway towards the street that would lead them to the Plaza, Margaret continued, "My mother has been ragging on me about my nonexistent relationship with John. Like I'm some kind of a dud for dating—which we are not—a man who may have been previously married. But it's none of her business. First, there is no relationship. Second, even if there were, I'm an adult and fully capable of handling relationships. Yes, maybe that goes against her need to control everyone—especially me. But I need some space to do what's right for me!"

Pam could not conceive of a mother being this controlling. Yes, Thai parents exerted a degree of control over whom their daughters married. But with rare exceptions, they didn't berate their daughters the way that Margaret's mother did. Pam would have never been allowed to study at KU—the University of Kansas—and stay to work in the states if her parents had been as controlling as Margaret's mother.

"I totally sympathize, but what else is bothering you?"

"Why, when I have to learn all the duties of being the Acting HIM Director and get the hospital HIPAA compliant, do I have to put together a running team, for God's sake—for the Hospital Hill Half Marathon? And train to run it on top of everything!"

"It's a compliment. Mahan is testing you to see whether you are management caliber. Can you handle an issue outside health information management? Can you work with the medical and support staffs in a non-HIM environment? Are you a team player? Did you lie on your resume? Things like that. If he's thinking of making you the real director, he needs to know how you'll hold up under pressure. Look—I'll help you. I ran track in Thailand. I'll be on your team and be your administrative assistant. With two foxes like us on the team, the young doctors will be frothing to run the half marathon with us—and train with us!"

"Sounds great, Pam. What would I do without you? So I suppose that, instead of shopping for spring and summer work outfits, we now have to go out to Garry Gribble's for new running shoes and sexy running shorts and tops and sweats."

"Not what I wanted to shop for this evening, but let's go!"

So they turned back up the hill and headed for the parking garage to get Pam's car and drive south of the Plaza. As they meandered down beautiful Ward Parkway and past the big fountain, they planned their strategy for Margaret's new assignment, taking dibs on which cute doctors they wanted to train with.

14

CEO's office, Kansas City Memorial Hospital

Stanley Deutsch stalked past the receptionist's desk without a word and opened the door to the CEO's office. Because they had attended Harvard together, Stanley didn't feel as if he had to knock even though Larry Albright was the head honcho of the hospital, responsible not only for the day-to-day running of the hospital but also, under the direction of the governing board, for setting strategic goals, recruiting physicians and other staff, budgeting with Ken Mahan's help, compliance with the myriad laws and regulations regulating hospitals, putting the arm on potential donors, and the like. But Stanley was slightly pissed at Larry, even though the six to seven figures of legal fees that Kansas City Memorial paid Stanley's firm ensured that Stanley's partner share was among the biggest at his firm. But Stu was pissed that Larry had not hired his firm to get the hospital HIPAA compliant. That task could have been an additional six figures of legal fees. And to have a so-called lawyer/consultant that had graduated from a bottom 20 percent law school get the job was just criminal. Stanley felt that the number one student at such a school was way beneath the bottom student at Harvard or any other prestigious school. And Stanley had hardly been at the bottom of his class at Harvard.

Nor had John's response to his question about who could be criminally liable for a HIPAA violation at the medical staff HIPAA meeting mollified him. He had acted satisfied at John's response, but it was only out of self-preservation. Only bottom fisher lawyers were expert in criminal law, so he could hardly be expected to take on someone who had obviously spent time in the pits of municipal, county, and state criminal court systems. Stanley figured that Thomas was probably more comfortable in the Cook County jail than in the Kansas City Bristol Seafood Grill. The last time that Stanley had taken a client there for dinner, George Stephanopoulos was sitting at the next table. Thomas probably didn't even know who George Stephanopoulos was, Stanley mused.

And Stanley certainly didn't want the medical staff of his biggest client to see some low-life lawyer get the best of him. So his irritation festered for a couple weeks until he got a copy of the risk analysis report from the committee and decided that he could use it to take over the HIPAA compliance project.

Larry's huge office was sumptuous—with mahogany wainscoting and crown molding and magnificently framed diplomas and pictures of Larry with various political and sports celebrities. After all, Larry had to be able to intimidate the doctors on the medical staff. But the diplomas and pictures didn't intimidate Stanley. The ones in his office way trumped Larry's.

"Good morning, Larry. I didn't have an appointment, but I thought that this issue was important enough to barge in."

"You know you are welcome anytime, Stan. What's the issue?"

Stanley bristled. He hated for anyone to call him Stan. Known as the standing Stan rule, the first piece of advice that anyone new to his law firm received was not to ever call him Stan. He liked money more than he hated being called Stan, however, so he grudgingly put up with it from clients, especially this client.

"I'm really concerned about this HIPAA risk analysis report and remediation proposal. I'm really concerned that this so-called HIPAA consultant, Thomas, doesn't really have a handle on it and that his approach will expose the hospital to tremendous liability."

"Ken Mahan recommended him highly, saying that HFMA had hired him to train their membership on HIPAA at ANI and had evaluated all the HIPAA products on the market and found his both the best and most cost-effective. And we checked his references—covered entities that he had consulted for. Finally, he's AV rated by Martindale-Hubbell. So what's the problem?"

Stanley could have cared less that John had spoken at the Healthcare Financial Management Association's Annual National Institute or that they had endorsed his products. Nor did his AV rating by Martindale-Hubbell impress Stanley. Yes, "A" meant pre-eminent in his field of law, and "V" meant highest ethics, but Stanley's firm was too prestigious to bother with rating services. In his view, only the small practices with the non-Harvard-Yale-Michigan-Chicago-Berkley graduates needed to bolster their credibility by such ratings. But he didn't articulate those objections. He didn't want to challenge Larry's decision to hire John. That tactic might piss him off. Rather, Stanley challenged what John was doing.

"Look, Larry, I'm sure you did due diligence in hiring him, and I'm not questioning that. I'm questioning the minimalist approach that he's taking to HIPAA compliance."

"How so?"

"Well, you know that I'm all for the hospital saving money in these days of government reimbursement delays and cutbacks and having to provide uncompensated emergency care to the uninsured under EMTALA. But his minimalist approach can cause the hospital tremendous criminal and civil liability if his security measures are not reasonable and appropriate. And I don't think that they are."

Larry was far from sure that Stanley was really concerned about saving the hospital money. His legal fees seemed big enough. But Larry was concerned about the hospital's finances, and Stanley was correct that cuts and delays in government reimbursement and the cost of uncompensated care under the Emergency Medical Treatment and Active Labor Act was a big problem for the hospital. And he certainly didn't want to be hit with a big HIPAA fine or other sanctions.

"So why aren't they sufficient?"

"Well, for one example, he is handling the risk of a patient hearing another patient's name in the waiting room by simply placing a sign at the reception desk saying, 'If you don't want us to call you by name, tell us, and we will make other arrangements.'"

"What's wrong with that?"

"Well, what if the patient is retarded or senile and/or misses the sign? And the patient complains to DHHS? The hospital could be fined and/or suffer bad publicity and loss of business if patients fear that the hospital is not protecting their privacy."

"So what should we do?"

"I'd suggest using beepers much like restaurants do when your table is ready. And for the intake clerks, I'd suggest white noise generators so that those waiting cannot overhear the intake questions and answers—you know, like the ones that the judges in the trial courts in Washington, DC, use for jury selection."

"That solution would certainly cost more than the signs."

"Yes, but if it saves a huge fine or bad publicity that loses the hospital business, it will be cost-effective."

"Is that the only example?"

"No, in the acute care clinic, the clinicians see the patients in cubicles with only six-foot high barriers on three sides. Other patients or family members could look over the barriers or overhear conversations about the patient's health and treatment. So we should wall off the cubicles with sound-proof walls."

"That solution seems pretty pricy."

"Maybe so, but again, it may be cost-effective when balanced against the harm that could result from a breach."

"So the upshot is that you will not find this risk analysis legally sufficient?"

"No."

Even though he had gone to school with Stanley and even though Stanley had taken him and his wife out to many great meals and events, such as dinner at the American Restaurant and skyboxes at the Chief's football games, Larry did not kid himself that this entertainment was just friendship. No, it was to ensure that Stanley's firm got the hospital's legal business. Larry took all this largesse with a grain of salt. But he was a consummate politician. You had to be to succeed as a hospital administrator. Thus, he didn't want to alienate Stanley. Who knew when he might need him? And even though Larry felt that they raped the hospital when they submitted their monthly bill (after all, does it take a partner and three associates 10 hours each to give an opinion on whether a physician compensation package violated the Anti-Kickback Act?), Stanley's firm did make significant contributions to the hospital's fundraising efforts. And Larry did enjoy the invitations to the skyboxes at the Chief's NFL games.

"Ok, I'll talk to Ken Mahan and the Chair of the HIPAA Steering Committee and evaluate your criticisms. Fair enough?"

Although this response was far less than what Stanley had wanted—he wanted John fired and his firm hired—he was also enough of a politician to know when he had gotten all that he could get at the time. One didn't make named partner at a national law firm without being a politician and without being able to placate clients even when you disagreed with them. "Ok, fair enough. Let me know what you decide."

"Will do. Don't be a stranger. I assume that you are coming to the fundraiser Friday night?"

"Wouldn't miss it. See you." There was nothing that Stanley wanted to do less Friday night than put on a tux and attend a formal dinner dance. But attending such boring functions was how one kept existing clients and met potential new clients. And his wife would like it. Maybe she would even stop ragging on him for a day or two for never taking her anywhere.

Larry waved at Stanley as he left. As soon as Stanley was out the door, Larry hit the button on his state-of-the-art phone and ordered his secretary to get Ken Mahan and the acting director of HIM—he couldn't remember her name—to his office immediately. He wanted to resolve this issue quickly. He had more important matters to attend to, such as who should be seated at his table at the fundraiser.

15

Acting Director of Health Information Management's Office
Kansas City Memorial Hospital

A hospital's G-2 (intelligence) system is as good as that in any military unit. Whether the hospital administrator's secretary eavesdropped on his conversation with Stanley Deutsch or whether she put two and two together when he ordered Ken Mahan and Margaret to his office, or whether some paranoid physician had bugged his office, it took only about five minutes before everyone in the hospital knew that outside counsel had trashed the HIPAA consultant. Maybe because Margaret was relatively new to the hospital, it took her ten minutes to get the word.

Pam appeared at the door of Margaret's office and blurted out, "The rumor is that Stanley met with Larry and tried to get John fired as the HIPAA consultant."

"So what did Mr. Albright do?" Even though Margaret knew that Mr. Albright encouraged management to call him "Larry," probably as a result of some b.s. civilian leadership course that had taught him to be informal with the little people, as a relative newbie, she was not comfortable doing so. And as much as she liked Pam, she didn't consider her to be management. But the thought of losing John as the HIPAA consultant drove those concerns out of her mind.

"The rumor is that Mr. Mahan and you have to persuade Larry that John knows what he's doing."

"Well, the politics of the matter aside, that task should be a no-brainer."

"Yes, but—no offense—as an idealistic wet behind the ears new college graduate, you have to realize that it is all about politics."

As if to prove Pam's point, Margaret's phone rang, and when she picked it up, the disembodied voice, who was probably Mr. Albright's secretary, ordered her to meet with Mr. Albright and Mr. Mahan in Albright's office in ten minutes. "I'll be there," Margaret responded. There was no answer other than the sound of a phone being disconnected.

"See?" Pam said, somehow cluing in to the other end of the call.

"Whatever. If it is purely political, there is nothing I can do about it. If Mr. Albright really cares about compliance issues, he will listen to reason. All I can do is lay it out on the line. But thanks for your input. I'll talk to you later." Margaret was actually a little irked at Pam's interjecting herself into this issue, but figured that she'd better not piss anyone off who might get embroiled in the matter. And Pam was, after all, her second-in-command and was the closest to being a friend on the staff even if she did call her wet behind the years. Maybe you needed a friend to tell you the hard truth. She vowed not to act like a wet-behind-the ears newbie.

Margaret gathered up her note pad and pen as if she were going directly to the meeting. But as soon as Pam left her office, she picked up the phone and called John, "John, I'm on the way to a meeting with the hospital administrator and Mr. Mahan. Apparently, outside counsel trashed your compliance effort, and we have to justify keeping you on board. I think Mr. Deutsch wants the HIPAA business for his firm."

John laughed, which Margaret found somewhat reassuring. "No big surprise. I tried to let Deutsch down easy when he tried to shoot me down in front of the doctors, but I knew that he was enough of an asshole that he might try something like this stunt. Mr. Mahan isn't about to fall over and play dead, hospital politics or not, and as the hospital financial guru, he has a lot of clout. He hired me, and he's not going to admit that he screwed up. You two just have to give Mr. Albright enough ammo to stand up to

Deutsch and sell the governing board if Deutsch tries to go over his head, which he won't. He doesn't want to lose the hospital's legal business. There are a lot of Kansas City firms that would love to take over from Deutsch's firm, and Deutsch knows it. Just hold back in the meeting. Let Mr. Mahan take the lead and only interject if Ken asks for your input or Mr. Albright asks you a question. That plan will work, and everything will be fine. And whatever happens, stay calm, cool, and collected. You said that your father was a retired Army officer. Did he ever tell you about lieutenant colonel pissing contests, excuse my French? You are not at their rank, so stay out of the argument. In this case, the pissing contest is between a CEO and a CFO. The contest is to see who can piss the farthest or in this case who has the most clout. It has very little to do with you or me."

Margaret let out a sigh of relief, "Ok. Thanks."

"And if an issue comes up that neither of you can handle, tell Mr. Albright to get me on the phone. I'll stay in my office until you call me after the meeting."

"Sounds good!"

"Ok. Hang in there, kid. If worse comes to worst, Mr. Albright fires me, I sue, and we no longer have a professional relationship, and I can take you out!"

"That really sounds good, although I suppose I should wish for getting the hospital HIPAA compliant before you are no longer our consultant."

"Yeah, you are probably right. Call me as soon as you know anything."

"Will do. And thanks again. Bye."

"Good bye."

Feeling somewhat more positive although somewhat conflicted about what John had meant about if he got fired they could go out, Margaret gathered up her notebook and pen again and, this time, walked out the door of her office. She walked out of the HIM Department and down the hall towards the executive officers feeling a lot more confident than she had before she called John.

When she arrived at Mr. Albright's office, Mr. Mahan was already waiting. The severe looking secretary—gray hair in a bun, no less—said, "Now that you're both here, you can go in," clearly implying that Margaret was dog meat for not having arrived earlier. Margaret followed Mr. Mahan in.

Mr. Albright greeted them effusively—as if he were going to promote them rather than question their judgment in hiring that dud, Thomas. After an exchange of pleasantries, he got to the point. "I had a somewhat disturbing meeting with Stan Deutsch today. He's concerned that our HIPAA consultant, this Thomas fellow, has a way too minimalist approach to compliance that will expose us to tremendous liability."

Ken didn't waste any time responding, "With all due respect to Mr. Deutsch, he's full of it. He just wants our HIPAA business and is pissed that some non-Harvard graduate got it instead of him. The federal government has hired Mr. Thomas to teach its covered entities HIPAA, not Deutsch's law firm, which should tell you something. He was the second speaker at HIPAA Road Map I in Boston, one of the first national HIPAA conventions, following Dr. Braithwaite, who wrote the Security Rule, and preceding the head of the Office of Civil Rights, which enforces the HIPAA Privacy Rule. The next year, at HIPAA Road Map II, he was the keynote speaker. Kind of tells you where he is in the HIPAA pecking order. My organization, HFMA, found Thomas's HIPAA products to be the best and most cost-effective on the market, and we financial types don't screw up that determination. The American Health Lawyers Association asked Thomas to write an article for its *Health Law Digest*. And where's Deutsch in the pecking order? Answer—nowhere. Yes, Mr. Thomas may have what one could call a minimalist approach to spending big bucks on HIPAA compliance. But most consultants try to justify their fees by making HIPAA way worse than it is. But Mr. Thomas realizes that HIPAA is just a 'reasonable and appropriate standard' for security. That's below best practices and way below best available security measures. He tries to justify his consulting fees by making HIPAA as cost-effective as possible and by seamlessly integrating it into a facility's practice of medicine rather than by making it a big barrier. So if you want to pay your bud, Deutsch, way more money than we are paying Mr. Thomas and you want to spend all sorts of money implementing unnecessary security measures, replace him with Deutsch. But don't expect me to endorse that decision."

A casual observer might not have expected the CFO to talk so sternly to the CEO. But Mahan was retirement eligible, and Albright had been darn near begging him not to retire. So Ken didn't really give a shit what Larry thought, and Ken was going to be honest. He did care passionately about the hospital and its financial condition, and Thomas was the best for HIPAA compliance.

"Do you have anything to add, Margaret?" Mr. Albright asked.

"No Sir, I think that Mr. Mahan has said it all."

"Ok, I think that I need to run this situation by the board. We have a meeting tonight. I'll let you know their decision tomorrow. Thanks for coming by."

After they were past the secretary and out in the hall, Margaret had to ask, "So what's going to happen?'

"Nothing. Albright just wanted ammunition to justify Thomas as our HIPAA consultant to the board so that he could tell Deutsch that he tried, but the board wanted to stay the course with Thomas. It's all politics. As CEO, Albright would be admitting to the board that he screwed up for following our recommendation to hire John, and he's not going to do that. This type of nonsense is why I'm ready to retire. With increasing governmental regulation, like HIPAA and incomprehensible Medicare reimbursement rules, with rapacious malpractice attorneys, and with hospital politics, I'm ready to kick back and just pull weeds and feed chickens on my small farm out of town."

Feeding chickens didn't sound all that exciting to Margaret, but she felt good that Mr. Mahan was so confident that she could keep John as her—the hospital's—HIPAA consultant. But she had a fleeting tremor of guilt when she rued losing the ability for that potential date that John had alluded to if he were no longer the HIPAA consultant.

All in all, however, Margaret felt really good about the situation—that is, until she went to work the next morning and found an email from Mr. Albright's secretary notifying her that she, Mr. Mahan, and John had been summoned to appear before the governing board to answer their questions about the HIPAA compliance effort in just one week. She emailed John to alert him and emailed Mr. Mahan to try to find out what this development meant. Ken responded that she shouldn't worry, that it was still just politics—the board covering themselves—and that they would agree to keep John on board. But she couldn't keep from worrying. Not only was she upset at how they were hassling John, how could she get the doctors and others on board with all the rumors going on about dumping her consultant? It was hard enough to get any cooperation as it was.

So she emailed Mr. Mahan back, "I thought that Mr. Albright was going to use the ammunition that you had given him to convince the board, and now it appears that we have to convince them. I don't mean to be disrespectful because you have always been supportive of me, but I'm worried that we have to go through this additional step."

"It's just more hospital politics. I thought that it might go away when Albright briefed the board, but they apparently want cover for their decision to keep John on board as the HIPAA consultant. I know that this CYA activity is hard for you to deal with as a relative newcomer who just wants to do the right thing. But you have to understand hospital politics to be able to do the right thing. A year from now, you will have this political posturing down and be able to recognize it for what it is. But for now, you just have to trust me. I'll talk to John, and we will nuke Deutsch and win over the governing board."

"Yes, Sir," Margaret emailed back. Now, she was less worried. As her military father had often said, "He's got your six." In other words, he was protecting her backside. But the board meeting would prove or disprove that theory.

16

Boardroom, Kansas City Memorial Hospital

If Margaret had thought that Conference Room A and Mr.
Albright's office were sumptuously appointed, she was blown
away by the Boardroom when she poked her head in to see where
the meeting would take place. She should have known, she
supposed, that they would take care of the governing board, who,
after all, represented the crème de la crème of Kansas City. She
had found the hospital's annual report and read the bios of the
board members so that she would have some idea about what to
expect at the meeting. When she complained to John, who had
flown in that morning for the 6:00 P.M. meeting, that the board
members were all such big shots so how could they possibly win
them over, she added, "And don't tell me it's all politics. I'm sick
of hearing it!" She smiled as she said that, however, to show John
that she wasn't mad at him.

"Ok, I won't say that it's all politics, even though it is," he
responded, obviously ignoring her admonition. "But I've won over
governing boards before—they just want documented CYA
protection. With Enron and other cases finding board member
liability, no board member in his or her right mind wants to make
an uninformed decision. So we have to do yet another dog-and-
pony show to give them a peg to hang their hats on."

"Well, despite your optimism, I'm still nervous. My best friend
on the staff, Pam, pointed out to me that I'm a newbie and don't
really understand hospital politics—and that's probably true. But I
know enough from listening to my father rail against bureaucracy

when he was an Army officer not to trust hospital bureaucrats. But at least, they are letting you give your executive briefing on HIPAA before they start raking you over the coals."

"Yeah, if I can win over the doctors, I ought to be able to win over these yo-yos."

Calling the board members "yo-yos" elicited a big smile from Margaret, and she managed to relax a little bit. It didn't seem as if John was at all cowed by the prestigious board members. But then another concern intruded. "But what about Ms. Niles? She is a partner at Mr. Deutsch's firm. Isn't she going to want to get rid of you so that they can get the HIPAA business?"

"Maybe, maybe not. Maybe she thinks that Deutsch is an asshole and doesn't want him to get a bigger new business generation bonus than she might otherwise get. Can't rule that out. Or maybe she doesn't want to look as if she has a conflict of interest as a board member and is afraid to vote against us because that would make her look biased. And we don't have to convince all of the board members, just a majority."

Before Margaret could fret any more, Mr. Albright led the board members into the waiting room outside the board room. He had had them brought to his office, where he could ply them with a libation, since they couldn't be seen to imbibe alcohol in the boardroom during a meeting. Mr. Mahan followed closely behind, looking not at all cowed by the pompous looking board members. Once the board members had settled themselves around the large mahogany conference table, with their nameplates displayed in front of their seats, and coffee, bottled water, and soft drinks set out in front of them, Mr. Albright motioned John, Ken, and Margaret in.

Right after they had entered, Stanley Deutsch showed up and followed them in. He smiled superciliously at them and said, "Nice to see you. No hard feelings?"

None of them answered. They stepped aside and let Mr. big-firm lawyer, Harvard grad, Stanley Deutsch precede them.

After they had found their seats, Margaret noted that John had already set up his PowerPoint presentation. So he went up and stood next to his computer and projector at the end of the table. Ken and Margaret sat behind him on the chairs set around the wall for those who were not in enough to sit around the table with the board members. Margaret looked at the board members. They did not, to put it mildly, look receptive.

But John winked at Margaret as he turned to the side to plug his computer into the power strip handily provided. Once it had powered up and he had called up the PowerPoint presentation, he nodded to Mr. Albright, who introduced him. "Members of the board, this is Mr. Thomas, the HIPAA consultant that Mr. Mahan hired to get us compliant."

"You asshole," Margaret thought, although she normally didn't use that kind of language. "You approved Mr. Mahan's recommendation to hire him."

But if this introduction had bothered John, he didn't show it. He merely thanked Mr. Albright for the introduction and for having hired him as the hospital's HIPAA consultant.

Slick, Margaret thought. He had thrown the ball back into Mr. Albright's court, letting them know that it wasn't Mr. Mahan's decision alone—that Albright had made the final decision. God, he's so good, she thought, then blushed furiously as she realized that she might be falling in love, or at least excessive like, with him. She hadn't previously admitted it even to herself, but under the pressure of trying to salvage the HIPAA compliance effort, her emotions were no longer constrained by the barriers between them—her mother's disapproval, his status as a consultant, and the difference between their ages and life experience. Fortunately, John started his presentation before Margaret could no longer restrain herself and do something stupid, like hug him on the pretext of wishing him good luck with his presentation.

And John just hammered the board, talking about management liability, including the board's liability, if the hospital was not HIPAA compliant. He recounted some disconcerting information that he had learned at a national HIPAA conference. The woman who had written the Privacy Rule—he called her a scary woman, which got a laugh out of the board members—had spoken at the conference and seemed to be frothing at the idea of indicting management if one of the workforce members committed a breach under principles of corporate criminal liability. She used Enron as her example. In other words, John stated, the board members and senior management could be liable for the criminal HIPAA violations of their subordinates if the hospital was not HIPAA compliant and if that noncompliance encouraged the perpetrator to commit the criminal HIPAA violation or failed to prevent it. John also recounted that he had talked to the Department of Justice Attorney that would be in charge of HIPAA prosecutions nationwide, who was also frothing at the thought of the chairman of the board or a hospital administrator doing the perp walk— being led away in handcuffs—for not being HIPAA compliant and for that noncompliance encouraging an employee to commit a HIPAA crime. John asked what message that scenario would send to the health care industry about the need to take HIPAA seriously.

The board members looked more than a little bit concerned at this information. But when John finished his executive briefing, that concern didn't prevent them from grilling him.

Ms. Niles fired up the grill: "Our outside counsel, who has been looking after our interests for more than a decade, is concerned that your 'minimalist' approach exposes the hospital to tremendous liability. What's your answer?"

"The first thing that you have to realize is that HIPAA actually has a fairly low standard, 'reasonable and appropriate.' That standard is lower than 'best practices,' and it's way lower than 'best available' security measures.

"But a lot of HIPAA consultants have made HIPAA way worse than it is to justify their big consulting fees." John looked directly at Stanley Deutsch as he continued, "And that's what we have here. You can fire me, you can hire a local Kansas City hot-shot law firm that doesn't know the difference between an RHIT, an RHIA, an ART, and an RRA, the difference between the chronological and the SOAP format for medical records, or when to put the defendant on the stand in a Medicare fraud trial and when to rest because the government hasn't proven its case and is hoping to prove it on cross-examination of the hospital administrator defendant. So instead of grilling me, why don't you ask Mr. Deutsch those questions and see whether he is qualified to be your HIPAA consultant?

"Now, I can waste your valuable time and detail all of the federal, state, and local governments that have hired me to get them compliant and who have purchased my HIPAA compliance products. And you should ask Mr. Deutsch how many HIPAA consultant cases his firm has done. But you know what, if it weren't for the hard work that Mr. Mahan and your brand-new Acting HIM Director, Margaret, here," pointing at Margaret, "have put in, I wouldn't have even showed up for this inquisition. Fire me. I've got more than enough HIPAA business without yours. And spend three times the consulting fees and ten times the cost of security measures for Mr. Deutsch to justify his fees and end up less compliant than if I took you there."

Although Margaret loved to hear this, she didn't think it was good politics—not that she knew anything about politics—to challenge the board like this. But what did she know as a newbie?

"So if there are no questions, I'm done," John concluded his rant.

Board member Marta Weagryn, a vice president of Cerner, who was in the business of selling electronic medical records, wasn't about to let John off the hook. "How do we know that you are right and the majority of consultants, who are saying things like you can't call out a patient's name in the waiting room without committing a HIPAA violation, are wrong?"

"Three ways. One, read the Security Rule and the Privacy Rule. They don't even mention calling out patient names in the waiting room or anywhere else. Two, remember that HIPAA puts some burden on the patients to object if they don't want their names called out. They can request restriction or alternate communications. You don't have to be psychic and intuit that they don't want to be called by name. Three, DHHS has not found any complaint about calling a patient by name in the waiting room to be valid. Ok, maybe I misspoke. There are four ways. DHHS and other federal agencies have hired me to train them on HIPAA compliance and have bought my products, not one of which says that you can't call a patient by name in the waiting room. So when the agency who wrote the regulations and other federal agencies use my materials, they must agree with my interpretation. Again, many so-called HIPAA experts made HIPAA way worse than it was to justify their consulting fees. But I don't operate that way. I try to justify my fees by saving my clients more money than I cost them. And by getting them compliant seamlessly—without changing how they practice medicine or conduct their business operations."

"Well, I've heard enough," Marta said. "I've got great confidence in Mr. Albright's and Mr. Mahan's ability to do what is right for the hospital and what I have heard about the Acting HIM Director has been very positive," nodding at Margaret. "So unless the rest of you want to go on some witch hunt or unless Mr. Deutsch has some compelling rebuttal to Mr. Thomas, I suggest that we excuse the non-board members, vote to keep Mr. Thomas as the HIPAA consultant, and get to the always great buffet that Mr. Albright will have waiting for us in his office. If you will excuse us? Any one so move?"

Margaret wondered whether they should leave without Ken's input and the chance to answer other board members' questions. But John had already unplugged his computer and projector and loaded them into his carrying case. Even as Stanley Deutsch, John, Ken, and Margaret were gathering up the items that they had brought with them to the meeting and were beginning to file out, the motion was moved and seconded.

Stanley looked as if he had been pole-axed. He hadn't expected John to attack him directly like that, and he certainly hadn't expected to be prevented from presenting his side of this issue. Damn that bitch Marta, he thought. How does she get away with ending the debate so quickly?

Once the non-board members had actually left the room, the vote passed with only one dissent—Stanley's partner, Ms. Niles.

After Stanley had beat a quick retreat down the hall in the opposite direction, John, Ken, and Margaret waited out in the hall for the elevator to arrive. They didn't know yet that the vote had passed, however, so Margaret asked John, "Did we do enough? Shouldn't we have had Ken speak in support of our effort?"

John replied, smiling, teasing her a little bit, "So you think that I didn't do enough?"

Margaret blushed and almost stammered, "N—No, I didn't mean that."

"No offense taken. If I have learned one thing as a lawyer, it's to recognize when you have won and shut up and sit down."

"How can you have known that you won when you came out so hostile to the board?"

"You've got to read your jury. And I decided to nullify Deutsch by confronting him rather than appearing weak by saying, 'He's got a good point, but . . . .' Trying to placate him didn't work at the session with the doctors. I gave him the opportunity to save face, and what did that gain us? No, it was time to play hardball."

"But isn't he going to be your mortal enemy forever now?"

"Yes, but he was going to be my mortal enemy anyway. But now he's going to have to question whether attacking his mortal enemy is going to result in his enemy savaging him again. And however it may have looked to you, I was toying with him. He may have learned to fight in a Harvard Law School classroom, but I learned on the ground in the jungles of Vietnam, in courts-martial around the world, in the bowels of the Cook County criminal justice system, in several federal district courts, and in four U.S. Courts of Appeals, to say nothing of years of Master An's tae kwon do classes. Let Deutsch bring it on. He hasn't a clue unless he has another partner and three associates backstopping him and probably not even then."

This sprezzatura was a side of John that Margaret hadn't yet experienced. Yes, she knew that he was what her military father would have called "hard core." But seeing it in action was something else. But she found it strangely attractive. Even though she was somewhat of a feminist, she found the Alpha male very compelling and appealing. She was pondering whether she should fall for this strong a man when Mr. Albright came out into the hall and announced that the board had voted to keep John as the hospital's HIPAA consultant. Margaret couldn't keep from clapping her hands. Ken looked pleased, but John simply said, "Thanks for your support," even though he hadn't really seen any support from Mr. Albright, and pressed the button for the elevator. When it arrived, he got on by himself, because Mr. Albright was asking Ken and Margaret about the next step in the compliance effort. The last thing John saw as the elevator door closed was Margaret's stricken face.

Margaret crumpled up the note that she had written and was about to pass to John, asking him to come over to her apartment for a drink to celebrate. If she had asked him in front of Mr. Mahan, they would have had to invite him, too. Why wasn't John waiting for her? Had she irritated him by questioning how he had handled the meeting? Or was Pam right when she said that he always flirts with women who, after all, are the vast majority of medical records types that buy his products and hire him and that Margaret was deluding herself in thinking that he had any real interest in her?

17

Health Information Management Department
Kansas City Memorial Hospital

Pam barged into Margaret's office unannounced and uninvited. Margaret looked up, prepared to be irritated, but when she saw that it was Pam, she relaxed and smiled. "Hi, Pam. What's up?" But her smile faded as she saw the pissed-off look on Pam's normally smiling Thai let's-avoid-confrontation face.

"It's you. You've been a real bitch ever since the board meeting last week, snapping at the staff, treating me like I'm not even there, and so forth. Should I go on?"

"No, you're right. I just didn't know that it showed. Thanks for so graciously pointing out my lack of control of my inner thoughts. I was so happy that the board had voted to keep John on, and I was going to invite him over to my apartment to celebrate, but he just vanished. And he hasn't called or emailed me since that evening. I can't figure out what I did. And I don't know what to do now."

"Oh, that explains it," Pam said as she shut the door and plopped down in the chair in front of Margaret's desk. "So your feelings are hurt that he didn't fall all over you. Any fool can tell that he's very attracted to you, but he's probably conflicted by the fact that he's an attorney, even if only a consultant, and you are the client. So take it as a compliment that he didn't just jump your bones, that he cared enough about you to pull back and evaluate the relationship. After all, what does it do to your position as Acting Director if Deutsch complains that the Chair of the HIPAA Steering Committee and the Privacy Officer is in a sexual relationship with the outside HIPAA consultant, a consultant that he would love to get some dirt on so he gets fired and Deutsch gets the HIPAA business?"

"That theory makes sense, but what do I do?"

"Nothing. You keep it professional. You just contact him and ask him to verify what you believe the next steps are to get into compliance by the compliance date. Don't hassle him about leaving after the meeting without saying good bye. If you hassle him about it, you will just come across as a weak, desperate woman, whether that's the case or not. It's time for you to play hard to get. And if he doesn't make the next move, it wasn't meant to be. And you are attractive enough and young enough and otherwise smart enough that you don't need to panic. In fact, if he does come back for more consulting, you ought to let him see you out with some other guy. Just listen to me, my friend, and I'll keep you straight."

"Ok, I can do that," Margaret responded. "And thanks. As what my career military father would call my second in command, you have the job of keeping me straight. If I turn into an absolute bitch, you have to square me away. Ok?"

"Deal. Let's go for a run after work today and do lunch tomorrow. Bye."

After had Pam left, Margaret composed the email to John detailing what she thought remained to be done by the compliance date. As she put the message together, she didn't know whether to be relieved or to be appalled at how little there was left to do. John might not even have to return to the hospital. He just had to approve the few remaining security measures that had not been fully implemented and review the policies that they had drafted. The Notice of Privacy Practices was ready to go. The authorization forms were ready. HIPAA training was 90 percent complete and would be finished in another two weeks except for new hires who would have to be trained when they came on board. The hospital had appointed her as Privacy Officer and the Director of Information Systems as the Security Officer. The hospital's Patient Advocate was the Complaint Official. John had suggested that she, as Privacy Officer, not also be the complaint official so that she could be above it all—impartially deciding whether a complaint was valid or not without having to personally deal with the complainant.

No, there wasn't much left to do. And Margaret hesitated before sending the email to John. But she decided to trust Pam's advice and decisively clicked on the send icon in her Microsoft Outlook. *I may never see John again,* she thought, *but at least they can't fire me for failing to get HIPAA compliant by the compliance date. And who knows, maybe the final Security Rule will have so many changes that we will have to rehire John to get compliant with security.*

John had made them implement the draft Security Rule because, although it applied only to electronic protected health information, the Privacy Rule applied to all PHI regardless of form or format and required appropriate safeguards for all PHI, whether electronic, paper, oral, or some other weird form or format. So he said that they had to protect their EPHI under the Privacy Rule even though the Security Rule was not in final yet. He was adamant that the final rule would not differ much from the draft rule, but that they might have to tweak some security measures. So, Margaret hoped, he would have to return to determine whether any changes in the Security Rule from draft to final required them to redo the risk analysis or modify their security measures. Her final thought, before sternly putting the absent-without-her-leave John out of her mind, was that she could always go to another Cross Country HIPAA seminar and see him. She shut her office door again, locking it this time, unzipped her running bag, and changed into her sweats and running shoes to go meet Pam for a training run. Margaret needed a long run indeed.

18

Health Information Management Department
Kansas City Memorial Hospital

Margaret was taking a rare moment of relaxation at her desk. A whole week to go until the Privacy Rule compliance date, and they were ready! All the documents were ready; all the policies were written, reviewed, and adopted; all the security measures were in place; and all the training was done. When she had briefed Mr. Mahan earlier in the day, he had given her a rare smile and commended her leadership in getting the hospital compliant.

She felt compelled to give John a lot of the credit, but Mr. Mahan turned it back on her by complimenting her on finding him and convincing the hospital to hire him. Anyway, Margaret was feeling pretty good about herself and about getting the hospital compliant. Pam, who had friends in other hospitals' health information management departments, had told Margaret that no other facility that she knew of was close to being compliant. Yes, they had their notices of privacy practices and their authorization forms, but they hadn't completed their risk analyses, finalized their policies, and implemented all their security measures.

So Margaret felt that she could relax for a few moments, sip a cup of tea, and bask in the glow of being compliant with the Privacy Rule with time to spare. Her pleasant reverie was interrupted, however, by the shrill ring of her phone. She didn't know how, but somehow she intuited that the call was not a congratulatory one. She was right. It was Doctor Hass, the Director of the Psych Ward. She had met Doctor Hass briefly, when she had gone around to all of the departments to introduce herself and offer her help if they had any problems with health information. She remembered Doctor Hass, a board-certified psychiatrist, as being quite pleasant but, according to Pam, not a doctor you wanted to get on the wrong side of.

"Ms. Nicks, this is Doctor Hass. Stay in your office. I'm coming down to see you."

"Yes, Sir." Margaret knew that Doctor Hass ran the hospital's Psych Ward with an iron fist. She felt like saying, "Yes, Sir, Doctor, Sir," as her military father would have prompted her to do, but wanting to maintain some dignity as a department director, even if not a clinical director, even if only an acting director, she refrained from groveling too much.

Doctor Hass showed up in less than four minutes, which was fast, considering the relatively slow elevators in the building. He barged into her office, slammed his fist down on her desk, making her tea slosh over the brim of her cup, and said, "Well, I'm not going to sugar-coat this. I'm really pissed. We had a psych patient escape from the ward last night. Once the staff had notified me, I immediately went to your department and asked for the patient's mother's address because I knew his most likely destination was to go home to mommy. If you remember, it was sleeting last night, and he was wearing only pajamas and a robe. I was concerned that he would die of hypothermia and wanted to alert law enforcement to watch the route that he was probably going to take on the way home so that they could police him up before he got into trouble in the cold. And the dud in your department, citing HIPAA, wouldn't tell me.

"So I called Mr. Deutsch, the hospital's legal counsel, and he agreed with your dud. Which is absolute b.s. So I ignored him.

"I finally got the address by coming down from the Psych Ward to your department, plowing past your employee, pulling the chart out over her protestations, and finding the mother's address. This whole thing really pissed me off because I've got better things to do than fight with medical records pukes and the hospital's outside counsel about when I, as the Department Director and the attending physician, can access my client's chart. And if I hadn't charged down there, he might have died of hypothermia, which would seem to cause the hospital greater liability—wrongful death—than the disclosure of what his mother's address was. And we are not even to the Privacy Rule compliance date for a few more days, for God's sake—so how is HIPAA an impediment to this disclosure?"

Margaret did not feel that this moment was the time to object to his calling her staff medical records pukes. Her retired military father always called the staff types—the personnel staff, the finance types, and the supply types pukes. Being a personnel puke was the kiss of death. She suspected that being a medical records puke was no better in Doctor Hass's estimation. She didn't know whether Doctor Hass had a military background that caused him to view any nonclinicians as pukes, like a medical records puke. So she responded in a manner that she hoped would defuse the situation, "You are absolutely right, Doctor Hass. HIPAA is not a barrier to this disclosure. My staff member should have given you the information immediately. Even if we were past the Privacy Rule compliance date, HIPAA would authorize this disclosure. First, HIPAA authorizes disclosures without patient consent for treatment, payment, and health care operations. Locating a missing patient so that the patient doesn't die of hypothermia is clearly treatment and probably also health care operations. Second, the Privacy Rule authorizes a disclosure without consent or authorization from the patient to prevent a serious and imminent threat to the health or safety of a named individual or the public. Death from hypothermia sounds like a serious and imminent threat to me. Third, the Privacy Rule authorizes disclosure without consent to law enforcement in order to locate a missing person. Sounds like all three of those grounds would have authorized the HIM Department worker to tell you the mother's address even if HIPAA had been in effect. And even if the disclosure were flaky and constituted a breach, which it wasn't, what's the harm? Disclosing the mother's address to law enforcement is not going to get anyone fired or result in bad publicity that leads to a lawsuit.

The workforce member should have followed the release of information policy but didn't. So as the Acting Director, I'll take the blame. I had trained the department's workforce and had implemented the disclosure policy, but that tactic obviously did not work in this situation. So I will retrain my staff and make certain that they follow the release of information policy so that this situation does not happen again. And if you run into a problem like this again, please call me immediately, whether it is after normal work hours for the support staff or not. My cell number is 816-523-3955. By the way, what happened to the patient?"

"Well, he was apparently not as mentally challenged as we had feared. He quickly realized that he was freezing his butt off, found a police car, and turned himself in to get back to where it was warm. But we can't rely on that happy ending every time. We've got to handle these situations right the first time. With an hour's delay, he might have died from hypothermia."

"Yes, Sir," Margaret responded, "I'll square away the person who put up the HIPAA barrier to your legitimate need for the information and retrain all my staff on how to make a proper disclosure. I really appreciate your coming to me with this complaint."

"Ok, Ms. Nicks, I'm impressed by your reaction to this incident and your willingness to accept responsibility and fix the problem. So I'm not going to report the issue to the hospital administrator or to the medical staff. But just see that you square this situation away."

"Yes, Sir. Thank you, Sir."

After Doctor Hass had stalked out, Margaret pulled up his bio on the hospital's website. Yes, he had been a combat surgeon for the Army in the first Gulf War. So he was prior military. That background explained his approach to this incident and his willingness to accept Margaret's act of taking responsibility and agreeing to fix it. Margaret's father had told her that, when it came to disciplining his troops, he always hoped for the response, "No excuse, Sir," rather than some b.s. excuse. The few times that the errant soldier had said that, he had said, "Fine. You've taken responsibility, so I'm not going to take any disciplinary action. Go back to your platoon. But don't screw up again, or I'm going to go nuclear on your ass."

So following that military leadership principle—don't offer some flaky, half-assed excuse—had saved Margaret from Doctor Hass's wrath, which might have gone up the chain-of-command and resulted in her termination, notwithstanding her success in getting the hospital compliant before the compliance date. But would falling on her sword—a military concept relating to taking the blame whether one was at fault or not—have saved her if Mr. Deutsch had complained about this issue to the hospital administrator? She didn't think so.

But even with her relief that the matter was settled to Doctor Hass's satisfaction, Margaret's warm and fuzzy feeling that she had gotten the hospital HIPAA compliant shortly before the compliance date was gone, replaced by the question of whether every day was going to have a hassle like this one—where someone who didn't understand HIPAA caused a complaint that she had to deal with. She wanted to call John and get his opinion as to whether she had handled Doctor Hass properly but didn't want to face Pam's calling her a wimp. So she suppressed her feelings and started on a PowerPoint presentation on how to make a proper disclosure for her HIM Department in-service training tomorrow so that Doctor Hass's particular complaint didn't occur again. But she wasn't very confident that, although she had dodged a bullet on this one, there wouldn't be more hassles, some of which would be a lot harder to defuse. John had told her that being Privacy Officer was job security—an important extra duty that made her more valuable. For the first time, she began to wonder whether he knew what he was talking about. Was being the Privacy Officer doing nothing more than putting her in the position where she would be hung out to dry if she didn't magically anticipate a HIPAA violation and forestall it? Or even worse, would the hospital administration hang her out to dry for a perceived HIPAA violation even if it wasn't one but rather was an overreaction to HIPAA? No, her warm fuzzy feeling about getting the hospital HIPAA compliant was colder than her cup of tea, replaced by a creeping feeling of dread about being hung out to dry as the Privacy Officer—a feeling that persisted after she went home and went to bed. She lay awake until after 2:00 A.M., worrying about her ability to succeed as the Privacy Officer and the Acting Director of HIM. Yeah, maybe John had won over the medical staff, but she sure hadn't. And where was he—that asshole—when she needed him?

19

Health Information Management Department
Kansas City Memorial Hospital

Margaret blanched when she saw the envelope on top of her stack of mail. It was addressed to the HIPAA Privacy Officer, Kansas City Memorial Hospital, but it was the return address that scared her:

Mr. Frank Carmody
Regional Manager, Region VII – Kansas City
Office for Civil Rights
U.S. Department of Health and Human Services
601 East 12th Street - Room 248
Kansas City, MO 64106

She could think of no good reason why OCR would be contacting the hospital Privacy Officer. With trembling fingers, she opened the envelope. Her trepidation was well placed. What a way to start a Monday morning. The letter read:

May 1, 2003

Dear Privacy Officer:
    One of your patients complained to us that she overheard two psychiatrists talking in the hall about another patient's diagnosis. The complainant was Ellen Rockowich, and the other patient that the doctors were taking about was named Jackie Baker.

The date and time of this incident was the afternoon of Monday, April 21, 2003. One of the doctors was named Hass, and she didn't know who the other one was, but it was a tall male who looked to be in his fifties. Ms. Rockowich also complained that the receptionist called her by name so that others in the waiting room could hear. Please investigate this complaint and provide a written response to me at the above address within 14 business days from your receipt of this letter. Based on your response, we will decide whether to investigate further.

Sincerely,

Mr. Frank Carmody
Regional Manager

If Margaret was miffed that OCR hadn't even bothered to look on the hospital's website and find out the name of the Privacy Officer to properly address the letter to her, that irritation paled compared to her fear that this situation would end up a valid complaint that she would undoubtedly take the fall for as the newbie Acting HIM Director and Privacy Officer. But as she read the letter again, she felt better. Apparently, no harm had resulted from the alleged breaches—if they even were breaches. Margaret remembered something that John had said about incidental disclosures not being HIPAA violations. But I've got to kick this upstairs, she thought. If management finds out that I knew about a complaint and didn't tell them, they would really freak. So she scanned the letter, drafted an email to Mr. Mahan, and attached a pdf of the letter.

From: Margaret Nicks [MNicks@KCMemHosp.org] Sent Mon 5/5/03
To: Kenneth Mahan [KMahan@KCMemHosp.org]
CC:
Subject: HIPAA Complaint

Attachment: ◉ HIPAA complaint letter from OCR.pdf.

Enclosed is a complaint made against us. I don't think that it is any big deal, but I thought that you should know ASAP. With your permission, I will conduct the investigation that OCR wants and provide you the results and my recommendations for how to respond. Margaret.

CONFIDENTIALITY NOTICE: This message, including any attachments, contains information from Kansas City Memorial Hospital that is confidential and privileged. The information is intended solely for the use of the addressee(s). If you are not an addressee, your disclosure, copying, distribution, or use of the contents of this message is prohibited. If this message has been sent to you in error, please notify the sender by return email and then delete this entire message. Thank you.

Just before hitting the send button, she paused. Pam will say that I'm a wimp, she thought, but I really ought to run this complaint by John and see what he thinks before I notify Ken. That step would give some support to my statement that it doesn't appear to be a big deal. But do I call him or email him? I'd better email him—that way, I can't say anything stupid out loud.

From: Margaret Nicks [MNicks@KCMemHosp.org] Sent Mon 5/5/03
To: : John Thomas [john@emrconsultants.com]
CC:
Subject: HIPAA Complaint
Attachment: ◉ HIPAA complaint letter from OCR.pdf.

Enclosed is a complaint made against us. I don't think that it is any big deal, but I'd like to know your thoughts ASAP—

before I forward it to Ken Mahan. Thanks. Margaret.

CONFIDENTIALITY NOTICE: This message, including any attachments, contains information from Kansas City Memorial Hospital that is confidential and privileged. The information is intended solely for the use of the addressee(s). If you are not an addressee, your disclosure, copying, distribution, or use of the contents of this message is prohibited. If this message has been sent to you in error, please notify the sender by return email and then delete this entire message. Thank you for your cooperation.

It didn't take long before she had a reply.

From: John Thomas [john@emrconsultants.com] Sent Mon 5/5/03
To: Margaret Nicks [MNicks@KCMemHosp.org]
CC:
Subject: OCR Complaint
Attachment: .

You are correct. Overhearing the conversation would be an incidental disclosure, which DHHS has said is not a violation if the covered entity is otherwise compliant. And you are. Nor is it a violation to call a patient by name in the waiting room unless (a) some other law prohibits it, such as the Illinois Mental Health and Developmental Disability Confidentiality Act, which makes it a crime to indicate that a named individual is the recipient of mental health care. So an Illinois mental health practice should not call a patient by name in the waiting room because doing so would clearly indicate that the individual was receiving mental health care. But Missouri does not have a similar law. So unless the patient had requested restriction or alternate communications—that you not call her by name—it was not a violation (unless perhaps she was a celebrity, which she wasn't.). So they will either accept your investigation's finding and dismiss the complaint or decide that it needs an investigation before dismissing the complaint. I wouldn't lose any sleep over it. John

CONFIDENTIALITY NOTICE: This message, including any attachments, contains information from EMR Legal that is confidential and privileged. The information is intended solely for the use of the addressee(s). If you are not an addressee, your disclosure, copying, distribution, or use of the contents of this message is prohibited. If this message has been sent to you in error, please notify the sender by return email and then delete this entire message. Thank you.

Margaret was pleased that John had agreed that it was no big deal, but she had to admit that she had hoped that he would have not been so totally business-like. But she put John out of her mind and sent the previously drafted email to Mr. Mahan, after having added that John agreed with her analysis.

A few minutes later, Ken Mahan replied, telling her to go forward with her investigation but to let him see her draft response no later than a week before they had to respond to OCR because they had to run it by outside counsel and the risk manager. He'd decide later whether she would sign the response or someone higher up in the hospital.

So she called Ms. Rockowich, "Ma'am, I'm Kansas City Memorial Hospital's Privacy Officer, and Health and Human Services has told me about your complaint and asked me to investigate before any investigation they may do. I assure you that we take your privacy seriously, and I just want to get all the facts. We will not retaliate against you in any way for complaining."

In a defensive voice, Mrs. Rockowich responded, "Well, I don't know. You'll probably just try to twist my words to get the hospital off the hook."

"No, Ma'am, as the Privacy Officer, I'm supposed to protect patient privacy. I'm not going to twist your words. Feel free to bring someone with you to the interview if it will make you more comfortable."

"Well, I suppose it's all right. How about tomorrow afternoon? About two. I'll be near the Plaza anyway."

"That will be fine. It shouldn't take too long."

A trained investigator would probably have interviewed the complainant before anyone else. But Margaret was hardly a trained interrogator. They had not taught her anything in her college health information management courses about how to conduct an investigation. So she had to wing it. So she called up the Psych Ward's receptionist to set up appointments to talk to the two psychiatrists that were allegedly discussing another client when Ms. Rockowich was in the area. She was a little nervous that Doctor Hass was one of them after the incident when one of her staff had refused to give him his client's mother's address. She felt that he was satisfied with her response, but would another HIPAA incident irritate him to the point of kicking it upstairs? But it was what it was. She had to deal with it. Then, another thought occurred to her and she asked the receptionist, "Do you call clients by name in the waiting area?"

"Yes, unless they ask me not to. Most of the clients have come to know each other from talking while waiting to be seen. We've only had a couple of new clients ask not to be called by name, and they usually give up on that after a couple of weeks. If we have a celebrity, which is rare, they don't come to the waiting room. We meet them at the doctor's entrance and escort them up a back way so that no one in the waiting room sees them. Did I do something wrong?"

"A patient complained about being called by name in the waiting room, but no, you didn't do anything wrong if she had never objected to being called by name."

"Who was it?"

"Ms. Rockowich."

"That old bat. She complains about everything. A couple of weeks ago, she complained that a vase full of flowers was too bedraggled. It looked fine to me. On another occasion, she complained that we had *Time* magazine instead of *Newsweek* and that our copy of *People* was mutilated. She said that we should have the magazines in plastic covers so that they don't get ripped. But she had never asked me not to call her by name, and she's been coming here for two years."

"Thank you for the information. You didn't do anything wrong. But if she comes in for another appointment, please ask her very quietly, so that no one else can hear, whether she wants to be assigned a number so that you don't have to call her by name."

"Ok, you got it. Should I tell the chief of the department about this?"

"No, I'll take care of that, and I'll tell him that you are doing a good job from a HIPAA privacy standpoint. Bye."

"Goodbye."

Margaret sent an email to the Chief of the Medical Staff, informing him of the two complaints and that the complaint that the receptionist had violated HIPAA by calling the client by her name in the waiting room was unfounded but that she still had to interview the two doctors that the complainant had overheard. She apologized for taking the doctors' valuable time, but said that Mr. Mahan had tasked her to investigate and that she would make her interviews short and sweet. She added that John Thomas had said that such an incidental disclosure was not a HIPAA violation, knowing that Thomas had earned a lot of credibility with the medical staff by getting the hospital HIPAA compliant without any serious disruption of their practices.

So a few minutes before her 3:00 P.M. appointment with Doctor Hass, Margaret left the HIM Department and went to the Psych Ward. After getting past the guard—they had mentally ill prisoners on the ward—she turned right into the administrative wing and found Doctor Hass's office. She knocked on the door frame and poked her head around the door as if afraid to intrude after the refusal by one of her staff to give him his client's mother's address. But he looked up from his work, smiled broadly, and waived her in. "So this is your revenge for my hassling you, huh, a HIPAA violation?" The smile and his sarcastic voice told Margaret that he was not mad but only teasing her. So she decided to play along.

"Yes, Doctor Hass, as the head of the hospital's Privacy Police, I have to interview you about your potential HIPAA violation. But first, I have to give you your rights."

"What rights?"

"None, except the right to bribe the Privacy Police head by offering her a cup of coffee so that she is pumped up enough on caffeine to question such an eminent physician."

"Sounds fair," he said, getting up to pour her a coffee from a coffee machine on the console behind his desk. Margaret looked at the cup, which was emblazoned, "Omaha Riverfront Marathon."

"I knew you were a runner because you are on our Hospital Hill Half Marathon team, but I didn't know that you were a marathoner."

"Yes, I have to stay in shape to outrun the Privacy Police."

"Great plan, but I'm between you and the door."

"So you are. I guess I'll have to answer your questions."

"A patient, Ms. Rockowich, overheard you and another doctor talking about patient Jackie Baker's condition in the hall and reported this so-called privacy breach to the Office of Civil Rights of DHHS, which required us to respond so that they could determine whether they needed to open a formal investigation or not. Now, I shouldn't tell you—it's inconsistent with my tough cop Privacy Police persona—but our HIPAA consultant, John Thomas, said that incidentally overhearing part of a conversation containing PHI is not a HIPAA violation if the covered entity is otherwise HIPAA compliant. So I probably have to take you off the suspect list. But it would be helpful if I knew more about the incident."

"First, you have to understand that Ms. Rockowich is a querulous old lady who's never satisfied with anything. And on the day in question, she was pissed that her psychiatrist would not increase her dosage of Zanax. So she was looking for a way to get back at the Psych Ward by complaining.

"Second, my assistant gave me a heads-up that you were on the way to talk to me about this complaint, so I talked to Doctor Revels to make certain that my recollection of the discussion was accurate. All that Ms. Rockowich could possibly have overheard was my agreeing that she met the criteria for discharge—that is, that she did not have a DSM-IV disorder. So I don't know what the harm would be for a stranger to overhear that a client didn't have a mental health problem. And from Thomas's lecture, I remember that an incidental disclosure is not a breach. So I'm not panicked by your Privacy Police tactics.

"But on the other hand, I'm aware that HIPAA is more concerned with privacy than even previous mental health law was and that compliance is even more difficult, even if your staff won't give me information that I'm entitled to. So I recommended to the Chief of the Medical Staff that he forbid any clinicians from discussing a case where the conversation might be overheard."

Considering that he smiled again when he mentioned the failure of her HIM Department worker to give him data that he needed and his admission that he had pushed for extra training to prevent future breaches, Margaret was more than satisfied with the HIPAA issue.

What with John's abrupt departure after the board meeting and his failure to add anything personal to her recent emails, Margaret didn't feel much constraint about continuing to flirt with Doctor Hass. "Ok, Doctor, I'm satisfied. I guess I don't get to handcuff you and make you do the perp walk out of the hospital. But I want another cup of coffee and not in your office in return for my not busting you."

Margaret's mother would have thrown a shit fit at Margaret for being that forward with any person of the male persuasion. But her mother wasn't there, and neither was John. And Pam had told her to go find a guy other than John. Besides, she did enjoy the banter and sassy repartee with the good doctor.

"As both a clinician who wants the hospital to automate its health records and a clinician who is very interested in client confidentiality, it would be my honor to buy you coffee or even dinner. And to avoid your arresting me, I suggest that I take you to the Classic Cup Friday or Saturday night."

Just as John had learned that women in Kansas City loved the Classic Cup and the Cheesecake Factory on the Plaza, Margaret had learned that guys liked the Hereford House, Ruth's Chris Steak House, or the Capital Grille on the Plaza. So she responded, "You are not getting off that easy, Doctor, I'm in the mood for some red meat. So find me some red meat on the Plaza Saturday night, and I'll leave the handcuffs at home. But I'm going to write up a summary of our conversation and ask you to sign it."

Doctor Hass positively glowed. "You've got it, Director. I'll email you the time and the arrangements for picking you up Saturday evening."

Margaret tried to avoid showing her pleasure. It was the first time that any clinician had called her "director." But she smiled as she said, "Thank you, Doctor. It's been a pleasure interrogating you."

Her "interrogation" of Doctor Revels added nothing. He couldn't even remember the conversation, but said that, if Doctor Hass had related the substance of the conversation, he was sure that it was correct. Nor was he anywhere near as cute as Doctor Hass, so Margaret left this interrogation satisfied without a dinner date. All that she had left to do was to interview the complainant, and she could wrap this complaint up.

20

Hospital Administrator's Office
Kansas City Memorial Hospital

When he saw Ken Mahan standing in the doorway, Larry Albright waved him in. "What's up, Ken?"

"I've got Margaret's report on the complaint to OCR by Ms. Rockowich. Margaret's done a very thorough job, and I think that she's right in concluding that neither incident was a HIPAA violation. John Thomas has reviewed her report and agrees. The question is who should sign it when we forward it to OCR. She can sign it, I can sign it as her supervisor, or you can sign it as the head honcho. There are probably pros and cons no matter who signs it. If you sign it, your title may give it an importance that it doesn't deserve and make OCR wonder why the hospital administrator would get involved in something that the hospital has to know isn't a violation. Or maybe your title would send the message that we've taken the complaint seriously and have run it up the flag pole."

"What's your recommendation?"

"Let's split the difference, and I'll sign it."

"Agreed, but I want to run it by Stan Deutsch first."

"I wouldn't. He doesn't know the difference between HIPAA and a hippo. But if you have to for your due diligence, it has to be quick. We have to submit the report no later than the day after tomorrow."

"Ok. I'll light a fire under him."

After Ken had left, Larry instructed his secretary to get Stan Deutsch on the line. Two minutes later, she had complied.

"Yes, Sir. What can I do for you?" Stanley was nothing but a sycophant when he smelled a chance to earn some legal fees. At a party, he might call the hospital administrator by his first name, but he was "Sir" when he might need legal services.

"One of the clients of our Psych Ward—an outpatient—made a complaint against us to OCR alleging two HIPAA violations, and OCR required us to investigate and provide the results by the day after tomorrow. Our Privacy Officer investigated and ran it by our HIPAA consultant, and he and Ken Mahan agree with her findings and conclusions that the two incidents were not HIPAA violations. But I want you to look it over and see whether you agree. We don't want to get sideways with OCR. I'll fax you the letter from OCR and our draft response."

"I'll get right on it. Goodbye, Sir."

After telling his secretary to fax the materials to Stan Deutsch, Larry went to his wet bar, poured himself a 25-year-old Macallan single malt scotch and began wondering whether it was a mistake to get Stan involved. But at least, if it blew up, he could tell the board that he had run it by outside counsel.

Sure enough, Stan called back less than an hour later. "This mess is the exact kind of thing that I was worried about when we took it to the governing board whether this Thomas character should be the HIPAA consultant. Maybe it's not the HIPAA violation of the decade, but do we really want to dismiss it quite so cavalierly? We don't want OCR to think that we are playing fast and loose with health information so that they impose a corrective action plan on us as they would do if we committed Medicare fraud."

The thought of a CAP was anathema to any hospital administrator—having to submit a plan of all their "fixes" to their noncompliance to DHHS and to agree to periodic audits to ensure compliance. But Larry Albright, remembering Ken's opinion of Stan's HIPAA knowledge, thought that Stan was somewhat overreacting. "But we're taking some corrective action, even though these incidents do not appear to be violations."

"But it's not enough. The receptionist and the doctors should be disciplined. They don't have to be fired, but a three-day suspension would show OCR that we take privacy seriously. And maybe your Privacy Officer should be reprimanded for not having forestalled this situation."

"Ok, Stan. I'll consider taking disciplinary action. But you just said that the incidents do not appear to be violations. So I want your legal opinion to that effect. But don't go any further. Don't suggest remedial actions or comment on whether our actions are adequate. I just want one sentence in writing from you that our investigation reveals that the two incidents were not HIPAA violations and that you concur."

"Yes, Sir." Now, Stanley was using "Sir" rather than Albright's first name because he was pissed. "Goodbye."

"Bye."

Even before he got the phone handset back into its cradle, Mr. Albright thought of the mutiny that he would have on his hands if he suspended two well-regarded doctors over this minor incident. And although he might hang a non-physician, like Margaret, out to dry to make a point, this incident was not one that called for it. It wasn't like anyone else in the HIM Department could function as the Privacy Officer. And Ken would probably get really pissed and retire if he disciplined Margaret when she had done a good job to date. No, it wasn't worth expending the political capital to take any discipline in this matter.

21

Cafeteria, Kansas City Memorial Hospital

As Margaret finished paying for her salad and iced tea, she looked around the crowded cafeteria for a place to sit down. She usually avoided the dreary cafeteria in favor of the many upscale eating places nearby on the Plaza, but ate in the cafeteria when pressed for time. The food was typical institutional food, but how much could they screw up a salad?

After standing there scanning the room for an open table for a couple minutes, she was about to give up and take the salad back to her office to eat when what appeared to be a nurse from her whites and nurse's cap beckoned to her and said, "Come join us. We've got room for one more."

Margaret complied. As she sat down, the nurse, a tall, forty-something black woman, said, "You're the HIPAA lady, aren't you?"

Margaret laughed, "I didn't know that I'd be called that, but yes, I'm the Acting HIM Director and the Privacy Officer. I guess that makes me the HIPAA lady."

The nurse introduced the others at the table, "This is Kathy Canon. She's on peds. Jade Kloss, neonatal ICU. And Cassandra Geyer. She effectively runs the outpatient surgery. And I'm Keliah Stevens. I'm on peds, too."

"Hi, I'm Margaret Nicks. Thanks for letting me join you."

Keliah answered, "No problem. Now we can hassle you about HIPAA. Even though that consultant did a good job in explaining

HIPAA and lessening our anxiety, we still have HIPAA issues come up all the time."

Kathy, a thirtyish blonde who was a little on the chunky side, added, "Yeah, and he was cute and funny too!"

To her horror, Margaret blushed. The table full of nurses raised their eyebrows in unison. Jade, who looked vaguely Asian—as if she were the daughter of an American and an Asian—blurted out, "You're blushing, HIPAA lady. Did you have the hots for your consultant?"

Well, this conversation was certainly not what Margaret had expected to have over her salad today or any other day, for that matter. Margaret's "no" didn't sound very convincing, but Keliah was at least kind enough to change the subject before the others could hassle Margaret too much. "Cassandra, tell Margaret about what the head of the outpatient surgery is making the receptionist do."

Cassandra, a heavy-set white woman with gray hair that looked like it was trying to be an Afro, responded, "Well, Doctor Butel, the head honcho, who, in my opinion is wrapped too tight, made the receptionist call all patients by their first name and the first letter of their last name. So you'd be Margaret N. I told him that HIPAA didn't prohibit calling a patient by name and that they could request that we not call them by name, but he said that he didn't want the chance of having a HIPAA violation. What do you think?"

Margaret thought about Ms. Rockowich's complaint that the receptionist had called her by name and wondered whether this HIPAA myth was so prevalent that she would be hassling with it forever. "You are correct, and you can tell him that I said so. But I think that you might want to add something that the supposedly cute HIPAA consultant used to illustrate that point in a seminar I went to. He said that, when you were doing your risk analysis to see whether a real risk existed in calling a patient by name in the waiting room, you also had to ask whether a risk existed in not calling a patient by name. In other words, does the security measure cause a greater risk than any HIPAA violation? How many surgical suites do you have?"

"Ten."

"So if the consultant was your patient, you would call him up to be taken back to be prepped by calling 'John T.' Could there be two 'John Ts' scheduled that morning?"

"Easily."

"What if one of them is in the restroom and doesn't hear the page? And you take the wrong John T back and prep him for the wrong surgery? In other words, do you risk medical error by not calling the patient by the patient's full name?"

"Well, the nurse is supposed to verify that she's got the right patient before she starts prepping."

"Is supposed to. John—Mr. Thomas—who used to be a malpractice attorney—says that a lot of malpractice occurs because of a slight slip that isn't caught and then mushrooms into a major adverse patient outcome. And what if the patient has some senile dementia or is so stressed out at facing the surgery that he doesn't even know his own name?

"Mr. Thomas would say," Margaret continued, but this time without making the mistake of calling him by his first name again, "that the real risk was an adverse patient outcome that would carry way more liability than letting others in the waiting room know what his name was and that he was there for some sort of surgery. As I told the receptionist on the Psych Ward, who had a patient complain that she had called her by name, why not just put up a sign saying, 'If you don't want us to call you by name, tell us, and we will make other arrangements?'"

As Cassandra nodded, apparently satisfied with Margaret's response, Kathy piped in, "Yeah, at my family doctor's office, they've way over-reacted to HIPAA. You know what they do? They assign you animals. And call your animal when they are ready for you. Last time, I was a hippo."

Everyone at the table laughed, but Cassandra didn't laugh with them as she said, "Part of me thought that was kind of funny—

hippo—HIPAA. But another part of me was insulted. As you can see, I'm overweight. So I resented being called a hippo."

"Can't say as I'd blame you," Keliah said. "I'd be pissed if they called me a polar bear or a snow leopard." She looked at Margaret and continued, laughing, "I don't know whether you noticed, but I'm not white."

Margaret had no clue how to answer this comment, so she just nodded and responded to the practice of calling patients by animal references. "Yes, I can see some ambulance chasing lawyer suing your family doctor's practice for intentional infliction of emotional distress for calling a patient some insulting animal name, like rat or snake or hippo."

Kathy interjected, "I can top that one. Do you know what my doctor's staff does? They've been told that they must protect the patients' names from being divulged under all circumstances. So they call you by your condition!"

More laughter.

"Really. Fortunately, I was in for a follow-up appointment to see whether my blood pressure medication needed to be adjusted. What if I had been there for syphilis?"

More laughter, as the nurses called out conditions:

"AIDS!"

Erectile dysfunction!"

"Enlarged prostate!"

"Senile dementia!"

Jade was next. "Yes, my OB-GYN doctor's receptionist gives us all those restaurant flasher/beepers that go off when your table is ready."

More laughter.

Kathy said, "Well, that's better than yelling out, 'Yeast infection!'"

"Yes, but the last time that I was there, I was engrossed in a game of Sudoku and about had a heart attack when my flasher/beeper went off."

To more laughter, Margaret added, "Another example of failing to recognize a risk inherent in a security measure!"

Keliah laughed and said, "You're all right, girl. We're going to make you an honorary nurse. Anytime we're eating here, you just come right on over and join us. Ok. We've heard from Jade and Cassandra. Who else has a HIPAA horror story. No one. Well, I've got one.

"My mother is in a long-term care facility. After visiting one day, I was chatting with one of the nurses. I try to bond with the nurses hoping that if they like me they will take better care of Mama. Somehow, the topic of AIDS came up, and I asked her whether any of the residents were HIV-positive or had full-blown AIDS. She told me she didn't know. This answer floored me. So I asked her why she didn't know. She said that their lawyer had said that, under HIPAA and under AIDS/HIV law, they couldn't document who had AIDS/HIV, and that they didn't need to document it anywhere because they observe universal precautions.

"I told the nurse that this advice was the dumbest thing that I had heard of in medicine. First, I've been there a lot, and I haven't seen universal precautions lately. Second, if a resident needs acute care, and they transfer him to a hospital, doesn't the hospital need to know that his immune system is compromised? I could go on and on. So for all I know or anyone else knows, my Mama has an HIV-positive roommate.

"And to make it worse, one of the residents is a biter. If you don't make eye contact with her and tell her what you are going to do, such as take her by the arm and take her back to her bed, and you touch her, she's faster than a striking cobra. And her bite breaks the skin. And no one knows whether she's HIV-positive or not.

"I told this conversation to my son, who's a lawyer. He said there would be no damages or only what he called nominal damages for any breach of confidentiality that one of the residents has AIDS. They won't lose a job because they will never work again anyway. But the now HIV-infected health care worker that the biter bit will have a hell of a case.

"The nurse said that she would pass my concerns along to management. So I'll follow up on my next visit."

Margaret, feeling pretty comfortable with the group as an honorary nurse, said, "This story isn't as funny as calling patients by animal names. This one is scary. But neither Congress nor the Department of Health and Human Services wanted HIPAA to be a barrier to providing good health care or to protecting health care workers. Some of the HIPAA provisions may not have been thought out very well and may have that kind of effect on occasion. But such should be a rare case."

"Yes," Cassandra added, "one of my patients in outpatient surgery told me that he could have cared less about confidentiality. All he cared about was whether he had a board certified anesthesiologist so that he woke up with the same brain cells that he went to sleep with."

"Amen," the other nurses chorused.

"Any others?" Keliah asked.

No one seemed to have anything to add, so Margaret said, "Folks, I don't have a HIPAA hassle story, but I do need your help. I got stuck organizing the hospital's team for the Hospital Hill Half Marathon, and I don't have enough runners yet. You don't have to be fast—just able to complete a half marathon. And Mr. Mahan has also asked me to round up some volunteers to staff a water station."

Keliah laughed, "Honey, the last time that I ran was to catch a bus in college. Isn't a marathon 26 miles? So half of that would be 13 miles, right? And up and down these hills? Do you see stupid tattooed on my forehead, girl? I think that I can safely speak for this group that none of us can run worth a shit. But because we are nurses, we probably could man a water station. How about it, girls?

The nurses nodded in agreement, so Margaret had her water station covered. She looked at her watch and said, "Thanks for helping out with the water station. This lunch has really been fun. It's nice to get to know all of you, and thanks for making me an honorary nurse. And it's been helpful to me to learn more about what's going on with HIPAA here and elsewhere. Wait! I just had an idea. Let's meet for lunch once a month or so and share our new HIPAA hassles. It would be fun and really help me out."

"Yeah," Keliah agreed. "Ok, girls?"

They nodded again in agreement, and Margaret said, "What if we call ourselves the HIPAA Hassle Informal Workgroup?"

More laughter and nodding. Margaret had a really good feeling about this group and was glad that she had not gone back to her office to gnaw on her salad in silence, alone with her paperwork again.

22

Crown Center, Pershing & Grand, Kansas City, Missouri

Margaret, although she had run track and cross-country in college, had run only a couple of road races since and was far from the team's leading runner. But she had certainly never started a race in such an upscale place as the street leading through Crown Center with Hallmark Cards corporate headquarters, its upscale shops, great restaurants, such as Morton's steak house and the Peppercorn Duck Club, and the Westin Crown Center Hotel with its indoor/outdoor pool, where you could swim in comfort when the temperature was in the twenties and snow was falling. And that area was where the race would finish after running up and down the hills that featured many of Kansas City's elite hospitals—hence the name of the race.

Margaret and Pam had met with the team a half-hour before the race, and Margaret had reiterated that they weren't going to start together as a team. She explained that doing so would hurt the better runners to start way too far back and might lead the weaker runners to go out too fast and crash and burn—especially on a course that *Runner's World* magazine had rated as one of the toughest in the country because of its hills. "Daunting," the magazine had called its hills. And Kansas City, even at 7:00 in the morning, was hot and humid this first Saturday of June 2003—the first Saturday in June being the historical date of the Hospital Hill Half Marathon, which had been run since 1974.

But even though she was nervous at running a half-marathon for the first time—13.1 miles—Margaret felt pretty good. Besides, if nothing else, she knew that she looked good in her silky running shorts and tank top with her hair in a ponytail poking out of the back of her Kansas City Royals baseball cap and her race number pinned over her midriff. She was glad that she had remembered to put BodyGlide on the tops of her thighs so that they wouldn't chafe. Pam, who had run a couple of Hospital Hill Half Marathons, had stressed this protective measure. She had told Margaret that she would be in enough pain going up the last long hill without chafed thighs.

Also, Margaret felt good that she had managed to get all of the team members to the race on time. It took some cajoling. It was one thing to show up for a training run after work. It was quite another to get up early enough to arrive an hour ahead of time to check in for a 7:00 A.M. half-marathon start time. But Margaret used the diplomatic skills that she was rapidly developing as the HIM Director and Privacy Officer to keep all of the team members focused and committed to running the race.

Finally, Margaret still had a nice warm fuzzy from her dinner date with Doctor Hass a few weeks earlier. They had gone to the Hereford House, a Kansas City institution, rather than one of the national chains, like Ruth's Chris Steak House or the Capital Grille. But she loved prime rib, and Ruth's and the Capital Grille did not have prime rib. And Doctor Hass—ok, he had said to call him Richard—had been a perfect date. He hadn't recounted his accomplishments, had asked flattering questions about her, and had regaled her with several hilarious stories about the other doctors on staff. When he dropped her off at her apartment, he simply took her hand, thanked her, and said that he hoped that they could do it again. She thought that it was a perfect first date. And this morning, he looked cute in his shorts as he walked up to the starting line in the first couple of rows with the more elite runners. "Nice buns," Pam had said. Yes, I could forget about John, Margaret thought.

As they waited through the prerace ceremonies, which always seemed interminable, Pam piped up, "You know that it's all over the hospital that you and Doctor Hass are an item."

"We're not an item. We had one dinner date. We don't even have another one scheduled!"

"Doesn't matter. I'm just passing on the perception. No one thinks that there is anything wrong with it. I'm just jealous!"

Margaret was about to respond, but just then, she saw John walking past in running shorts and singlet, with his race number pinned to his shorts on top of his right thigh. She had sent him the hospital's invitation to be on its team with a race application, but he hadn't replied to her. But here he was. And his race number was one of the numbers reserved for the hospital's team. Uncharacteristically, Margaret, the information management major, didn't know how to process, much less manage, this information. It was as if her inner computer had seized up and couldn't compute. Fortunately, she was saved from this cognitive dissonance by the starting gun going off. Like Scarlett O'Hara in *Gone with the Wind,* she'd have to think about it tomorrow. Amid hundreds of runners, some slower, some faster, she had to concentrate just to keep her footing and keep moving until they had passed Crown Center and had turned east up a steep hill that led to the first hospital. It was more than a half mile before she could begin to run and breathe normally.

As they settled into a pace that they could maintain, Pam asked, "Did you know that John was going to run?"

"No."

"Why is he here?"

"I don't know. I sent him a race application, but I didn't know that he had registered."

"He's here because he's hot for you."

"He has hardly been showing it."

"He has nice buns, too."

"Pam, I'm having enough trouble breathing on these hills without discussing my nonexistent love life and various runners' buns. Can we table it until after the race?"

"Sure, whatever. I wouldn't want to handicap such a competitive runner!" Pam's laugh belied her somewhat snippy words, and they ran on in companionable silence, as running friends often do.

Even after getting past the first steep hills going south from Crown Center, the race was tough. It was hot and humid. At about the 8-mile mark, Margaret really began wondering what in the world she was doing running a hilly half marathon in June when the longest race she had ever run was a 10-K—a lot of difference between 6.2 miles and 13.1. And 10 miles was the longest that she had gone in training. Oh, she knew that she was going to finish, but that the last few uphill miles were going to be tough. And they were.

She was starting to fade when she heard, "Come on, HIPAA lady! Push it!" It was Keliah. With her head down, focusing on the next step, Margaret hadn't noticed that she was approaching the Kansas City Memorial Hospital water station with its big banner advertising its health services to probably the healthiest batch of people in the city. The others on the HIPAA Hassle Informal Workgroup also yelled words of encouragement, which picked Margaret up considerably. She was even more energized when Keliah poured a paper cup of ice water over her. It was a shock at first, but then felt pretty good.

With that encouragement, she picked up her pace, sprinted the last quarter mile, which mercifully was a downhill after a mile-long hill leading up to the finish, and finished in less than two hours, which was just over eight minutes a mile—pretty good for a mediocre competitive runner who had had only a few weeks to train for her first half marathon. Pam had finished about a minute ahead—disloyally sprinting away from Margaret with a half mile to go. What good is it being the boss if your second-in-command beats you at the finish? But Margaret didn't really mind. She was just glad to get her medal, some cheers, a gulp of cold water, and a couple of orange wedges at the finish.

After she had recuperated somewhat and was relieved to discover that she was not going to throw up after all at the finish line the way that some of the other runners were doing, she looked around for the other members of her team. She saw Doctor Hass massaging the calves of a runner who was apparently cramping up. "Here, drink some of this sports drink," he said. "You need to replace some potassium." After watching to make sure that the runner followed his instructions, he looked up and smiled at Margaret. "How did you do?"

"Just under two hours. Yourself?"

"One twenty-nine and change."

"Wow, that's a little under seven minutes a mile, isn't it?"

"Yeah. Not a great time for any other half marathon, but with these hills and in this heat, not bad for an over-the-hill doctor. You're around eight minutes a mile. That's pretty awesome. Are you sure you don't need some mouth-to-mouth resuscitation from a qualified M.D.?"

Margaret blushed but managed to say, "I probably did when I crossed the finish line, but I've recovered now. But maybe you should stay close to monitor my condition to make sure that I don't suffer a relapse. Let's round up the rest of the team."

Pretty soon, all the team members except John assembled in the area to the east of the finish line where Crown Center had an ice-skating rink in the winter. After having found out everyone's time, except John's, Margaret announced that she thought that they might even place in the team competition. So they had to stay for the awards ceremony.

The race organizers presented the individual awards first. The male winner finished in 1:12:06. The first female finished in 1:19:37. Margaret didn't pay a lot of attention until she heard "John Thomas, third place, 35-40 age group, 1:27:42." She didn't know what to think about his beating Doctor Hass but felt that his time would help the hospital team win because the team competition totaled the time of the top five finishers from the team and had to include two females' times. And hospital teams had to consist of full-time hospital employees or independent contractors who had done a significant amount of work for the hospital, so that no hospital could hire a ringer, a part-timer, or "consultant" from Kenya who had run barefoot ten miles to school at a sub-five-mile pace back in his or her homeland and who had qualified for the

Olympic marathon. So John, as the hospital's HIPAA consultant, who had spent considerable time as their consultant in the past year, qualified. But regardless of her conflicting feelings about John and his last-minute appearance, Margaret joined Doctor Hass and the other team members in clapping enthusiastically for John's medal.

When John got down from the blocks that the race staff had set up to mimic an Olympic medal ceremony stand, Richard waved him over to the group, "We're over here, John. Congratulations! With your great time, we now have a chance for a team medal!"

John walked over, smiling wanly. He looked wiped. He shook everyone's outstretched hand, thanking them for their congratulations. Maybe it was fatigue, but John didn't react when Richard possessively put his arm around Margaret's shoulders and said that, except for her hard work, they wouldn't have had a team. Margaret would have liked some reaction from John. A widening of the eyes. A raised eyebrow. A frown. Something. But John just nodded and said, "Right," and turned away.

So Margaret risked incurring Pam's wrath for violating Pam's guidance to play it cool with John and ducked out from under Richard's arm, walked after John, and said, "John, thanks for coming. We're glad you're here. Why didn't you tell me you were coming and going to race with us?"

"It was a last-minute decision. I finished up with a consulting gig earlier than I had thought that I would, so I faxed in my entry form."

"Why didn't you tell me? I'd have picked you up at the airport so that you wouldn't need to pay for a rental car."

"With all my frequent flyer, hotel stayer, and rental car points, the rental car was free. But thank you for the thought. Listen! They are about to announce the team winners.

To no one's surprise, the University of Kansas Medical Center's team won first place in the hospital team competition. KU Med Center was a huge teaching and research hospital and had zillions of members of the workforce, so they had to have many excellent runners. The third place male finisher in the open category was a KU Med student from Ethiopia who had placed in a number of African and European marathons.

Baptist Hospital's team came in second. One of their female runners had finished in second place in the 30-35 age women's category, which gave them a huge lift in adding the time of the top five finishers so that they had the second lowest aggregate time.

Kansas City Memorial Hospital came in third. Between John and Richard's times and both Margaret and Pam finishing in less than two hours, coupled with a sub-1:20 time of some kid fresh out of college two weeks earlier who had worked every summer at the hospital and who now worked full-time in patient accounts, they had the third best total time. Margaret was thrilled. She knew that Ken would be so happy that the last-minute team that she had pulled together had won a trophy, even if only third place, and beat out all but two of the thirteen other hospitals that had entered a team. Now, he wouldn't have to take any shit at the local Healthcare Financial Management Association chapter meetings about his slow, over-the-hill, half-marathon team. And he could even dish it out to most of the other hospitals' HFMA types that hadn't medaled at this year's Hospital Hill Half Marathon.

Although Margaret doubted that any potential patient would choose a hospital based on its half-marathon performance, the publicity of its third-place finish couldn't hurt. Who knows, maybe if patients think that their hospital staff is fit and healthy, that notion could induce them to trust the hospital and go there for health care. Margaret's medical marketing course in college had stressed that any publicity—good or neutral—was better than no publicity. The only bad publicity was an unfavorable report, and having a team of doctors and support staff win third place in one of the country's most challenging half marathons was better than neutral, even if it wasn't in the same category as a clinician winning a Nobel Prize for medicine. Yes, Ken Mahan and probably even Mr. Albright would surely be pleased.

Gloating in the glow of these positive thoughts, Margaret almost missed John walking away again. Where was he going now? Didn't he care that they had come in third in the team competition?

So Margaret again risked Pam's displeasure and ran after him. "Wait, John. We are going to Fiorella's Jack Stack Barbecue to celebrate our third-place finish. And there is a cocktail party at Ken Mahan's home tonight to celebrate our getting HIPAA compliant. I emailed you an invitation. Aren't you coming now that you are in town anyway?"

"I don't know, Margaret. I'm pretty wiped from all my travel consulting and giving HIPAA seminars around the country, and to be frank, the race took something out of me. So I'm inclined to catch my late afternoon United flight back to Chicago."

"Oh, come on, John. Everybody appreciates what you did for us getting us compliant with a minimum of hassle and very cost-effectively. And they want to tell you so at the party. If I had not been so busy, I'd have paid better attention to your having failed to R.S.V.P. and bugged you to come. So please stay overnight and come to the party. I'll try to reimburse you for any change fee for your airline ticket and for a hotel room for the night."

"I don't care about the cost. Again, I've got enough frequent traveler points that I won't have to pay anyway. And I suppose that I am grateful to all the people who worked so well with me to get you guys compliant. Sorry I didn't R.S.V.P. I was always getting in trouble in the Army for failing in my social obligations. Somehow, I thought that being a good combat leader or a kick-ass military lawyer was more important than remembering to R.S.V.P. or leaving an engraved calling card in the silver tray in the colonel's foyer when one attended a social function at this house. Ok, I'll be there. Where and when is it?"

"It's at Ken Mahan's house in Brookside, about two miles south of here. Call my cell, and I'll give you directions from your hotel when you have something to takes notes with. It starts at six, but you can come anytime after that."

"Ok. I'm going back to my hotel and shower and catch a nap. I never sleep well before a competitive early-morning road race. I'm always afraid that the hotel will screw up the wake-up call and that I'll miss the start time. As you saw, I barely got there as it was."

Margaret thought that she'd better cut it off while she was ahead. She hadn't made a total fool of herself, and he had agreed to come to the party. "Well, thanks again for racing and being largely responsible for our third-place finish. See you at the party."

"Do you need a ride?"

"No, I've already got one." She had accepted Richard's offer of a ride before she knew that John was here. But maybe it wouldn't hurt him to see that other men were interested in her, especially one as formidable as Doctor Hass. And she certainly wasn't going to dump Doctor Hass when asking whether she needed a ride was the height of John's apparent interest.

"See you there, then," John said, as he turned and started walking away.

"See you."

Margaret groaned as she saw Pam scurrying up. "Well? I saw you start to throw yourself at him, but it appeared that you played it pretty cool. Did he come on to you?"

"No, but he's coming to the party. He offered to pick me up, but I told him that I already had a ride."

"Did you tell him that it was with Doctor Hass?"

"No, he'll see that soon enough."

"Girl, you are finally starting to get devious. I'm proud of you. You are handling it well, playing one off against the other."

But Margaret wasn't so sure.

23

Health Information Management Department
Kansas City Memorial Hospital

Margaret was sitting in her office, rereading the letter from the regional Office of Civil Rights that they were not going to further investigate Ms. Rockowich's complaint and that they were going to notify her that no HIPAA violation had occurred but that the hospital was taking steps to ensure that her privacy was protected. Margaret was congratulating herself and enjoying the pleasant surprise on a Monday morning when Pam barged in without knocking, making Margaret wonder, not for the first time, whether she was being too familiar with someone that she supervised. Pam didn't really take advantage of their friendship in any significant way, but she was a little too familiar at work. And Pam's question didn't alleviate Margaret's concern. "So what happened at the party? I saw you arrive with Doctor Hass, but didn't see whether John saw that or not, so I couldn't tell his reaction. Don't keep me in suspense. What happened?"

Margaret was saved from having to recount all of the events of the party by one of the medical records clerks paging her that a patient was waiting to make a complaint about a HIPAA violation. "I've got to handle this right now, Pam, as the Privacy Officer. If I don't deal with it immediately, the patient may complain to the Office of Civil Rights, and then we'll have another hassle on our hands."

"Ok," Pam said as she left the office, "but don't think that this HIPAA thing gets you out of telling me what happened!"

Margaret rolled her eyes, but not so that Pam could see her, and got out a yellow legal tablet to take notes of the complaint. The clerk brought a young, attractive woman to Margaret's door. Margaret smiled and said, "Come in. I understand that you have a complaint. What's your name?"

"I'm Alice McCaffery."

"And whom are you a patient of?"

"Doctor Hass."

Oh, no, Margaret thought. I'm screwed. Another complaint involving Doctor Hass, and now, he's going to get me fired regardless of whether we went to dinner and then the party together. "Whom is the complaint against—Doctor Hass?"

"No, your pharmacy."

Whew. Thank God, Margaret thought. Not against Doctor Hass. "What happened?"

"Well, I work at a company that does quality assurance for prescription drugs. On Friday, I went to lunch with three of my coworkers. After lunch, I asked them whether they would mind if I drove through your pharmacy drive-through to pick up a prescription. I didn't tell them what the prescription was for. It was an antidepressant drug that Doctor Hass had prescribed for me. My coworkers said that they didn't mind, so I pulled up to the drive-through window. There was an overweight woman with black hair standing in the window. She made eye contact with me, but ignored me. Finally, she looked at me again and pointed to my left rear with a pissed-off look on her face. I looked back and saw a sign that said, 'Press the button.' If I had seen the sign, I wouldn't have pressed it anyway, because one of the pharmacy workers was in the window and had made eye contact with me. So I wouldn't have felt a need to press the button to summon a pharmacy worker when one already knew that I was there. But I backed up to where I could press the button. And she responded, again in a pissed-off voice, 'Yes?' I gave her my name, which should have been sufficient, but she said, 'Do you have a prescription to pick up?' I wanted to say, 'Yes, you stupid cow. Why else would I have driven up to the drive-through-and-pick-up-your-prescription window and given you my name,' but with my coworkers in the car, I just said, 'Yes.'

"So after she had given me a withering glance, she turned away, went to the boxes where the filled prescriptions were stored alphabetically, and returned to the window. She put the prescription in the little dumbwaiter type thing that extends out to your car window and said, with a sneer on her face, 'Do you have any questions about your antidepressants?' I almost fell through the floor board to the pavement, stunned that she would say such a thing in front of three other people—people who could tell management that I was on antidepressant drugs, which might get me fired as not being competent to do quality control of experimental drugs, much less being qualified for the promotion that I had just applied for. None of the three spoke to me on the way back to the office. So far, I don't know whether any of them said anything to management, but no adverse employment action that I know of has occurred as yet. But I'm waiting on pins and needles for the other shoe to drop. I haven't been able to sleep very well ever since. I want action taken against this bitch. She asked that question just to humiliate me in front of the others in my car because I didn't press her stupid button."

"Well, Ms. McCaffery, you certainly did the right thing to bring this complaint to me. I'm going to do a thorough investigation, and I'll get back to you as soon as possible. I may have some more questions for you after I have investigated. Did you put your contact information on the complaint form that you filled out?"

"Yes, and I'll be happy to provide any more information that you need."

Margaret stood up, extended her hand, shook hands, and repeated, "Thank you for making this compliant, and I assure you that I will take it seriously."

"Thank you. I feel a little better already. My boyfriend thought that I should complain to Health and Human Services, but I thought that I'd see whether you could handle it first."

"I'm glad that you did. If I can't wrap it up to your satisfaction, you still have the option of complaining to them. Thanks again."

After she had left, Margaret first heaved a sigh of relief that the complainant hadn't gone to OCR first—too many complaints, even invalid ones, could cause them to think that they needed to audit the hospital. Then, she thought about the complaint. It just rang true to her. How would someone make this story up? It wasn't like Ms. Rockowich's complaint in which she had failed to complain about being called by name many times before she was irritated at her doctor's refusal to adjust her drug regimen the way that she wanted. And it was clearly an incidental disclosure when she overheard Doctor Hass and another doctor talking about a client in the hall. But this disclosure didn't seem incidental—it seemed malicious and purposeful. Margaret knew, however, that she couldn't prejudge this complaint. She had to investigate it thoroughly before coming to a conclusion. She made herself a mental note to write to her alma mater and suggest that they offer an elective in how to handle complaints, including how to do a thorough investigation.

First, Margaret called the pharmacist and asked him whether he had a female employee who was overweight with black hair. He did. Jane Birkin.

"Any others that fit that description?"

"No."

"And can you tell me whether she was working last Friday at lunchtime?"

"Wait a minute." A few moments later, Margaret had her suspect. "Yes, she was working at that time, and there was only one other worker was there, and she was a black woman."

"Can you arrange for Ms. Birkin to come to my office for an interview tomorrow?"

"Certainly."

"Thank you. I'll brief you on why I'm asking these questions after I have gathered some more information."

"Great. If this involves some breach of confidentiality, I assure you that I take patient confidentiality seriously. Keep me in the loop."

"Will do. Bye."

So Margaret had the identity of her suspect. She was beginning to feel like a detective.

When Ms. Birkin showed up for her interview the next day, she wasn't very good at defending herself. If she had said something like, "I didn't notice the others in the car," Margaret might have not been able to determine that the disclosure was something other than incidental. But Ms. Birkin recounted how this stupid woman had driven up and neglected to press the button—a failure to follow instructions that had which pissed her off. She was tired of demanding pharmacy patients who crossed the HIPAA line— "Don't cross the HIPAA line inside the pharmacy and approach the counter until the person ahead of you has picked up his/her prescription and left"—and who phoned in their prescriptions and expected them to be filled within an hour. So she recounted that, yes, she had asked the patient whether she understood the instructions as to how to take her antidepressant drugs knowing that the others in the car could hear. But she concluded by saying that, if the dipshit woman was dumb enough to pick up antidepressant drugs with others in her car, she had no grounds for complaint, especially if she was too stupid to follow instructions to push the button for a drive-through pickup. And if the woman had wanted privacy, she could have left her friends in the car and come inside to the counter where everyone else would be behind the HIPAA line.

So Margaret's investigation was wrapped up. If Ms. Birkin had not basically confessed, Margaret would have asked the complainant who was in the car with her and whether she could interview them. And the complainant might not have wanted her coworkers to be interviewed and have any more reminders that she was on antidepressants. But now, there was no need to question them. Margaret had all that she needed. She felt pretty good about the investigation. Maybe she was a detective after all. But she still emailed John for his opinion whether this incident was a HIPAA violation and what, if any, disciplinary action was appropriate. His opinion was that this intentional breach was gross enough that a severe sanction was necessary to deter Ms. Birkin and others from committing such a malicious breach. He suggested at least a suspension without pay, and not just a three-day suspension, but at least a week and preferably two or three weeks.

So Margaret emailed back, "How do I suggest a sanction to select and support that sanction?"

"Well, the sanction policy that I drafted and that you got the hospital to adopt said that the hospital would select a sanction based on the past record of the offender and the seriousness of the offense. Did Ms. Birkin have any prior disciplinary problems?"

"I checked with HR, and she has a clean record—that is, no disciplinary actions—but her employee evaluations sometimes criticize her for being rude to pharmacy customers."

John emailed back, "Call me." Margaret did.

After the exchange of hellos, John said, "This conversation was getting too long to type in emails. With no past disciplinary actions, unless the complainant gets fired from her job or some other severe harm results, I don't think that the pharmacy worker needs to be fired. You don't want to fire everyone who commits a fairly minor HIPAA violation because that boxes you in to where you have to fire everyone, and if you don't fire the people who committed a serious violation, the people you did fire for a minor violation have a pretty good employment lawsuit. For example, in a hospital in Texas, three low-level worker bees committed a minor violation. Two forgot to log-off, in violation of the hospital's policy on workstation use, which required log-off if one left the work station. In both cases, the supervisor caught it quickly, and no unauthorized person viewed what was on the screen. The third employee made a borderline unauthorized disclosure to a family member in an emergency situation. Yes, he should have checked with the Privacy Officer, but it was an emergency. The patient wasn't mad, nor was the family. But the hospital did a knee-jerk reaction—which I've seen a lot of—'Oh, no! HIPAA violation—fire them!' So they fired all three of them. Then later, every doctor and nurse on staff accessed a celebrity's chart when only two doctors and five nurses had any patient responsibility. So were they going to fire virtually their entire medical and nursing staffs? Not likely. But that's their precedent. If they had reprimanded the worker bees, they would have had some room to operate with the real HIPAA violation. It's not a HIPAA crime to forget to log off. It is a crime to improperly access a chart. If they had reprimanded the worker bees, they could have suspended the doctors for three days or reprimanded them and required them to come to my HIPAA seminar as cruel and unusual punishment."

Margaret laughed, "I didn't view coming to your seminar as a violation of—is it the Eighth Amendment?"

"Pretty good for a medical records type!" John responded. "I've got another call. Catch you later. Bye."

"Bye."

So Margaret wrote up her report, recommending a three-week suspension without pay, specifying that, although Ms. Birkin had a good record except for having been warned about being rude to customers, this incident was a malicious, purposeful breach that required a stern sanction to protect the hospital and its management from liability for creating an atmosphere in which HIPAA security could be ignored by the workforce. Margaret put it into an envelope to go to Mr. Mahan as well as a copy of the letter from the OCR. Maybe that letter would put management in a good enough mood that they would accept her recommendation on what discipline was appropriate for Ms. Birkin.

But did John's "Catch you later" mean that John wanted to talk to me some more, she wondered, or was it just his way of quickly ending a phone call? I don't want to throw myself at him, but Pam's play-hard-to-get approach doesn't seem to be working. Maybe he got jealous of Doctor Hass hanging all over me at the party, and that's why he left early without saying goodbye. Or maybe he's simply lost interest in me if indeed he ever had any interest in me. Maybe he was just being nice to me to get the consulting contract. Well, I don't need him except for his legal opinion now and then. So I'll catch you later, too, Bub.

24

Corner Office, Badami, Lower, Huffman, & Deutsch
Crown Center Office Building, 2301 McGee, Kansas City

As a named equity partner, Stanley had a large corner office in the large building that the law firm leased very close to Crown Center. His office rivaled, if not topped, Larry Albright's at the hospital. His firm had what Stanley thought was a stupid policy that you could not hang your diplomas and awards on the walls of your office, so he had to fall back on hanging close to a half-million dollars worth of art on his walls. Any true art connoisseur would have said that he, or the firm, had overpaid for the mediocre works by famous artists that "graced"—using the word loosely—his walls with discreet spotlights highlighting each work. He liked to point out to any visitor to his office that was polite enough to compliment the art that his Picasso was a drawing—the only image—not an etching or a lithograph that had dozens or hundreds of identical images. But anyone who knew Picasso's work would have immediately seen that it was a very minor drawing—much like the scribbles that Picasso used to draw on napkins to leave for a particularly helpful waiter in lieu of a tip. Nor was it as valuable as one of Picasso's major graphic works that, although it might be in a large edition, was far superior esthetically to Deutsch's framed scribble that didn't seem to fit within any of Picasso's genres. Yes, a crafty art dealer could smell Deutsch's ego a mile away and could get rid of third-rate works by major artists at inflated prices. But if anyone had dared point this fact out to Stanley, he would have dismissed it as mere jealousy.

Stanley was sitting at his desk, gathering up files, and stuffing them into his designer leather briefcase to take home when his secretary buzzed him, "Mr. Deutsch, Mr. Albright is on the line."

"I'll take it."

Stanley didn't want to take it. He wanted to get home early for once. His wife was going to be at a board meeting of one of the interminable charities that she spent her time and his money contributing to. So he would have the house to himself and could pour a stiff drink, relax in his recliner, and read or watch television, or look at his clients' documents in blessed peace and quiet, while occasionally feasting his eyes on the (also mediocre) Picasso hanging beside his recliner. But Kansas City Memorial Hospital, through Albright, brought the law firm high six figures of legal fees in a bad year and more than a million in a good one. And Stanley got compensated both for initially originating the business and for handling much of the hourly rate work. He knew that the hospital contributed several hundred thousand dollars to his partnership share, so he was hardly going to fail to take the call. In fact, he would miss his wife's funeral if necessary to keep Albright's business.

"Yes, Sir. How's your family?" Stanley couldn't have given a rat's ass about Albright's family, but you had to play the game to keep good—that is, high-paying—clients.

"They're fine. And yours?" Albright didn't really care either, but one had to be polite.

"They're fine. So what can I do for you?"

"Remember that I told you about the breach in which the pharmacy worker asked the patient in front of others whether she had any questions about her antidepressant prescription?"

"Yes, I remember."

"Well, our Privacy Officer has completed her investigation, and it's pretty clear that the worker did so maliciously. Margaret recommends that we suspend her without pay for three weeks. What's your take?"

"Well, I still think that you should have disciplined Doctor Hass and that other physician, and the receptionist, as well, even if

OCR did dismiss the complaint. So I think that you'd better take some strong action this time, or you'll be setting yourself up for management liability for not enforcing your security measures. I'd fire her."

"But the worker has a clean record, and no real harm has resulted, other than some embarrassment."

"I'd still fire her. Send out a strong message."

"My Privacy Officer recommended a three-week suspension without pay, and Ken Mahan thought that two weeks was enough. I'd like to support them and not go way worse. Besides, firing her might result in an employment lawsuit, which you are constantly warning me about. You've told me many times that Kansas City is a good jurisdiction for plaintiffs who allege some discrimination in their termination because, under the Missouri Civil Rights Act, the winning plaintiff can get attorney's fees if the plaintiff wins even just one dollar."

"Ok, I've given you my opinion. And yes, there would be some chance of litigation if you fired her. But there's certainly some chance of an adverse action if you don't take severe enough discipline against one who intentionally violated patient privacy."

"Thanks for your input, Stan. I'll talk to Ken, Margaret, and HR and make a decision. This situation isn't one that I need to run by the board, is it?"

"No, I'd advise the board but not seek their approval. You have the authority to terminate employees, don't you?"

"Yes, but just checking. I don't want to hear from you down the road that I should have gotten board approval."

"Fine. Call again if anything else develops."

"Will do. Bye."

"Bye."

What a loser, Stanley thought. How in the world did he become a hospital administrator? As a Harvard Brahmin, Stanley wasn't wise enough in the ways of the world, having grown up with a silver spoon in his mouth, to know that, if everyone were perfect like him, no need for lawyers would exist. And Stanley wouldn't have made much of a carpenter or a truck driver. Having to delay his departure home for the call made Stanley decide to have his stiff drink sooner rather than later. So he went to his sumptuous wet bar and poured a stiff shot of 25 year-old Macallan single malt scotch whiskey into a brandy snifter—no shot glasses for Stanley—and downed it before once again preparing to leave. Oh well, he thought as he walked out the door, that 15-minute phone call delay was another couple hundred dollars of billable time.

25

Boardroom, Kansas City Memorial Hospital

Board member Stu Bowman was pissed at having to attend a board meeting on a Friday afternoon when he could have left his duties as the president of a local bank early and played golf, especially the Friday before Memorial Day weekend. But it was important to getting business for the bank that he appeared to be of service to the community by serving on the governing board of the local hospital, so he showed up and acted attentive as Mr. Albright called the board meeting to order: "We have only one item of new business, so if we can approve the minutes of the last meeting, which are before you, we ought to be able to get out of here in twenty minutes or so."

This plan sounded good to the board members, so Ms. Niles's motion to approve the minutes of the last meeting was quickly seconded and unanimously approved.

"So to our one item of new business," Mr. Albright began. "We need board approval to shift funds from other departments to the Oncology Department. To show you how the patient load in oncology has increased to the point that the department needs more funding, you have the required reports that have gone to the Cancer Registry for the past year in front of you to assess."

Each of the board members removed the reports from the manila envelopes that they were sealed in and perused them. The reports had the name of the cancer patient, what kind of cancer the patient had, what stage the patient's cancer was in, and the prognosis.

Stu Bowman removed the contents of the packet in front of him and blanched as he realized that he had struck gold right there in his envelope. It told him what bank clients were credit risks because they had stage IV—that is, terminal—cancer, cancer that had metastasized into other organs and was not curable.

So after the board had unanimously accepted the hospital administrator's recommendation to increase the Oncology Department's budget by 40 percent, Stu Bowman did not hand the report back in as the other board members did. Rather, he surreptitiously slipped it into his briefcase, took it back to the bank, skipped golf, powered up his computer, drafted a form letter, searched the bank's database, and, when he found a match between the report to the Cancer Registry and the list of bank customers who had home loans or car loans with the bank, he sent that borrower the following letter: "You have cancer. You are a credit risk. Under paragraph 12 of the note, when you become a credit risk, the entire amount of the note is immediately due and payable. So pay off your [mortgage] [car loan] in full, or we will [foreclose] [repossess]."

As it turned out, some of these patients got irritated at this letter and went to their friendly local lawyer. After having been contacted by a number of lawyers, pretty soon the bank sent out letter number two to the effect of "Please ignore letter number one from our idiot president. We're your friendly local bank, and we are here to help you. If you need to miss a few payments, we will work with you during your time of need." A cynic would say that they were more concerned with the bad publicity than with the potential legal liability for a breach of confidentiality, but regardless, the bank president had screwed up big time.

Several of the patients who had received such a letter also complained to the hospital. Some complained to Margaret as the Privacy Officer, but others, who were up there in Kansas City society, complained directly to Larry Albright. When the complaints started arriving, Ken Mahan was out of town on business, so Margaret had to go directly to Mr. Albright, who told her that, because the subject of the complaints was a board member, he would take care of it personally. As if in an effort to placate her, he also said, "Good job being in charge of the Kansas City Memorial Hospital team for this year's Hospital Hill Half-Marathon and getting our team to place the second year in a row. It's unprecedented around here. Thanks for all of your hard work. You may as well plan now to lead the team again next year."

"Thank you, Sir, my pleasure. Will you notify me of what action you take, Sir, regarding the board member? I have to prepare a security incident report and maintain it for the six-year HIPAA retention period."

"Yes, Margaret. I'll keep you in the loop." But the hospital administrator had no intention of keeping Margaret in the loop. This situation concerned a board member, after all, and the board set his salary. Unless Stan Deutsch had some real objection, he would just suggest to Stu Bowman that the ambitious bitch federal prosecutor could view his disclosure to constitute the crime of improperly using individually identifiable health information for either personal gain or commercial advantage. But he would add that the matter stopped right there, and perhaps Stu would even be grateful enough to support a big raise or end-of-the-year bonus for his loyal hospital administrator.

But to cover his ass, Larry called Stan, recounted the story, and asked whether he could sweep it under the rug because it was a board member. Stanley responded that, although it was somewhat inconsistent with his prior advice in which he had argued that suspending the pharmacy worker who had disclosed the patient's antidepressant prescription was too lenient, they had to protect the board members. So Stanley agreed that just pointing out the folly of Stu Bowman's breach to him was probably enough and would put Stu Bowman in the position of owing Larry Albright.

So that's exactly what Albright did. And sure enough, Stu appeared appropriately contrite. He even agreed to watch the HIPAA training video that John Thomas had produced so that he would know what he could and could not do with patient identifiable health information. Albright took all of this change of heart with a grain of salt, but did believe that Stu Bowman felt that he owed him—good news for Albright's compensation package.

So Albright simply sent Margaret an email saying that the breach had been mitigated by the letter from the bank to ignore the first letter and that he had imposed a confidential sanction on the board member involved, including extra training on permissible uses and disclosures of individually identifiable health information. Margaret was hardly satisfied by this report, but in her short time as a hospital management official, she had learned that you didn't screw with the governing board. She emailed Albright saying that she needed the details of the training and the sanction, but was hardly surprised when she never received an answer. But at least, as John had taught her, she had a paper trail demonstrating that she had tried to ensure that the sanction policy had been properly followed, board member or not.

She had emailed John to get his take on the situation, to see whether she should do anything else, and to say that they had missed him at this year's Hospital Hill Run. He replied, "Thanks. Nothing else you could've done."

Margaret resigned herself to the notion that Pam may have been right all along about John's intentions—or lack thereof.

26

Patient Accounts Department
Kansas City Memorial Hospital

As bored as Bart Gibbons was with his job—entering CPT
codes into billing documents in the Patient Accounts Department
of the hospital, he perked up when he saw the next billing
document. The patient's codes were 162.5, lower lobe bronchus or
lung, metastasized to the brain (198.3), liver (197.7), and adrenal
glands (198.7). This patient was clearly stage IV and terminal.
Some hospital workers might have had some compassion for a
patient in such dire straits. But not Bart. Ever since the previous
weekend, when he and his best bud, Joe, had gotten kicked out of a
Royals baseball game for merely moving down from the cheap
seats to empty seats in the second row behind the visitors' dugout
at Kauffman Stadium, he had been waiting for the perfect patient.
He and his friend were irate at having been kicked out. The jerk
sitting in front of him had asked them to stop blowing beer and
obscenities in his ears and his ten-year-old daughter's ears. Bart
had told him to shut up before he suffered physical injury. The old
dude didn't shut up. He stood up and said, "Come on, asshole."
Bart thought that he could take the old dude, but hesitated a little
because the old dude seemed pretty confident. So Bart had
responded, "Better be careful, dude, you'll stroke out." The old
dude just smiled and said, "You wish." Bart was spared seeing
where this conversation was going to go by an usher appearing.
Bart had the usher about ready to kick the old dude out when the
old dude said, "Here's my ticket. I'm in this section. Look at their

tickets. So Bart and Joe had to beat a quick retreat, but not quickly enough for them to avoid being escorted out of the stadium by armed security guards. So Bart wanted money—money so that he could buy something better than the cheap seats.

So Bart and Joe stopped at the first bar that they saw to lick their wounds and commiserate as to how their lives sucked. After a few brews with a chaser, they started talking.

"Why can't we watch a fucking Royals game? The hospital isn't paying me jack, and I can't make ends met," Bart whined in his beer. "My girlfriend's always ragging on me for never taking her out and never buying her anything. So she won't put out. But I don't have the scratch to get anywhere with her."

Joe had no idea how Bart even had a girlfriend. He wasn't exactly Brad Pitt. Rather, he was overweight with a scraggly beard that didn't compensate for his thinning hair. But Joe wanted to help one of his few friends. "Dude, you can get the scratch. Easy. Look at all that financial data that you have access to where you work. Get the Social and other data of a patient who is going to croak quickly and apply for credit cards in the patient's name. Get them, run them up, and when the patient dies, the executor of the estate won't know any better and will pay them off, and you'll get away with it."

"Hey, asshole, you may have had a good idea for a change."

They sat there in boozy silence for a while. Bart mulled Joe's idea over and decided that it would work. But he didn't want Joe to think that he was going to do it. Joe was a friend, but Bart didn't feel that he could trust him not to rat him out if the police started nosing around. Joe was on probation from a possession charge and might want some consideration from the cops when it was time to ask the judge to lift the probation or, God forbid, give him ammo to get the judge to reinstate the probation after he had violated it.

"Yeah, good idea, Joe, but I can't risk losing my job, or I've got no scratch, and my girl would dump me the second that she found out that I was unemployed."

"Ok, just a thought."

But it was a thought that Bart hadn't just filed away and forgotten about. So when he saw the data that indicated that Ben Carter was terminal with stage IV lung cancer, he knew that he had his chance. So he used his almost universal access as a Patient Accounts employee and obtained Carter's name, address, phone number, Social Security number, and credit card numbers that had been used to pay the copays—more than enough information to get credit cards sent to Bart's home in the patient's name that Bart could run up in the, hopefully, few weeks before the patient died.

So that night, at home, Bart logged on to several credit card sites and applied for credit cards as Ben Carter, using all of Ben's data except for his home address, substituting his own home address for Ben's. He also filled out several applications to the girlie magazines that he bought periodically and put them out in the mailbox. And lo and behold, less than a week later, he had five Visa and MasterCard Gold Cards in Carter's name in his mailbox.

So he ran them up: video games, jewelry for his girlfriend, cases of beer, and good Royals tickets. Yes, it was a brilliant criminal plan. And his girlfriend was much friendlier after he had taken her to the Olive Garden and Red Lobster on his new credit cards and had given her a diamond tennis bracelet for her birthday. Yes, life was good.

27

407 W. 62nd Street, Kansas City

Ben Carter heaved a big sigh as he closed his front door behind him. After four months as an inpatient in the Cancer Ward at Kansas City Memorial Hospital, he was ready to be home. At least for a while, he would have some privacy, some decent meals, and, most importantly, uninterrupted sleep. No nurse waking him up right after he had finally fallen asleep to take his temperature or to give him a sleeping pill. No lying awake listening to the moans or snoring of whoever was sharing his semiprivate room. No more shuffling to the restroom towing the stand to which his IV drip was attached with his hospital gown flapping open behind him showing his flabby cheeks. Ben wasn't super religious. He didn't quite understand how a loving God could permit lung cancer. But he thanked God for his remission and that it was a good enough remission to let him go home, at least for a while. He vowed to make the most of whatever time he had left before the Big C decided that he had had enough of a remission and that it was time to get medieval on him. He had always remembered that line from the Quentin Tarantino movie, *Pulp Fiction,* in which the black gangster told Bruce Willis that he was going to get medieval on the asses of the two "home boys" who had raped him. Ben knew that the Big C would get medieval on him before it was all over, remission or not.

For a few long moments, he just stood there in the entry hall, with the staircase leading up to his bedroom and office on the second floor with the living room to his right, and the dining room to his left, just taking in the atmosphere of home. He didn't even lose his happiness at being home when he looked to his left and saw the huge stack of mail on his dining room table. He had paid the neighbor boy to collect it and bring it inside so that his house wouldn't appear unoccupied.

He set his bag down. It was a small bag. He hadn't taken much to the hospital, and he certainly had not accumulated much there to bring back home with him, other than some fond memories of some of the nurses and other support staff who had been more than kind to him. He walked through the dining room to his kitchen in the rear of the house. He had cleaned out the refrigerator before going to the hospital, but had left some things in the freezer that had to be better than the hospital food. As he opened the refrigerator door, he glanced over at the phone on the counter. Its message light was blinking, and the little window showed the number "27." He had 27 messages. He looked in the freezer and saw a frozen steak and two beef pot pies. Grilling the frozen steak seemed like too much hassle, even though it might make a better meal, so he removed the pot pies, which he did like a lot, and they were certainly better than hospital food, stabbed holes in the top so that they would vent, and placed them on a metal tray, which he put into the oven. He set the temperature and time and decided that he would listen to his messages while waiting for the pot pies to cook. But he had spotted a bottle of Amstel Light in the fridge when he had opened it up to see whether there was magically something unspoiled and good to eat in there. He wasn't supposed to drink while on his chemo, but he was on borrowed time anyway, he thought, and one cold beer could hardly kill him. So he popped the cap and took a long pull at the cold beer as he hit the play button on his answering machine.

He immediately sat the beer down as he heard the last message. He had programmed his machine to play the most recent first.

"This is Bev from MasterCard. You are seriously behind in your account. You have run up over three thousand dollars and have yet to make any payment. Call me at 1-800-788-3000 to arrange for payment so we don't have to turn this over to a collection company."

I don't even have a MasterCard, Ben thought. What is this shit?

The next message was a similar one from Visa. Then another from Visa. Apparently, a different account. By now, Ben had the feeling that this mess wasn't some mistake. It looked like identity theft. While he had been in the Cancer Ward, someone had stolen his identity. What kind of asshole would do something like that?

So he replayed the messages and wrote down all of the information so that he could call law enforcement, which he did immediately. The desk sergeant who took the complaint said that they would send a detective over in the morning. Would he be there? Yes.

The detective came, listened attentively, and said that he would contact the credit card companies, try to get them off Ben's back as being an identify theft victim, and see whether he could figure out who the perpetrator was. When the detective left, Ben felt pretty good. Law enforcement was on it.

But as the days passed and the detective never had anything positive to report, Ben got more and more irritated as the nastygrams continued to fill up his answering machine. How hard could it be to track the perp down? So finally, Ben decided that he had had enough. He would find the perp himself. It was not hard to get Visa and MasterCard to provide him copies of the credit card slips that the perp had signed as Ben. He simply told them that he wanted to make sure that he hadn't signed any of them so that he could pay them if they were his charges. They fell for that theory, hook, line, and sinker, and faxed them to him immediately.

So he played detective. He went to every vendor where a charge slip had been executed and asked questions. "Do you remember this transaction? What did the buyer look like? Did you see what kind of car he drove?" and the like. He didn't get anywhere until he stopped at Noble House Jewelry on Metcalf in Overland Park.

"Yes, I remember this transaction. I don't sell a diamond tennis bracelet every day. But I don't remember much about the buyer other than he was a chubby young guy. That's half of the below 30 population of Kansas City. But wait a minute. Let me see if we still have the security video for that day and, if so, that it hasn't been overwritten."

"Please do."

After a few minutes, "Yes, we've still got it. And we haven't reused it. I've loaded it up, and it will appear on the monitor in a few seconds."

Ben watched intently. The manager fast-forwarded the video, which had the date and time running across the bottom of the screen, until it got to the time on the credit card receipt.

When he saw the perpetrator's face, Ben was elated. He knew that he had seen him before and more than once. And the only place that he had been recently so that he could have seen someone more than once was the hospital. Because the local cops had not been helpful, he persuaded the jewelry store manager to give him the tape rather than just reporting his findings to the cops. And he took it to the hospital.

As he returned to Kansas City Memorial Hospital, which he had never wanted to do, but would happily do this time to catch the asshole that had stolen his identity, he wondered whom to take the tape to. As he looked at the hospital directory, he seized on the Privacy Officer and the Complaint Official. One of them ought to be able to help him. He decided to start with the Privacy Officer, so he asked the receptionist for directions to the Health Information Management Department.

28

Health Information Management Department
Kansas City Memorial Hospital

Pam actually knocked on the side of Margaret's open door, which pleased Margaret. Pam was finally cluing in to the fact that she couldn't be too familiar at work.

"What's up, Pam?"

"A patient wants to see you. He says that he thinks that a hospital employee stole his identity and ran up credit cards in his name. He wants to show you the evidence. His name's Ben Carter."

"Oh my God."

"Yeah. This one could be serious."

"Ok, send him in."

After Ben, a fairly distinguished gray-haired man, had been shown in and had introduced himself, Margaret asked him what had happened. As he told the story, she got more and more concerned. This situation could be huge: an identity theft at the hospital. And Ben had a video of the perpetrator using the card.

"Sir, I take your complaint very seriously. Let's go to Conference Room A, which has is a media center, so that we can play your tape and see whether the person on the tape is a hospital employee or not."

They did. But Margaret, while agreeing that the perpetrator looked familiar, could not identify him. So she buzzed Pam over the intercom and had her come to the room. When Pam saw the tape, she immediately said that it was Bart Gibbons in Patient

Accounts. She knew him well because he had tried to hit on her several times. Several unsuccessful times, that is, because he struck her as such a slug that she would remain unmarried and even unloved for the rest of her life before she would go out with him. After all, what was the chance that she was going to accept a date to go out and play paintball with a loser?

So Margaret addressed Ben, "Sir, it appears that it was a hospital employee that my assistant here has identified. We can proceed in either of two ways. I can contact the FBI, or you can. I assure you that we will not sweep this situation under the rug. Regardless of which of us notifies the FBI, I will strongly suggest that the Security Officer suspend Mr. Gibbons's access to health information immediately and that Human Resources suspend him from employment pending investigation so that he cannot commit any more identity theft. Do you want me to contact the FBI, or do you want to?"

"Let's do it together."

"Sounds good to me. I just have to run it by my boss. Give me a half hour, and I'll have an answer. Pam will get you some coffee if you'd like some while you wait."

Margaret ran it by Ken Mahan, who ran it by Mr. Albright, who ran it by Stanley Deutsch. All agreed that they had no choice but to notify the FBI. Both the Security Rule and the Privacy Rule had a duty to mitigate—to lessen the harm of—a breach. So promptly notifying law enforcement of potential identity theft was mandatory in such a case so that the offender couldn't commit any more such crimes. And the duty to mitigate also made it necessary for the Security Officer to immediately suspend Gibbons's access.

So Margaret took Ben back to her office and had Pam get the local FBI Field Office on the line. Special Agent Alexander took the call. Margaret put the phone on speaker and introduced herself as Kansas City Memorial Hospital's Acting Director of Health Information Management and Privacy Officer and Ben Carter as a patient and a victim of identity theft committed by a hospital employee in violation of HIPAA if not also other federal laws.

Margaret said, "He has a security video of a hospital employee using a credit card in his name."

"Great work, Mr. Carter," the agent said. "Sounds like your investigation—getting the security video—has him dead to rights. I'm going to come right over and take your statements. Then, we will have probable cause to arrest him. Sound ok?"

"Yes," both Margaret and Ben responded.

Margaret immediately called James McManus, the IT Director and the HIPAA Security Officer, and told him that they needed to suspend Bart Gibbons's access immediately so that he couldn't commit any more identity theft before he was arrested or afterwards if he was released on bail.

James responded, "If I suspend his access, he might figure out that something is wrong. What if I send him an email telling him that his workstation may have a virus and that I've got to shut it down until we can identify and remove the virus? That way, we've effectively shut down his access without alerting him to the fact that he's suspected of something. If he doesn't read the email immediately, I'll call him and tell him what I'm doing."

"Sounds great!" Margaret replied. "Thanks, James. We have to protect this information from any further breach."

Less than five minutes later, Margaret had an email from James, "Mission accomplished."

Less than an hour later, the agent arrived. He looked like an FBI agent was supposed to look. Ruggedly good-looking, well dressed in a suit and a conservative tie. After showing them his credentials, he took their statements, took custody of the tape and the credit card receipt copies, and announced that he was prepared to arrest Mr. Gibbons.

"Thank God," Ben exhaled and then said louder, "The local cops wouldn't do anything, so I had to investigate on my own."

"Well, don't worry, Mr. Carter, I'm going to turn this case over to the U.S. Attorney, and I predict that Mr. Gibbons will end up facing significant jail time. Again, I hope to arrest him before the day is over."

Margaret and Ben were not there to see the arrest. Ben went home, and Margaret stayed in the HIM Department working on the next year's budget. But she quickly heard—it went around the hospital like wildfire—that the FBI agent, accompanied by another agent, had walked into Patient Accounts, asked Bart whether he was Mr. Bart Gibbons, and, when he said that he was, told him that he was under arrest for using individually identifiable health information for personal gain, for identity theft, and for mail fraud. Other workers in Patient Accounts said that Bart had turned white, pissed himself, and croaked, "What do you mean?"

Agent Alexander ordered the suspect to turn around, place his hands against the wall, and spread his legs. He tapped Bart's legs further apart, forcing him to support his weight on his hands—what law enforcement called positive control. Bart couldn't rise up and make an aggressive move from that position. Then Agent Alexander expertly frisked Bart after putting on a pair of disposable latex gloves. He didn't particularly want to pat down Bart's thighs which were wet from his urine without hand protection. Then, he drew his prisoner's hands behind his back one at a time and cuffed him. He pulled him upright and said, "I've got to read you your rights, asshole. Shut up until I'm finished." The agent normally wouldn't use that kind of language. Why give defense counsel something to work with as they had done so well in the O.J. Simpson case? But he thought that stealing the identity of a terminal cancer patient made one an asshole, so he couldn't restrain himself.

After having been read his rights and having answered that he understood them, Bart tried to protest his innocence. But Agent Alexander told him to button up until they got to the office. Then, the two agents led the totally humiliated, handcuffed prisoner, out of Patient Accounts in front of all of his shocked, although not necessarily sympathetic, coworkers.

29

FBI Field Office, Kansas City, Missouri

The two FBI agents shoved Bart Gibbons, still handcuffed, into the interrogation room. "Sit down, asshole." The room was bleak, with a discolored linoleum floor, no windows, and faded beige wallpaper. The only furniture consisted of a battered table with one chair on the back side as you walked into the room and two chairs facing the lone chair across the table and a table with a TV and a tape player on it. A recessed light shone down on the lone chair.

Totally cowed, with his urine-stained underwear having turned icky and clammy, Bart sat down in the lone chair.

Special Agent Alexander fastened Bart's handcuffs to the arms of Bart's chair. Without saying another word, the two agents left Bart alone to stew about his suddenly threatened future. If it wasn't the worst wait of his life, it came close. I really fucked up this time, he thought. His mind ran wild with what might happen to him. He had several friends, such as Joe, who had been in prison, and he knew he had much to fear from the other prisoners. Much as he liked thinking about sex, he had no interest in being some gang-bangers' bitch in a cell in Leavenworth.

The only respite that he had from thinking about his potential incarceration was when he remembered his humiliation at being arrested at work, in front of his coworkers, after having pissed himself. Even if this mess magically went away, he could never go back there.

An hour and a half later, the agents returned. Bart was not a happy camper, what with sitting there worrying about his immediate future for so long. Agent Alexander shoved a form at Bart. "Sign this. It's a statement that you understand your rights, like you already said that you did."

Agent Alexander uncuffed Bart, and he signed. Then Agent Alexander cuffed him back to the chair.

"And you are willing to talk without a lawyer being present?"

"Yes, I didn't do anything, so why would I need a lawyer?"

"Ok, tell us how you stole Mr. Ben Carter's identity and ran up credit cards that you got in his name to the tune of more than $9,000."

"I don't know what you are talking about."

"Come on, asshole, we've got you dead to rights. Why did you piss yourself if you're so fucking innocent? If you want to help yourself, you have to come clean. If you b.s. us, we'll just tell the U.S. Attorney that you weren't cooperative, wouldn't accept responsibility, and don't deserve a good plea bargain. And she'll listen to me. So keep b.s.-ing me, asshole. See what it gets you. You know, we can just write this as a HIPAA violation and identity theft. Or I can write it up as those crimes and add about a dozen others, like computer fraud, mail fraud, theft by deception, and the like, and you'll face about 100 years in federal prison."

The agents could tell from Bart's stricken expression—no poker face here—that they were getting to him. But his ego wouldn't let him cave just yet, so he kept denying the charges.

"Ok, let's try this." Agent Alexander pressed the play button on the video. The security video of Bart buying jewelry for his girlfriend appeared. Alexander then handed Bart a copy of the credit card receipt that showed the same date and time as the date and time running across the bottom of the video.

"So how do you explain this, asshole?"

"This tape doesn't prove anything. It could have been doctored."

At this, Agent Alexander slammed his fist down on the table right in front of Bart, almost making him piss himself again, and said, "I've had enough of this asshole's bullshit. Fuck him. Let the U.S. Attorney put him under the jail. He won't help himself."

Alexander stalked out.

The other agent, Agent Millar, smiled at Bart and said, "Chill. He won't be back for a while. Would you like a cup of coffee?"

Bart nodded, not trusting himself to speak. Agent Millar, who was barely 5' 10, slender, with a pleasant face, appeared to Bart to be a kindly soul, unlike Agent Alexander. Bart didn't know that Millar was a stone-faced interrogator who would pull out his fingernails one by one if he could get away with it, smiling and talking pleasantly while doing so. But he and Agent Alexander had pulled the Mutt and Jeff routine many times, and they knew that Alexander couldn't pull off the good cop role. But Bill Millar could. And did.

Agent Millar picked up the phone on the wall in the back of the room and ordered two coffees. When another agent delivered two plastic cups of what turned out to be truly bitter, awful coffee, Agent Millar unlocked one of Bart's handcuffs so that he could pick up the coffee, leaving the other one locked to the chair. Bart felt almost pathetically grateful for this slight improvement in his freedom of action.

"Ok, Bart," Agent Millar began. "How do you want to play it? We've got only a few minutes before Agent Alexander returns, and you don't want that. His last job was interrogating terrorist suspects in a secret location in Poland, including water-boarding them, and I don't think that I could control him, so you had better come clean. The Attorney General is investigating his techniques to get confessions, but Agent Alexander doesn't give a shit. He just wants results. And I don't want to be caught up in any prosecution if Agent Alexander goes overboard with you. So when he returns, I'm out of here. I'll wash my hands of you."

Bart had read enough spy and detective novels that he recognized that this scene was the classic Mutt and Jeff—good cop, bad cop—routine. But it was one thing to know it intellectually and quite another to effectively deal with it when you were its target. And with what he—as a spy/detective junkie whose main physical activity was paintball so that he could pretend to be a secret agent/assassin—knew about interrogations, he could not rule out that Agent Alexander would put him through what the spy novels called a hostile interrogation. And Bart, delusional as he was about some aspects of his life, such as his attractiveness to women, knew deep down that he was a physical coward. So he didn't really want to find out whether this threat was a good cop, bad cop bluff or the real thing. So he caved after one more piece of persuasion from Agent Millar.

"Look, Mr. Gibbons, this questioning is your last chance to get your side of the story out before the file goes to the U.S. Attorney. If there are some extenuating circumstances, you need to tell us now so that it will go into our report. That way, the U.S. Attorney will see that you're not a hardened criminal and that you have some mitigating factors. That scenario could cause her to charge this case as a misdemeanor rather than a felony. Or it could even predispose her to consider a plea bargain that doesn't include jail time. And your cooperation, or lack thereof, plays into whether the U.S. Attorney will oppose bail. And I'll even go to court and tell the Magistrate Judge that you cooperated, had no prior criminal record, and should be released on your own recognizance or on a reasonable bail. I've even got a list of bail bondsmen that I can give you. But once we end this interview, you've lost those chances. What do you say?"

Bill knew that the suspect had not used the stolen credit cards to buy bread and milk for his starving family. He was single and had no family, as Bill had learned from Bart's personnel records at the hospital. And from the credit card receipts, he knew that Bart was buying video games and diamond tennis bracelets for his girlfriend—identity theft purchases that just about guaranteed that the U.S. Attorney would want to put him under the jail, particularly when the victim was a vulnerable, terminal, cancer patient. But Bill also knew that the criminal procedure laws governing confessions prohibited him from lying to the suspect to get a waiver of his right against self-incrimination or to get him to waive his right to an attorney. But once he had waived his rights as Bart had done, he was fair game, and the agent could lie through his teeth to get a confession. The most common lie was that the suspect's accomplice had confessed and had said that it was the suspect's fault when the accomplice had, in fact, remained silent. But there was no evidence that Bart had an accomplice, so Bill resorted to the tried and true lie, "You'd better get ahead of this mess and get your side of the story out before it's too late."

And it worked yet again. What a great line. After Bill had persuaded Bart to agree that the rest of the interview could be recorded, Bart spilled his guts, but tried to make himself sound less culpable by blaming the hospital. "Yeah, I shouldn't have done it. But the hospital doesn't take confidentiality seriously. Two doctors on the Psych Ward blabbed about a patient's condition in front of another patient, and they didn't do anything to the high-and-mighty doctors or to a receptionist who called a mental health patient by name in the waiting room. And a pharmacy worker divulged that a prescription was for antidepressants right in front of the patient's fellow workers and got only a two-week suspension. It was like the hospital was encouraging us to play fast and loose with health information. And I know of other breaches that were never even discovered. There was no real enforcement. I may be guilty, but the hospital encouraged me to commit the crime by its lax enforcement."

Bill didn't think that this line of reasoning was the best mitigation argument that he had ever heard, but, hey, it got the taped confession. And although Bill took Bart's story with a grain of salt, maybe the U.S. Attorney would be interested in the hospital's alleged failure to enforce HIPAA. Bill and the other agents in the FBI Field Office had read the Department of Justice Memorandum issued just the week before stating that, in an appropriate case, management could be criminally liable, under principles of corporate criminal liability (Enron, he had thought), when the facility was not HIPAA compliant and that noncompliance either encouraged the actual perpetrator or failed to prevent the crime. Bill knew that the U.S. Attorney for the Western District of Missouri was very ambitious and wanted to move way up in the Justice Department, maybe even to the Attorney General position eventually, or run for some high political office, and getting the first HIPAA scalp on her belt for successfully prosecuting management for what an employee did would be a big feather in her cap. Bill could just see the U.S. Attorney's joy when watching the six o'clock news showing the hospital administrator doing the perp walk. TV images of a hospital administrator being led off in handcuffs would get her national notoriety and further her image as a crusader against the evil health care industry's management.

"What happens now that I've cooperated?" Bart asked.

"We will take you to the Jackson County jail, where we have an agreement that they will hold our pretrial prisoners because we don't have a federal lockup in Kansas City. Although the U.S. Penitentiary in Leavenworth is only 40 miles away, it houses only sentenced prisoners. The Jackson County jail will in-process you for us, and because you cooperated, I'll arrange to have you brought before the Magistrate Judge tomorrow. If you can't afford a lawyer, he will appoint a federal public defender for you and either release you on your own recognizance or set bail, or if the U.S. Attorney objects to your release, he will set a hearing to determine whether you should be released. With no prior record, even if the U.S. Attorney objects, you probably will be released. Do you have an attorney or enough money to hire one?

"Not really."

"Well, the Magistrate Judge will determine whether you qualify for a federal public defender or not. If you do, he will appoint one. Hang loose and finish your coffee while I arrange to transport you to Jackson County."

After the FBI had transported Bart to the lockup, where he was photographed, fingerprinted, given prisoner's coveralls to wear, and locked in a holding cell, he actually felt a little better. It was largely out of his hands now, and at least he had dry pants on.

30

U.S. Attorney's Office
Federal Courthouse
Kansas City, Missouri

FBI agents Alexander and Millar cooled their heels in the
nicely appointed waiting room outside the U.S. Attorney for the
Western District of Missouri's office, in Room 5510 of the Charles
Evans Whittaker Federal Courthouse, 400 E. 9th Street, Kansas
City, Missouri, just east of downtown proper.

The courthouse was a somewhat strange, white, round,
concrete and glass, eleven-story structure that was obviously
designed more for security than for esthetics. But the interior was
nicely finished off, from the courtrooms to the judges' chambers,
and from other offices to the jury rooms and witness waiting
rooms.

Finally, the receptionist looked up from her computer screen
and announced that the agents could go in.

The office might not have been as sumptuous as those of the
partners Badami, Lower, Huffman, & Deutsch, particularly
Stanley's with his Picasso, but it was not too shabby. Among the
framed diplomas were well-framed photographs of the U.S.
Attorney with local and national celebrities, including the
President. The U.S. Attorney was, after all, a presidential
appointee. She was, perhaps, too blonde, youthful, and attractive to
come across as the chief federal prosecutor in the western half of
Missouri, but her looks belied the litigation skills of a shark with
the political ambition to match.

"Come in, Gentlemen." She rose and walked around her large desk, with its large nameplate, "Marsha Thorp, U.S. Attorney," predominately displayed, extending her hand. "Nice to see you two again." After a firm handshake, she motioned them to the two chairs sitting in front of her desk.

"Yes, Ma'am," Bill responded as she sat down behind her desk and picked up the file that Bill had set in front of her. "I think that we may have your HIPAA conviction all wrapped up. It's all in that file, including a transcript of the perp's confession."

For a long time, Marsha had wanted to be the first U.S. Attorney to get a HIPAA scalp to hang on her belt, to become the people's medical privacy champion to add another credential to her already over-filled resume. But another U.S. Attorney had beaten her to it. She knew, however, that she could still get a lot of good publicity with the second conviction.

The agents sat there stoically while Ms. Thorp reviewed the documents in the file. After she had finished, she looked up and smiled. Not a pleasant smile, but a smile nonetheless. "Well, you've got the perpetrator dead to rights. But I'm intrigued by his statement that the lax enforcement of HIPAA motivated him to commit the crime. Did you see the recent memo from the Department of Justice concerning who may be liable for a violation of section 1320d-6?"

"Yes, Ma'am."

"Remember this part?" She picked up a copy of the memo that was lying on her desk and read, "In addition, depending on the facts of a given case, certain directors, officers, and employees of these entities may be liable directly under section 1320d-6, in accordance with general principles of corporate criminal liability, as these principles are developed in the course of particular prosecutions." If Marsha couldn't get the first HIPAA conviction, she could get the first conviction of a member of a covered entity's management.

"So you know what I want. I want you to investigate and see whether we can indict management for encouraging this asshole by not being HIPAA compliant or by not enforcing their policies. Can you do that for me before you wrap this case up? Or do I have to call the SAC?"

Neither agent wanted her to call the Special Agent in Charge of the Kansas City Field Office, so both of them quickly assented to her request.

"And I'm going to indict Mr. Gibbons with every charge that I can think of—HIPAA, mail fraud, identity theft, theft by deception, computer fraud, and so on—to put the screws to him to make him cooperate if we need him to testify against management. Ok, that will be all."

Once the two agents were safely well away from the federal courthouse, both of them shook their heads at the same time. "Shit," Bill said, "I sure don't have much enthusiasm for hanging some poor hospital administrator out to dry so that the U.S. Attorney can get a management scalp on her belt to further her career."

"Me, neither. She just wants to do the press release while some poor member of management is filmed doing the perp walk for the six o'clock news. But if we don't do it, she'll go to the SAC, and he'll hang our scalps out to dry."

31

Law Offices of Tim Mogridge
Downtown Kansas City, Missouri

The receptionist, who apparently had never heard of HIPAA, nor should she have because it was a law office, not a hospital or another HIPAA covered entity, called Bart Gibbons by his full name. Of course, even if it had been a hospital, it would have been a no-harm, no-foul, no HIPAA violation because no one else was in the waiting room to overhear.

Attorney Tim Mogridge had a white collar criminal defense practice. So he seldom had a waiting room full of defendants wanting representation for their DUIs, drug busts, bad-check offenses, and the like that the run-of-the mill criminal defense attorneys handled. Instead, Tim defended the hospital administrator on Medicare fraud charges, the corporate president on securities violations, the corporate vice-president who was stupid enough to accept an internet offer to meet with a minor at a hotel out of state who turned out to be an anything-but-a-minor vice cop, and the like. So unlike the typical criminal practice mill, he handled at any given time only a dozen or so cases, and his waiting room was seldom occupied.

And anyone waiting to see Tim in his waiting room couldn't give a shit less whether his walls sported original Picassos or cheap reproductions. All they cared about was whether this hired gun attorney could pull off some magic and keep them out of jail.

If one were to rank offices, Tim's would fall well behind Stanley Deutsch's office and the U.S. Attorney's office. Even though Tim was very successful with his white collar defense, he couldn't afford the $100 per square foot of Stanley Deutsch's firm's palatial digs. So Tim's office had no Picassos, no pictures of him with the President, no marble floors, no crown molding, just framed diplomas and certificates showing that Tim was a member of all of the prestigious defense lawyer associations and that he had taught at their national conferences. As for photographs, if one looked closely, he would see a photograph of the Commanding General of Fort Knox, Kentucky, awarding the Judge Advocate General's Corps officer, Captain Mogridge, the Meritorious Service Medal with Captain John Thomas in the background. Other than the few pictures of Mr. Mogridge with lower level dignitaries than the ones that the U.S. attorney's wall sported, his office's walls were graced only by framed reproductions of English fox-hunting scenes—common décor for law offices that represented individuals, not corporations. And by the time that his clients got to his office, their offense had already been all over the six o'clock news, so they didn't care much about confidentiality other than having a strong desire that their attorney not tell the prosecutor how guilty they really were.

So when the receptionist called Bart by his full name, any breach of confidentiality was the least of his worries. He was worried about getting a lawyer who could either get him out of the mess that he had found himself in or, at least, get him a deal so that he didn't have to spend years in federal prison. Yes, Leavenworth was close, so his mother could visit, but he didn't really want to get acquainted with a Hell's Angels cellmate with an alternate sexual lifestyle. And nothing prevented the federal Bureau of Prisons from assigning him to a prison that was as far away from his mother as possible. So he had gone online and researched who the best criminal defense counsel in Kansas City was, and apparently, Mr. Mogridge was the man. And, thank God, his mother, after having chewed him out for several hours for his stupidity, agreed to finance his defense.

Bart, stupid as he was for committing identity theft and getting caught, had enough animal cunning to realize that he'd better get his act together and minimize his potential sentence by working with his lawyer. He had even read an article that he had found online about working with one's criminal defense lawyer. The main thing that he took away from the article was that you couldn't b.s. your lawyer. You had to come clean with what really happened. If you said that you weren't at the scene of the crime but a security video showed otherwise, the judge wouldn't sentence you just for your crime, but also for your deceptive stupidity. And the prosecutor might just indict you for perjury if you didn't get a stiff enough sentence from your original crime and lied about your involvement on the witness stand. The article pointed out that Martha Stewart didn't go to jail for the original crime but rather for obstruction of justice for allegedly covering it up. So Bart was going to be straight with Mr. Mogridge.

As he entered, he didn't immediately feel that Mr. Mogridge was a shark. He was about 5'10" tall, with a pleasant face. Although he was a former FBI agent, he looked somewhat like a southern gentleman farmer. Many opposing counsel had learned to their chagrin that Tim's pleasant face masked his legal brilliance. No one was better on the facts.

But Bart was convinced from all the accolades online that Mr. Mogridge was the lawyer for him, so when Mr. Mogridge asked Bart what he could do for him, Bart told the truth about what he had done and then added, "As your secretary instructed when I called to make this appointment, here is a cashier's check for $10,000 made out to your trust account to get you to agree to represent me."

It had taken Tim only about two deadbeat clients to learn to get a big hunk of money up front or not take the case. A client sentenced to 20 years in the big house had limited ability to pay his outstanding legal fees and probably even less interest in doing so. Tim obeyed this rule even with his white collar clients, like the president of a large hospital chain. If they didn't like it, they could obtain less qualified counsel desperate enough to work on the come.

After Bart had handed him the check and Tim had briefly inspected it, Tim launched into his new client spiel: "Ok, you are not my client until this check clears. Do not, however, discuss this case with anyone other than me or my staff. Not your mother, not your wife or girlfriend, not your best bud, and not even your minister if you have one. Yes, a spousal or a clergy privilege may exist, but do you want to risk it and waste your presumably limited defense fund paying me to litigate whether the privilege applies, or do you simply want to keep your fucking mouth shut?"

With his high level corporate white collar clients, Tim wouldn't have talked quite like that, but he had quickly clued in to what kind of language would make an impression on Bart's pea-sized brain.

"Now, I want you to make me a list of anyone who may be willing to testify that you are a decent guy, that this was a one-time lapse of judgment that is unlikely to happen again, and that they would hire you notwithstanding this offense." Tim believed in giving clients something to do so that they would, with any luck, stay out of any further trouble and perhaps even help out in their own defense.

"And it's a good sign that the AUSA—the Assistant United States Attorney—agreed to such a low bail. It may mean that they want something from you or at least aren't trying to put you under the jail and give you a decent plea bargain. But if you fail to show up for any court appearance, the judge will revoke your bail, and you'll await trial behind bars."

On that cheery note, Mr. Mogridge terminated the meeting after reminding Bart of the date and time of his next court appearance. After Bart had left, Tim called the AUSA to find out what was really going on. Something about the case didn't smell right to Tim's educated senses of how federal criminal law played out. And he was right.

32

CEO's Office, Kansas City Memorial Hospital

Larry Albright felt nauseous as he paged his secretary to get
Stan Deutsch on the line. Ken Mahan had just informed him that
the FBI was coming to the hospital to see whether Gibbons was the
only one culpable or whether management's failure to be HIPAA
compliant or its failure to deter HIPAA violations by failing to
enforce its policies and procedures had somehow encouraged
Gibbons or, at least, had failed to prevent his crime when it was
preventable. Larry felt pretty confident about the hospital's HIPAA
compliance. And if they weren't compliant, he could blame it on
the national expert that they had hired as their consultant. But
nonetheless, any hospital administrator who didn't darn near piss
himself at the thought of the FBI investigating his facility—for
anything—was clueless. Look at the Baptist Hospital Medicare
fraud case—the CEO went to jail for four and a half years for
entering into an arrangement whereby two doctors who owned
nursing homes were hired to train hospital staff on geriatric issues,
which the jury found to be an illegal kickback. The Anti-Kickback
Statute made it a crime to offer and so forth remuneration to induce
business paid for by health insurance. The prosecution's theory of
the case was that, because the compensation that the hospital paid
the doctors for their training duties was excessive, the arrangement
was, in part, an illegal kickback. What made this case so scary to
Larry and every other hospital administrator in the country was
that the CEO had obtained two legal opinions from two different
law firms that the arrangement did not violate the Anti-Kickback

Act. So Larry was not paranoid for sweating bullets at the thought of any FBI investigation. Even though he thought that John and Margaret had done a good job of getting the hospital compliant, he wanted Stan's input *now*.

"Mr. Deutsch is on the line, Mr. Albright."

"Thank you, Joannie."

Larry got up and shut the door before hitting the button to connect to Stan. "Stan, we've got a serious situation. I need your advice. Remember that Patient Accounts worker who committed identity theft? Well, he's apparently trying to exculpate himself by saying that our failure to be HIPAA compliant and/or our failure to sanction members of our workforce led to a permissive climate about HIPAA that encouraged him to commit the crime. And the FBI has notified us that they are coming to interview management about this issue. Quite frankly, considering the Baptist Hospital case, I'm scared shitless."

Stanley couldn't resist. "Calm down. I'll get you through this mess. You're not going to jail like the Baptist Hospital CEO. But you should have listened to me when I said that you needed to hire my firm rather than that minimalist consultant, Thomas or whatever his name was. And as I suggested, you needed to take sterner measures when you had breaches. I said that you should fire that pharmacy worker who breached confidentiality, but you were too worried about supporting Ken Mahan and that clueless woman that you have as your Privacy Officer.

"What you have to do is lawyer up. You don't talk to the FBI. You refer them to me. I'll find out what is really going on. My guess is that the U.S. Attorney, who is nothing if not a political animal, wants a management scalp to hang out to dry. So we will find someone other than you or a board member to sacrifice to her ambition. Maybe the Privacy Officer. Just leave it to me and don't argue with my suggestions if you want yourself and the hospital to get out of this thing in one piece."

"Thanks, Stan. I should have listened to you. Just tell me what to do."

"Well, I'm not a criminal attorney, but I do know that you cannot tell any members of the hospital's workforce not to talk to the FBI because doing so would be obstruction of justice. You may tell them that hospital counsel—that is, me—does not represent them, that they may want to get independent counsel, and that it's up to them whether to talk to the FBI or not."

"Will do."

"I know Marsha Thorp, the U.S. Attorney. I'll call her and find out exactly what she wants, and maybe we can work out a deal that protects you, the hospital, and the governing board."

"Sounds great, Stan. I knew that I could rely on you."

Stanley felt that he had made his point and that he didn't need to beat up on Larry any more for his alleged failures to cut Thomas out and have Stanley's firm handle HIPAA compliance. So he thanked Larry and told him that he had his back. The unstated part of that declaration was that Margaret was going to be hung out to dry to protect Larry, senior management, the governing board, and the hospital.

33

Cafeteria, Kansas City Memorial Hospital

The HIPAA Hassle Informal Workgroup again met in the cafeteria—but this time after the 7:30 to 3:30 shift. So no lunch. No salads. Just coffee and tea except for Margaret, who had a Diet Dr. Pepper. Margaret, who normally didn't drink anything stronger than an occasional glass of wine with dinner or on a date when she didn't want to seem too much of a prude, wanted something way stronger than a Dr. Pepper. Like a Maker's Mark and soda. Her military retiree father had been a bourbon drinker, having picked up the taste while he was stationed at Fort Knox, Kentucky. And Margaret had tried occasionally to enjoy a drink with him but had to water down the good, but strong, bourbon with some soda. And if learning that the FBI was going to investigate you for not being HIPAA compliant didn't make you want a stiff belt, what would?

Before the group could engage in its usual idle gossip about what doctors were hitting on what nurses, Margaret took the floor. Although Mr. Albright had tried to keep Margaret out of the loop, she was now in quite well with the hospital intelligence network, particularly through her now well-established friendship with the nurses in the HIPAA Hassle Informal Workgroup. Margaret said, "Ladies, I've got a problem. Remember that jerk in Patient Accounts who used PHI to commit identity theft? Well, he's trying to defend himself by saying that the hospital's failure to discipline two doctors who discussed a patient's mental health status in the hall and a receptionist who called a patient by name in the waiting room and only suspending another employee who purposely breached confidentiality by stating that a patient was on antidepressants in front of her coworkers set up a climate in which the hospital was not taking HIPAA compliance seriously. So Ken Mahan just told me that the FBI is going to investigate the hospital to see whether our lax enforcement of HIPAA caused or contributed to Gibbons's decision to commit identity theft using patient identifiable information. And finally, the fact that we didn't take any public action against the board member who improperly used the report to the Cancer Registry to require cancer patients to pay off their home loans or car loans because having the Big C made them a credit risk supposedly further encouraged Gibbons to commit identity theft. So what's your feeling? Has our enforcement been so lax that you feel that we don't take HIPAA seriously?"

"No way, HIPAA lady," Keliah answered. "No offense, but some nurses think that you are wrapped too tight about HIPAA. There's no way that any sane member of the hospital workforce thinks that you and the rest of management aren't serious about HIPAA compliance."

"Yeah, you're a real HIPAA bitch," Cassandra added, laughing. "Just kidding! But I agree with Keliah that you've done all that you could to make us take HIPAA seriously. So we've got your back, girl. Send those feds to us. We'll square them away."

Keliah asked, "What does your consultant say about this mess?"

"I haven't called him yet."

Keliah lapsed into the language that she would have used in the 'hood. "Look, bitch, are you stupid or what? This is the F.B. FUCKING I. You don't mess around with the Fibbies. You call that guy now. Didn't he used to do criminal defense?"

"Yes, but I didn't do anything wrong. So why can't I just talk to the FBI?"

"HIPAA lady, you may be very smart with your college degrees and your health information credentials, but you don't know squat about the real world. It doesn't matter a damn bit whether you did something wrong or not. What matters is who the administration hangs out to dry to keep the heat off them. And that may well be you, girl. So I don't care if you're pissed because your consultant inappropriately groped you before you were ready to be groped or failed to grope you when you thought it was about time for some serious groping, or whether you're pissed at him for failing to recognize your charms and fall all over you and profess his undying love. He's about the only person you can trust to tell you what to do. So call the mother-fucker."

The other members of the HIPAA Hassle Informal Workgroup emphatically agreed. So not without some misgivings, Margaret agreed to call him.

Margaret changed the subject. "Ok, that's my problem. What other HIPAA hassles have happened since the last time that we met that I need to know about? And in case you are concerned, if you tell me that's it's off the record, it's off the record."

"I've got one," Kathy said. "This one happened at KU Med Center. A man was in an auto accident and wasn't wearing a seat belt. So he crashed his head into the windshield and was taken to Saint Luke's trauma center. Turns out he was brain dead, but he had one of those driver's licenses that donates his organs as needed. Turns out KU had a cardiac patient who desperately needed a heart transplant and was a good match. So they harvested his heart at Saint Luke's and shipped it on ice across town to KU. The transplant surgeon calls the harvesting surgeon and says, 'Doctor, what meds did you have your patient on to stabilize him until you took his heart? I need to know so that we don't have a bad interaction with the antirejection drugs I want to administer.' The harvesting surgeon, citing HIPAA and the dead man's privacy rights, refused to tell him!"

To shocked gasps and exclamations, Kathy continued. "They eventually got the lawyers involved and worked it out. But it took about 20 minutes. And the heart could have deteriorated in that 20 minutes."

"Yeah, then we'd have two dead patients," Jade interjected.

"What about it, HIPAA lady? Wouldn't that be a proper disclosure for treatment purposes?"

"Absolutely. Yes, deceased patients keep their privacy rights after their death—"

"That's really likely to be my last comforting thought on my deathbed," Cassandra interrupted to laughter.

Margaret laughed, too, not minding the interruption. She was very glad that these pretty impressive nurses had let her join their group. She continued, "But it was absolutely a proper disclosure without patient consent for treatment, payment, and health care operations. And even if it wasn't, I'd argue that his consent to transplant his organs carried with it implied consent to share such information as necessary to facilitate the transplants."

"HIPAA lady, you really know this shit," Keliah observed. "Now, I can see why they made you the Privacy Officer."

"I agree," Jade said. "But think how stupid this situation was. What would the damages have been for one doctor improperly telling another that he had administered Mannitol to control brain swelling of a patient who was later found to be brain-dead? Compare that disclosure to damages if the transplant recipient dies!"

No one else had any HIPAA incidents to recount, so after a few minutes of gossiping about the doctors' follies and sexual misconduct, like the OR doctor who was being sued for saying to a student nurse, "Get your tits out of my operating field," which reminded Margaret of what her nurse aunt had told her many years earlier, the group broke up, but not until after Keliah had once again admonished Margaret to call her consultant.

But Margaret didn't.

34

Health Information Management Department
Kansas City Memorial Hospital

Pam, whom Margaret had briefed that the FBI was going to question her and maybe others, buzzed Margaret on the intercom and said, "They're here." She didn't have to tell Margaret who was here.

"Send them in."

Agents Alexander and Millar entered, dressed in blue suits with white shirts and conservative ties. "Good afternoon, Ma'am," they intoned together.

"Hello."

Agent Alexander continued, "I'm Special Agent Alexander of the FBI. This is Agent Millar." He flashed his credentials. Margaret couldn't have told whether the badge read "Roy Rogers Deputy Ranger," so she held out her hand for the badge.

Agent Alexander handed her the badge. It appeared authentic. If the two agents had showed up out of the blue asking for access under the law enforcement access to health information of a victim of a crime or abuse exception to the consent requirement, she would have called the FBI Field Office for verification of their status. But because she had gotten the word from multiple sources that the FBI was coming at this particular time, she didn't want to piss them off by hassling them too much.

"Well, I'm no expert on FBI badges, but it looks good to me. What can I do for you gentlemen? Please have a seat."

They sat down. They had talked about whether to summon her down to their office or to go to her and decided on the latter. They didn't want to do a Mutt and Jeff on her the way that they had done with Gibbons. They wanted to take a subtler approach. She would be more relaxed in her own office and, hence, more off guard.

"We want to talk to you about the state of the hospital's HIPAA compliance," Bill answered.

"Ok. But do I need a lawyer?"

"We can't advise you whether you need a lawyer," Bill responded. "But you are not a suspect in anything, and you will note that we did not read you your rights. But if you want to consult an attorney, we certainly don't mind."

"Why are you interested in whether the hospital is HIPAA compliant?"

"The perp—the perpetrator—this Gibbons fellow is trying either to defend himself or to get a lighter sentence by saying that the hospital's failure to comply fully with HIPAA encouraged him to commit the crime. So the U.S. Attorney wants to find out whether that accusation is true or not so that she can decide how favorable a plea bargain to give him. He's going to plead guilty. He has no real defense."

"Ok. What questions do you have of me?"

"You are both the Acting Director of Health Information Management and the Privacy Officer, right?"

"Yes."

"In your opinion, is the hospital HIPAA compliant?"

"Yes, we hired a very well qualified HIPAA consultant who took us through the process, and he certified us as compliant when he finished." Because Margaret had not called John, she had not been told to answer questions, if indeed she answered them at all, with the "shortest truthful answer." Long answers just gave agents more information to ask questions about.

"Who was this consultant?"

"Here, I've got one of his cards," handing it to Agent Millar.

"Ok, we'll check up on him." This comment made Margaret feel nauseous. Had she just involved John in some criminal FBI hassle? Maybe not calling him wasn't such a bright idea after all.

"Have you had any HIPAA violations since the compliance date?"

"We have had a couple."

"This HIPAA law requires you to document security incidents, does it not—something called a security incident report?" Bill had done his homework before the interview. "Do you have reports on these incidents?"

"Yes, Sir." Margaret was starting to get nervous enough to call the agents "Sir." "I'll get them for you." She got up and walked to a file cabinet and extracted the Security Incident Reports folder. She walked to the door and handed the folder to Pam who was trying not to listen too obviously. "Please copy the reports in this folder for the agents."

The agents didn't miss that Margaret was now calling them "Sir." They had gotten the upper hand and knew how to use it. Bill continued, "Ok, but let's talk about them. What was the first breach?"

"Well, it wasn't really a breach. A patient complained that she was called by name in the waiting room and that she overheard two doctors discussing another patient's case in the hall. The local Office of Civil Rights of the Department of Health and Human Services investigated and found no violation. But we took some remedial action just to avoid irritated patients who think that we don't care about their privacy."

"Were you satisfied with this outcome?"

"Yes."

"And the security incident report for that incident is among the ones that you are providing us?"

"Yes, Sir."

"What other ones occurred?"

"A pharmacy worker improperly disclosed that a prescription was for antidepressants. She was suspended for two weeks."

"Did you think that time was sufficient?"

"I had recommended three weeks, but could live with management's decision."

"You didn't recommend that she be terminated?"

"No. She had a clean record."

"And the report on this incident is one that you are providing us?"

"Yes, Sir."

"Any others?"

"One more, but I don't know much about it. It involved a board member. Way above, as my military father used to say, my pay grade. The scuttlebutt was that he had somehow improperly used a report to the Cancer Registry to call in loans that the cancer patients had made at his bank."

"All right, we'll ask management about that. Any others?"

"No, Sir."

"Was the hospital's failure to comply with HIPAA or discipline HIPAA violators a contributing factor in Gibbons's crimes?"

Margaret wasn't going to show it too overtly, but she was starting to get irritated at this line of questioning. "I don't see how. The hospital had done a criminal background check before hiring him. We had properly trained him and the rest of our staff. We required him to sign a confidentiality pledge. We had done a written risk analysis and implemented reasonable, cost-effective security measures as HIPAA requires. We had disciplined others who had committed violations, albeit they were less serious than his. I don't know what more we could have done. For God's sake, employees at Los Alamos had taken our nuclear secrets home on their laptops, and I'd like to think that situation would have involved way more security than HIPAA requires."

The two agents looked at each other and both arrived at the conclusion, that it was time to terminate the interview. They had enough to follow up on. They could interview her again if necessary.

"I think that we are done, Ma'am. Thanks for your cooperation. If we need something else, we'll be in touch."

"Thank you," Margaret responded because she didn't know what else to say. She didn't have a warm fuzzy feeling about the interview, but had no idea why. She just knew that it hadn't gone well.

After the agents had left, Margaret wanted to say aloud what she remembered from the Jackie Gleason show, *The Honeymooners,* which she had always watched with her father. When Jackie, playing Ralph Cramden, got caught by his wife, Alice, in a web of lies, he would always end the scene by yelling, "I've got a b-i-g mouth!!!" And now I know that I should have called John, she thought, but it's probably too late now.

35

FBI Field Office, Kansas City, Missouri

Agent Millar brought two Starbucks coffees to the office that
he shared with Agent Alexander. It was the basic Starbucks, not
some wimpy cinnamon soy light latte. FBI agents couldn't drink
wimpy coffee even if they liked it because they would have to take
so much shit from the other agents. Even female FBI agents had to
avoid anything more frou-frou than basic Starbucks. The office
coffee sucked, so Bill, knowing that they had a serious issue to
discuss, thought he'd try to get his partner and friend in as good a
mood as possible. So he had stopped at Starbucks on his way to
work and sprung for two vente—large—black coffees and brought
them to the somewhat dreary office that they shared with a mixture
of paper files and computers. Each desk had a computer, but stacks
of paper records took up all of the remaining space, along with
empty coffee cups, sandwich wrappers, and other detritus of less-
than-concerned-about-neatness agents who would rather be out in
the field doing something interesting than filling out the myriad
reports required for something as simple as a surveillance or, God
forbid, for a search warrant to be issued by a federal Magistrate
Judge.

"Thanks, Bill. Some decent fucking coffee for a change. So
you are trying to butter me up before we discuss the HIPAA case."

"You can read me like a book. We've got to figure out what to
do. It's a mess."

"Ok, let's go over what we've got and make sure that we both
assess the evidence the same way."

"All right. Let's start at the top and work down. That asshole Deutsch, although he did get the hospital's permission to waive the attorney-client privilege about what he had advised management about their compliance efforts, pretty much tried to hang Margaret out to dry. He said that her failure to insist on severe sanctions for the violations that they had experienced contributed to an atmosphere that the Privacy Officer and, hence, the whole hospital, did not care about HIPAA and patient privacy. And that she was light on Doctor Hass because she was dating him."

Agent Alexander agreed with Bill's assessment of the interview and the circumstances of the interview, especially that Deutsch was an asshole. And Bill had accurately summarized the interview with the self-important Harvard Brahmin. But agreeing with the summarization of the interview was a far cry from agreeing with the substance of the matter. "So what about Albright?"

"Well, I think that he tried to hang his Privacy Officer out to dry to avoid upper management liability, as well. He said that she had not forcefully recommended severe sanctions against Doctor Hass and the other physician who had discussed the patient's mental health problems in the hall. He said that he hadn't known that she was dating Doctor Hass when he accepted her recommendation but would have taken a much closer look at it if he had."

"She wasn't dating him then, was she?"

"I don't think so, but maybe she was attracted to him before going out with him."

"So we need to get the time-line straight."

"And even if she were dating him, because the Office of Civil Rights found no violation, it's going to be hard to hang her out to dry for not recommending severe discipline for a nonviolation whether she was hot for him or not."

They went through the other board members' interviews and the rest of the hospital administration's interviews.

"So," Bill said, "the only board member who supported Margaret was Marta Weagryn, who basically supported my belief that Deutsch was an asshole and added that he was against the compliance effort because the hospital had hired an outside consultant instead of his firm."

"So we agree that he has a motive to hang Margaret out to dry?"

Bill took a long pull at his coffee before responding, "Absolutely."

"And the only management team member who supported Margaret was Mr. Mahan?"

"But his credibility is suspect because he hired the consultant that she had recommended. And he didn't want to admit that doing so might have been a mistake. But no one else had any real personal knowledge and seemed to be just supporting Albright out of self-preservation."

Agent Alexander turned to the worker bees. "Correct me if I'm wrong, but every worker bee we talked to—the Health Information Management Department staff, the nurses, the doctors, and the other workers—all unanimously supported her, even the ones who called her the HIPAA bitch. And Nurse Keliah Stevens got positively hostile at the implication that Margaret wasn't committed to HIPAA compliance."

Bill removed the transcript of Keliah's interview. "Yeah, she made her position pretty clear." He read her answer to his question verbatim, "'Yes, Mr. FBI, you bust in here and start hassling us that we aren't HIPAA compliant. Well, let me tell you, Mr. FBI, the HIPAA lady, that's what we call her, is doing a fine, a super-fine, job. It's the assholes in management that are trying to hang her out to dry to save their sorry asses. Why don't you go catch a terrorist or something rather than hassling this fine woman? I've got nothing more to say to you.'"

"Little doubt where she stands."

"Yeah, that would be pretty powerful testimony in front of a majority black Missouri federal court jury."

"What about the board member who breached the confidentiality of the report to the Cancer Registry?"

Bill pulled that security incident report out of the file and scanned it. "The administration pretty much kept the Privacy Officer out of the loop. Margaret said that it was above her pay grade, and that assessment seems to be true. I can make a case that she did all that she could and that it's the hospital administrator and Deutsch who were lax, if anyone."

"Well, we are going to get crucified, but I agree. Let's write it up recommending no indictment. But Ms. Thorp isn't going to like it."

"Agreed. And other than the fact that shit rolls downhill, who cares whether she likes it or not? If she gets us fired, we can open a private security firm and make some real money without all this bureaucratic bullshit." Both of them took a long pull of their strong coffee, nodded as if they had accomplished their mission, and agreed that it was after five o'clock and time for something stronger than Starbuck's house brew coffee. Like one (or more) of the dozens of fine bourbons at the new Maker's Mark restaurant in the Power and Light District. And if stopped for erratic driving that could lead to a DUI test, their FBI credentials would get them professional courtesy.

36

Lakeview Patio, Lake of the Ozarks Resort

Stanley Deutsch was bored. He hated attending the annual
Missouri Bench and Bar Conference, but his firm thought that it
was important to go schmooze with the judges. Because Stanley
was not a litigator, he thought that any influence that he might
have on a judge was fairly tenuous, but the firm's thought was that,
if the firm contributed to the judges' campaigns and named
partners of the firm, such as Stanley, buttered them up at a legal—
that is, not in violation of legal ethics—buttering-up event, such as
this conference, these activities might make the difference in a
close case. And the firm might want the judge's support if a
member of the firm were being considered for moving from the bar
to the bench. Even if a judge who had come from the firm had to
recuse himself or herself from a case because it would be a conflict
of interest to judge a case in which his or her former firm
represented a party, judges asked other judges their opinion of
issues being litigated before them. So the former firm member
might influence the judge who was actually deciding the case
favorably to the firm's position. And it also helped recruiting the
best and brightest out of law school to be able to say that the most
recent appointee to the U.S. District Court for the Western District
of Missouri or the District of Kansas or even a state trial court had
come from the firm.

Stanley, unlike others, didn't come to this annual June
conference for the bass fishing guide, the trap shooting, the boating
from the marina on the Lake of the Ozarks, the golf or tennis, or

even the free (except for the cost of the conference and the hotel) continuing legal education, which made the conference tax-deductible. He didn't have to squeeze in his annual mandatory CLE course hours, including ethics, before the end of June to keep his law license because his firm provided all of the required CLE courses that he needed right there in the law firm's offices. And this year, he wasn't a presenter at any of the CLE courses being offered at the conference. So Stanley was pleased that he did not have to waste his time in a room full of loser attorneys who had waited till the last minute to get their CLEs in and who always seemed to fail to understand why they should be impressed with him.

No, this year, he had come to the Lakeview Patio just for the meet and greet, which at least had a cash bar. He carefully exchanged pleasantries with enough judges that at least some of them would remember that he was there for the conference if they ever had to decide whether his firm was supportive of their judicial careers—as if the firm's large campaign contributions wouldn't be remembered.

And after having dutifully mingled for almost an hour, he spied Marsha Thorp, standing by herself a few feet away from one of the cash bars so that it looked as if she were waiting for a chance to refresh her glass of white wine rather than because she was antisocial or bored out of her skull at the event. She was a little overdressed for the Lake of the Ozarks in a basic black dress. U.S. Attorneys had to butter up the judges just as large firms did, but as a presidential appointee, Marsha thought herself at least the equal of any federal district judge for the Western District of Missouri. After all, there were more than a dozen judges and magistrates in the District, but she was the one and only—the one U.S. Attorney for the Western District of Missouri. No, they could schmooze her. Ok, they didn't have to kiss her ass, but she didn't have to grovel to them, either. So she wasn't going to be too obvious about kissing their judicial asses to the point that they thought that they were superior to the U.S. Attorney for the Western District of Missouri.

So even though she, like the FBI agents, thought that Stanley was basically an asshole, she was glad when he approached. Talking to him would make it look as if she weren't ignoring the judges or so beyond the pale that no one would talk to her. Or even worse, that she couldn't bring herself to move more than five feet away from the cash bar.

"Hi, Stanley. What's up? You look about as thrilled to be here as I am."

"Madame U.S. Attorney, to put it into an appropriate dialect for this backwoods Missouri setting, you've got that right."

Marsha laughed, "Stanley, you're so predictable. Always the elitist."

To his credit, Stanley responded in kind but with an insincere smile, "When you are elite, what can you do?"

"Nothing, I guess. But should we be seen talking when I'm investigating the hospital that you represent for a criminal HIPAA violation?"

"Why not? I represent the hospital, not any of its officers, employees, or agents. And I don't believe that you are seeking a criminal indictment against the hospital as a corporate person."

"No, but I am looking at management to determine whether they are liable for not being HIPAA compliant, which may have encouraged Gibbons to commit identify theft or failed to prevent it."

"I understand your desire to be the first U.S. Attorney to get a management scalp for a criminal HIPAA violation. But none of the upper echelons of the hospital's management came close to encouraging Gibbons or failing to prevent his identity theft.

"Look, Marsha, you know that my firm has always supported you. We pressured the Democratic National Committee to support you when the President was going through the short list for your U.S. Attorney position. And if you run for the House or the Senate, you know that we will contribute to your campaign. Or if you have a chance to move up in the U.S. Attorney's Office, or the Solicitor General's Office, or the Attorney General's Office, we will do what we can to support you. But I'm not trying to buy you off in this case. I'm just suggesting that both of us can come out ahead if your investigation finds that the Acting Director of Health Information Management, because of her relationship with the HIPAA consultant and a doctor who should have been disciplined for a HIPAA violation, should be indicted, not the hospital itself or senior management."

Marsha set her empty wine glass down on the tray that a passing waiter was carrying. "What you propose is not that far from what I have been thinking. I don't know whether you're aware of it yet, but earlier this month, DOJ issued a memo regarding who may be liable for HIPAA violations, particularly management, and I know that the Department of Justice would like us to go after management-level HIPAA violators for criminal penalties. If I indict the young woman and don't indict Albright or any other upper level management, will the hospital cooperate?"

"Absolutely. One hundred percent."

"Ok. Let me think about it. I won't take any action against anyone else at the hospital without contacting you first to get your take on it."

"Sounds fair to me."

"I'll take another glass of Chardonnay now." Marsha wanted to let Stanley know who was in charge.

He didn't mind. "My pleasure," he said as he walked toward the bar. He knew that he had gotten what he wanted. He didn't have much against Margaret personally, but she had cost him significant legal fees by hiring Thomas, and he needed to get rid of her to take HIPAA compliance back to his firm. Maybe the Bench and Bar Conference wasn't such a waste of time after all. So he roughed it and got a glass of Chivas Regal—not the single malt scotch that he normally drank, but it was drinkable in a pinch—along with Marsha's Chardonnay, which he handed to her with a more sincere smile than he usually managed to manifest.

"Thank you, Stanley," Marsha smiled. Both of them smiled like Cheshire cats—both getting what they had wanted in their impromptu negotiations. "Come on, it's time to go in for dinner. I know that you are just dying for barbeque. I'll even sit next to you so that you don't have to mingle with the red-necks."

"I'd better not take your arm to escort you in," Stanley laughed. "Some asshole will take a picture on his cell phone, and when you run for office, it will surface to torpedo your campaign that you were escorted to dinner by a married named partner of a major law firm."

"Stanley, you should have been a politician. Your instincts are impeccable."

As they walked into the banquet hall, he responded, "I am a politician. I thought that you knew."

37

U.S. Attorney's Office
Federal Courthouse
Kansas City, Missouri

U.S. Attorney Thorp's secretary buzzed her. "Mr. Mogridge on the phone. He says that he represents Gibbons and wants to see whether you are interested in a plea bargain. He says that the Assistant U.S. Attorney assigned to the case is too wet behind the ears and clueless to discuss a plea bargain with."

"All right. I'll take the call." Pushing the connect button on her complicated phone system, which looked like the bridge of the Starship Enterprise, and removing her large earring, which would interfere with her headset, she answered, "Hello, Tim. What can I do for you?"

"As you undoubtedly know, I represent Gibbons. I was wondering whether we could agree on a plea bargain. Your AUSA keeps reiterating that he confessed, so you've got him dead to rights, so why deal."

"I'm listening."

"Well, I admit that you've got a pretty good case. But remember the last case that I tried against one of your newbie AUSAs in which you had a confession and my guilty-as-hell client walked. You know, the one in which the arresting FBI agent, showing off his knowledge of arcane terms, wrote up the confession such that my high-school graduate client confessed to fellation—an arcane variant on the term 'fellatio.' And I convinced the jury that my client had confessed to a crime that he had no clue what it was. He had no clue what fellatio was, much less fallation. Not that he didn't ever engage in it, just that he didn't know that terminology for it. So the agent wrote out the confession and said, 'Sign here.' If the confession had read, 'I made her give me a blow job,' or even 'We had oral sex,' the jury might have bought it. But they didn't believe the confession from my uneducated client with this arcane term. They believed that the agent wrote the confession and forced my client to sign it when he had no clue what it said."

"Ok Tim, I know you're good. We don't have to engage in this posturing as to who has the bigger dick, which, admittedly is only metamorphic in my case. As it turns out, I might be willing to offer your client a sweetheart deal in this case."

"How sweetheart?" Tim said, thinking to himself, let the posturing begin.

"Only one year's imprisonment and the jail time suspended. Repay the identity theft losses to the victim. Pay a fine that he can have the period of suspension to repay. And I'll dismiss the mail fraud, identity theft, and other charges with prejudice if he meets all of the conditions of the plea bargain, counts that would have him facing decades in prison."

"What's the catch?"

"As he did in his confession, he rolls over on the Acting Director of Health Information Management, whose relationship with the hospital's HIPAA consultant and a doctor who committed a HIPAA violation caused her not to discipline HIPAA violators appropriately, which encouraged Gibbons to commit his crimes on the theory that the hospital was not serious about HIPAA compliance. We will write the deal that, if his cooperation leads to a conviction, his jail time will be suspended. He will be put on supervised probation instead. If he's not helpful, his jail time is limited to one year. This deal is a gift from God. What do you say?"

"Well, reserving the right to quibble over some of the details, I can recommend this deal to my client. I've read the new Department of Justice Memorandum suggesting that management may be criminally liable for what someone like Gibbons does if the entity is not HIPAA compliant. But I don't think that the Acting HIM Director did anything that would make her criminally culpable under any theory of corporate criminal liability, but she's not my client. Gibbons is. And I've got to do what I can to zealously defend him even if we have to help hang her out to dry."

"Good. But I need a quick decision."

"No later than close of business tomorrow."

"That's fine. And feel free to jack up your fee for this sweetheart deal. But if your client doesn't agree, he's going down. Even if I have to step in, replace my newbie AUSA, and try the case myself. You may even be a better trial attorney than I am. But I've got the law and the facts on this one, and I'm not so far behind you in trial experience that I could lose this one, no matter how good you are. So you had better be at your most persuasive with your client, or in the absence of a guilty plea, I'll get a twenty-year sentence for all of the crimes that he's facing."

"Marsha, I've never said that I'm a better trial attorney than you. But neither one of us wants a protracted trial in this case. I don't want my client to end up under the jail because of my big ego as a trial attorney. And you don't want the 10 percent chance that I pull off a miracle against an inexperienced AUSA. Nor do you want to take the time away from your supervisory duties to try this case yourself. It's not trying Osama Bin Ladin that would make you the legal/political star of the century. It's just trying some low-life loser for identity theft. So let's work together and resolve this situation in a mutually beneficial manner."

"Agreed. I'll get you a written plea agreement and a stipulation by the close of business today for your review and edit."

"I agree, too. I'll get with my client and get back to you no later than tomorrow afternoon."

"Thanks, Tim. It's always nice to deal with an experienced criminal defense attorney such as yourself. Even though you kick our butt in court a little bit more than I'd like, at least I can deal with you. Unlike some of the wet-behind-the-ears new defense counsel who haven't got a clue or have such a big ego that they think that they can defeat the might and majesty of the U.S. government, you have a strong enough ego that you can do what's best for your client even if you would love to take me on. In other words, you don't need to get press releases for tearing up the U.S. Attorney's office when that feeds your ego, but doesn't help your client."

"Gee, thanks. I'll be in touch. Bye."

"Bye."

Tim was somewhat taken aback by this compliment. The U.S. Attorney had never said anything complimentary about him before. He took it with a grain of salt, as perhaps being a ploy to make him lower his guard and accept a plea bargain when he might have a decent defense. But agreeing with her and ending the conversation was the best way to lock in the favorable plea bargain. And he knew that he wasn't going to get an acquittal in this case even against a brand-new AUSA. Even if he beat the HIPAA charge, the identity theft and the mail fraud looked solid. The government had just too much evidence, including the videos of Gibbons using the credit cards, the handwriting exemplars showing that he had signed credit cards in the cancer patient's name, and his confession, for him to convince a jury that the government had not proved its case beyond a reasonable doubt. No, while he would try to improve the deal for his client, he had to put it to bed.

Tim immediately sent an email to Marsha summarizing his recollection of the proposed deal. That way, if she didn't follow up, he would have a paper trail that he could use to move to compel the government to honor the plea bargain. And so much the better if she answered back, confirming their understanding.

Then, Tim called Bart, who was surfing for porn on his home computer system. In the hierarchy of room décor, he was so far behind the lawyers that it wasn't even funny. Rather than Picassos, he had seminude posters of teenage TV and movie stars taped to his walls with masking tape. But the pictures went well with the empty Coke and beer cans, the pizza boxes with the crusts molding in them, and the Cheetos, which, even in their packaging, had long since passed the fresh test.

Upon taking Tim's call, Bart was quite relieved to hear that he could avoid jail time by pleading guilty, paying a fine and restitution, and agreeing to testify against the Acting Director of Health Information Management. If she went under the jail for the rest of her life, that was better than him spending another night in jail. The short period that he had spent in custody before being bailed out was enough. No beer. No video games. No internet porn. How was a guy supposed to survive in prison? Especially for a crime that really hurt no one. It didn't really hurt the cancer patient. It only "hurt" the credit card companies that were ripping off consumers anyway with their exorbitant interest rates and fees. So if he had to roll over on anyone in the health care industry to avoid jail, so be it. So he thanked Mr. Mogridge profusely, promised to cooperate, and went back to his porn website, feeling very much better now that he was most likely going to avoid jail. In fact, he felt good imagining a female, like Margaret, the Acting HIM Director, led off bound, in handcuffs, to jail, where she would be sexually assaulted by lesbian cellmates. He found this imagery so exciting that he refined his search and spent the rest of the evening on a website specializing in women in confinement. To his warped mind, it was an awesome website.

While Bart was surfing for porn, the U.S. Attorney was on the phone with Stanley Deutsch, letting him know that she was going to indict Margaret but that the hospital and upper level management were off the hook.

38

CEO's office, Kansas City Memorial Hospital

Margaret couldn't imagine why she had been summoned to the CEO's office. The HIPAA compliance date for the Security Rule was long since past, and she knew that the hospital was more than substantially compliant. And there had been no major breaches that she knew of other than the board member, a breach that she had been kept out of the loop on, and now Gibbons. When there was a health information management issue other than a major HIPAA breach, she dealt with Ken Mahan—not with Albright, the head honcho. And for the third year in a row under her leadership, the hospital's team of runners had placed in the Hospital Hill Run, so he should have been happy about her work in that regard. So she didn't have a warm fuzzy feeling about being summoned to his office. She sat in his waiting room nervously worrying her bracelet. She stopped only when her wrist started turning red from her twisting the beaded bracelet around and around.

Finally, Albright's secretary told her to go in. Her lack of a warm fuzzy feeling immediately turned into a feeling of cold actual dread when she saw Stanley Deutsch sitting there to Albright's right. She remembered how he had tried to get rid of John Thomas and immediately knew that his presence bode no good for her.

"Sit down, Margaret," Mr. Albright said.

She did.

"Margaret, I've got some bad news. But before we lay it on you, I want you to know that the hospital is going to stand behind you."

"What are you talking about? What have I done that you need to stand behind me?

"Let me handle his," Stanley interjected. "Margaret, I don't know any way of telling you this easily other than just spitting it out. The U.S. Attorney has indicted you for a criminal HIPAA violation."

Even though she was in shock, Margaret responded, "What are you talking about? I've not breached confidentiality. I've done everything that I could do to protect our patients' privacy. And you know it."

"Be that as it may, and that may be your defense, the U.S. Attorney is convinced that you encouraged Gibbons by failing to appropriately recommend discipline on a doctor that you dated and because you didn't implement proper security measures because you, to put it indelicately, had the hots for the HIPAA consultant. And that, in her opinion, qualifies as corporate or management criminal liability."

Margaret started to cry, "I can't believe this. I tried to do my best."

Mr. Albright stepped in, "I'm sure that you did, my dear. And the hospital will stand behind you. We have to put you on administrative leave until this issue is resolved, but we will make it with pay. And we will pay up to $10,000 towards your legal fees. I'm sure that this situation is all a misunderstanding and that it will all go away." He pulled out a tissue from the box on his desk and handed it to Margaret, who grabbed it as if it were a life preserver and she were drowning. As she was.

Stanley did nothing to make her feel better, although his words might have sounded compassionate. "Look, I've arranged with the U.S. Attorney and the FBI that you can surrender yourself with your lawyer. So they won't come to the hospital and arrest you and take you way in handcuffs. Have your attorney contact Assistant U.S. Attorney Smith to arrange your surrender. My firm, which represents the hospital, has an obvious conflict of interest, so we can't handle your case. But I can recommend some criminal lawyers for you. The U.S. Attorney's office has agreed that you can be released on your own recognizance, so you won't have to make bail and so you won't have to spend a day or two in confinement waiting for a bail hearing. But don't delay. Get an attorney who can arrange your surrender ASAP. If you wait too long, they will issue an arrest warrant and drag you off in handcuffs."

If this information were meant to be comforting—that she could avoid being publicly humiliated by being arrested and led off doing the perp walk—its effect on Margaret was hardly comforting and resulted in even more sobbing. Even Stanley began to feel slightly guilty at what he was doing to this basically innocent young woman. Even though he had never done criminal defense, he knew how stressful facing federal prosecution was. But he didn't feel guilty enough to step up to the plate and stop this travesty of justice. Nor was Larry Albright so inclined, thinking of his butt and the hospital's. But he did, charitably perhaps but more likely out of guilt, hand Margaret another tissue. He did, however, find her grateful look at this small courtesy to be heart-rending.

If Margaret hadn't been so shocked and blind-sided by the whole matter, she might have wondered how Mr. Deutsch knew that the U.S Attorney would let her lawyer surrender her if he was too conflicted for his firm to represent her.

Deutsch continued. "You have to clean out your desk and be out of the hospital by close of business. Pam will be appointed Acting HIM Director. If you need to come to the hospital for any reason, you need to call Mr. Mahan and get permission. Have the attorney that you hire provide me his contact information so that we can arrange for the hospital to pay up to $10,000 of your legal fees. If you are found not guilty, we will request the board for permission to pay all of your legal fees. But we will pay up to $10,000 regardless of the outcome. Any questions?"

"No, Sir," Margaret answered in an almost inaudible voice.

"Any other questions, Margaret?" Mr. Albright asked.

Again, in a low voice, "No, Sir."

"Margaret, we all hope that this mess goes away and feel bad that you have to go through this situation. Call me if there's anything that I can do." The last thing that Albright wanted was any more involvement in this mess, but he was starting to feel some guilt at his part in hanging Margaret out to dry.

He felt even worse as Margaret walked out, with her shoulders slumped and tears and mascara running down her cheeks. After she was out of hearing, he turned to Deutsch and said, "Stan, do we really want to do this thing to Margaret? She isn't responsible as management or otherwise for what Gibbons did. Gibbons is responsible, and you told me that he has a pretrial agreement wherein he won't even serve any jail time."

Stanley answered, quite forcefully, "Look, regardless of whether the U.S. Attorney could ultimately get a conviction or not, do you really want yourself and the board members on the six o'clock news doing the perp walk for being arrested for a criminal HIPAA violation? And this U.S. Attorney is the one that convicted the president of Baptist Hospital for Medicare fraud and sent him to jail for four and a half years—for an illegal kickback involving an employment arrangement that two separate law firms had advised the president were legal.

"This solution is the trade-off. Yes, it sucks that this apparently fine young woman is being hung out to dry to protect you and the board members. But she's not going to go to jail in a case in which she did not get any personal gain from Gibbons's breach, has no prior criminal record, and will have a lot of support from the hospital staff that she did her best."

"But she's going to have a federal conviction and have to perform community service or serve house arrest and for what?"

"To keep you, the other upper level management, and the board members from doing the perp walk. And it's basically a done deal now. The U.S. Attorney has already indicted her. Ok?"

"I guess. But it makes me wonder why in the world I ever decided to be a hospital administrator."

Stanley ended the conversation, "I can't answer that. Maybe you need to find a new profession. But what I can tell you is that you need this mess to go away. What are your job hunting prospects if the media should publicize that you or the governing board that you work for have been arrested for identity theft or for failing to prevent it?"

"All right Stan, I'll play along. But I don't want Margaret hung out to dry any more than is necessary. And if we have to let her go, I want you to put together a generous severance package."

"Yes, Sir," Stanley said as he left, well pleased. After the resolution of this criminal case, he could add the hospital's HIPAA compliance to his list of fees upon which his partnership total compensation was calculated.

As the two Harvard grads discussed her future or lack thereof, Margaret went into the executive restroom down the hall from Albright's office. She wasn't upper level management and, consequently, wasn't authorized to use it. But what were they going to do? Send her to jail? Fire her? Even if she were not convicted, her career as an HIM professional was probably shot. After she had checked to make sure that she was the only one in the restroom, she cried a little more, prayed out loud a lot, repaired her face as best she could with wet paper towels, and tried to prepare herself to go down to the HIM Department and clean out her desk. Don't let the bastards get you down, she thought, remembering what her father had always told her as an ex-military man. So she left the restroom, walked down the hall with her head held high, and took the elevator down to the basement to the HIM Department. She strode through the swinging doors to the department and hurried to her office. She was shoving her personal effects into a heavy-duty garbage bag that the department always had on hand to cover paper medical records if the sprinkler system went off or a pipe broke above them when Pam walked in. "What in the world are you doing?"

"Cleaning out my office."

"Why? You've been fired?"

"Worse."

"What could be worse?"

"The U.S. Attorney has indicted me for a criminal HIPAA violation."

"Oh, my God! What the hell for?"

"My nonexistent relationships."

"That makes no sense. Come on, girl. I can't help you if I don't know what's going on."

"They're saying that, because I dated Doctor Hass and because I had the hots for John, I didn't take strong enough disciplinary actions against Doctor Hass and others for HIPAA violations and that this failure encouraged Gibbons to commit his identity theft."

"That's bullshit."

"Tell it to the U.S. Attorney. Anyway, I have to leave the department until the matter is resolved. So the good news is that you are now the Acting Director. Although why you'd want the job when they'll hang you out to dry in a heartbeat is somewhat beyond me."

"I'll tell you, Margaret, this sucks so bad that if I didn't have to send money home to my family in Thailand to support them, I'd resign in protest."

"Don't do that even if you don't need the money. It wouldn't accomplish anything, and they'd probably ruin you for other HIM employment. And I may need a friend on the inside."

"You've got a spy on the inside, girl."

"But don't contact me from work. I can't come to the hospital without getting Mr. Mahan's permission, so who knows what they might do if I called you or you called me or emailed me from the hospital. We can email each other on our home email addresses, but please don't email me using any hospital computer system. Call me from your cell if you want to meet for coffee."

"What are you going to live on?"

"They are continuing my salary until the matter is resolved. So I'm ok for the moment for money. And the hospital will pay up to $10,000 for my legal fees."

"Sounds like they aren't totally hanging you out to dry."

"Yes, they are. They are just assuaging their consciences by throwing me some bones." At that, Margaret lost it and burst into tears again. So Pam came around Margaret's desk and hugged her. They both cried together for a few minutes before Margaret disengaged herself and said, "Enough crying. Help me get my stuff out of your office."

Pam said. "You pack. I'm going to load all the HIPAA compliance files onto a flash memory device so that the evidence that you did all that you could doesn't magically disappear."

"You're a good friend, Pam. And you appear to have what it takes to be a great inside spy. I'd have never thought of taking copies of those files so that the hospital can't ditch them. And to the extent that those files have patient identifiable information, taking a copy would not be a breach of confidentiality because it is an authorized use or disclosure to use such information to defend oneself against an allegation of misconduct. Will you explain to the department why I've left and thank them for their support?"

"Absolutely. All of us will stand behind you. Count on it."

Twenty minutes later, after Pam had made her repair her face again before walking past the HIM Department workers, Margaret walked out of the hospital burdened with her computer bag, purse, a large garbage bag filled with her personal effects, including her two framed college diplomas and her framed RHIT certification, and a flash memory device and hailed a cab to her apartment. She wondered how in the world she was going to tell her mother about this mess and, more importantly, how to prevent her mother from going postal on the hospital, barging in on Mr. Albright, and beating him about the head and shoulders with her umbrella. Although he might deserve it, Margaret wasn't sure that she wanted to piss the hospital off, at least not until the case was over and she was exonerated. After that, she might want to beat Albright and especially Deutsch about the head and shoulders herself with her computer bag—with the heavy computer in it. She hadn't figured out what to do about her mother by the time she got home, so she tabled that issue. She had more pressing concerns. She had to quit crying, get it together, face these charges, find an attorney, and defend herself. She didn't want to use any attorneys that Mr. Deutsch recommended. He would probably recommend the dud defense counsel of Kansas City or one who was the significant other of the U.S. Attorney who wanted her to have a 100 percent conviction rate. She wanted to call John, but wasn't sure that she should. After all, part of the allegations against her was that she was hot for him. As she mulled over this dilemma, quite undecided what to do, the phone rang.

39

EMR Legal, Monadnock Building
53 W. Jackson Boulevard, Downtown Chicago

Almost quittin' time, John thought, as he was about to pack up his briefcase and walk due west for a half mile or so to his apartment at Presidential Towers, an upscale high-rise apartment complex just west of the Loop. He was wondering whether he should stop at Bally's just off State Street for a workout on the way home or simply work out at the Presidential Towers fitness center and then order take-out from Pago Pago, one of his favorite restaurants in the complex, when he had a flash—call Margaret.

Where did that thought come from, he wondered. He had actually thought about Margaret quite a bit since he had finished his consulting gig with the hospital a couple of years earlier. He had concluded that, because she was no longer a client, he could now ask her out. And he really wanted to ask her out. Even though he had met hundreds of women at his seminars and at his consulting gigs—after all, most health information management types were women—she was the most attractive that he had met, both pretty and brainy. He had hidden his attraction to her fairly well while she was a client, but she was no longer a client. But he didn't think that she would agree to his flying her to Chicago and putting her up at a hotel for a date, even though he certainly had enough frequent flier miles from his HIPAA consulting and seminars to do both without even denting his frequent flier total. She would undoubtedly view that arrangement as way too committal for a first date.

But he had a strong feeling that he had to call her. Upon reflection, he couldn't see any real downside. Maybe if he called her, they could reconnect, and it might lead to a date when he was on some neutral ground, like back in Kansas City or giving a seminar in Topeka, Omaha, or even St. Louis. So he dialed her cell phone, figuring that, because it was after five, she might have left the HIM Department for the day.

"Hello," she answered in an almost inaudible voice.

"Margaret? It's John."

John instantly became way more alert as he heard her burst into tears. "What's wrong?"

It was several moments before Margaret was able to compose herself enough to answer. "I'm so glad that you called. I was just thinking about calling you. I don't know whether you can help me, but I'm in big trouble."

John wanted to say that it should be a no-brainer for her to call him if she was in trouble but didn't want to be critical if she was stressed out by her problems. So he merely said, "What kind of trouble?"

Sounding more like a sob than a normal sentence, she replied, "I've been indicted for management liability for one of our employee's identity theft."

"You have to be shitting me."

"I wish."

"Have you been arrested yet?"

"No, Stanley Deutsch said that it had been arranged that my lawyer could surrender me so that I wouldn't be subjected to being arrested and led off in handcuffs from the hospital. He said that his firm was conflicted and that they could not represent me but that he would recommend some criminal lawyers. I don't trust him and hoped that you knew of some good criminal lawyers here. I know that I'm not guilty, but I'm so scared."

"Well, you are absolutely right not to trust Deutsch. This scenario stinks to high heaven. I'll bet my HIPAA earnings for the next year that he is behind this nonsense. He's hanging you out to dry to protect Albright and the board members from being indicted. But calm down. I've got you covered. First, you don't have to look for an attorney. I'm licensed in Illinois, Missouri, Kansas, and Oklahoma, so I can represent you in the U.S. District Court for the Western District of Missouri. Second, although I've never made this promise to a client before, you will not be convicted. I guarantee it."

"I don't think that I can afford you. The hospital has authorized only $10,000 for my legal fees."

John wanted to start his answer with, "You silly goose," but in light of her apparently fragile emotional state omitted that language and cut to the chase, "Margaret, my fee is a big hug when all of this mess is over and done with and you are exonerated. We may have to use some of that money to pay local counsel to surrender you, because I can't get there for a couple days, and to handle status calls when it's not efficient for me to fly to Kansas City for a two-minute court appearance. And I've got great local counsel whom you can absolutely rely on. Dick Dvorak, one of my former students when I taught law school, is a former Marine drill instructor who, if you are one of my clients, will fall on a grenade to protect you. So he's going to call you tomorrow. Do what he says. Did the hospital tell you whom your lawyer should contact to arrange for your surrender?"

"Assistant U.S. Attorney Smith."

"Got it. And I'm not going to turn my cell off no matter if I'm giving a HIPAA speech at a national convention. If you need to call me, you call me any time, and I will answer 24/7."

"Oh, John, thank you. I feel so much better. I never dreamed that after you had completed your consulting contract that you would represent me in a criminal matter for free."

John wasn't sure that he should go there, but felt that, if it would comfort Margaret during her time of trouble to know that he did care about her, he could risk it. "Margaret, I know that I was pretty distant while I was consulting for the hospital and since then. But I have an inviolate rule that I never get involved with a client during a case or consulting contract. It's against legal ethics and always leads to trouble. And I respected you too much to put you in that position. But I've been thinking about asking you out. That pleasant thought is off the table for now because you are my client again. But don't think that I haven't cared about you the entire time since we met at the Cross Country seminar. So as I said earlier, I've got you covered. After this mess is all over, we'll see where we want to go. Ok?"

"Ok. God bless you."

John, as the next thing to a heathen, was slightly uncomfortable with the "God bless you," but again just went along. "Thank you. I'll do better than my best for you."

"What can I do to help?"

John, like Gibbons's attorney, Mogridge, knew the importance of keeping clients busy so that they couldn't quite so easily get into more trouble. So he told Margaret to write up a report in chronological order of everything that she had been involved in with regards to HIPAA compliance.

Then Margaret remembered. "Oh, Pam, my assistant, whom you met at the compliance party a couple of years ago, downloaded all of the HIPAA compliance files onto a memory stick so that I'd have them if the hospital or the FBI lost, destroyed, or modified them."

"Are you sure that she just copied them? That she didn't destroy them?"

"Yes, I checked. They are still saved on our server and backed up by our remote backup. Why do you ask?"

"Because if she had destroyed records, that destruction would constitute obstruction of justice. Remember, Martha Stewart wasn't convicted of insider trading, but rather of obstruction of justice for lying about what she had done. Deleting potential evidence also constitutes obstruction of justice. So I needed to know whether you were an accomplice to obstruction of justice. That charge would really complicate your defense. But it sounds as if you are not involved in that crime. But give me the memory stick so that, if they search your apartment, it is not there."

Margaret took the flash drive out of the inner pocket of her purse, from which she had retrieved her cell phone when it rang, and made a mental note to FedEx it to John.

"I'll FedEx it to you tomorrow for next-day morning delivery to your office. Will someone be there to sign for it?"

"Yes, thanks," he said. "Now, tell me, did the FBI interview you before you were indicted?"

"Yes."

"Did they read you your rights?"

"No, but I asked them if I needed a lawyer, and they said that they couldn't advise me on that, but if I wanted one, I could have one."

"Did you answer their questions?"

"Yes, I know now that it was stupid, but I did. Some of the staff here told me that I shouldn't talk to them until after I had talked to you. But I was stupid and didn't want to bug you when I hadn't heard from you since you finished the consulting contract. Again, it was stupid. But I thought that, because I hadn't done anything wrong, there was no harm in answering their questions."

"Law enforcement plays on the guilt inherent in the Judeo-Christian tradition, the desire to expiate your guilt by confessing. The Muslim religion is based on shame—it is better to lie to your interrogator than to confess and thereby bring shame on one's family. So out of a sense of guilt, even though you hadn't done anything wrong, or out of a sense of duty—I've got to cooperate with law enforcement—you talked. I'll have to get the tape or transcript of the interview to see whether they got anything out of you that cooks your goose."

"Oh, John, I feel so dumb. I should have called you as soon as I learned that the FBI wanted to interview me."

Again, John didn't want to tell her that she was right—that she was a dumb shit at least at that point—so he said, "I doubt that you told them anything that contributed to this b.s. charge unless you told them that Doctor Hass and/or I were humping your bones."

Margaret blushed and actually laughed, "No. Nothing like that. But compared to being indicted for a federal felony, humping even your sorry old bones sounds positively fun."

"That's my girl," John said, pleased that she was starting to lighten up and see some humor in the conversation, but perhaps a little jealous of Doctor Hass. "But were you humping Doctor Hass's bones?"

"No, silly, I was just flirting with him in a misguided attempt to make you jealous. Did it work?"

Margaret couldn't see it, because neither of them had a high-tech phone that showed the callers' faces, but John smiled at this revelation. Unfortunately, learning that Margaret might be just as attracted to him as he was to her just increased the pressure to get her out from under these ridiculous charges. John had always felt that it was much more difficult to defend an innocent client than a guilty one, not that he had had a lot of innocent clients. Sometimes, they weren't guilty of what they were charged with because the prosecutor had screwed up in the charging decision and charged the wrong crime. But they were usually guilty of something. So if they were convicted, it wasn't a total travesty of justice. But if he screwed up and an innocent client, like Margaret, was convicted, it was a travesty of justice that he had a hard time living with. And having a client that he cared about made it even worse. So both her innocence and his attraction really increased the pressure on him.

So he ignored her question and drove on, "Ok, Margaret, I've got to go. I've got to call Mr. Dvorak right now to get him laid on to surrender you so that you aren't subjected to any more hassle than absolutely necessary. And he and I have to formulate an action plan as to how we are going to aggressively attack this indictment. We're not going to lie back and react. We are going to aggressively defend you and put the pressure on the U.S. Attorney to make her respond to our motions rather than preparing her case. So I know that it is easy for me to give this advice and much harder for you to do it, but you've got to stop worrying. Dog Dvorak—which is what we call him because in one case he functioned as a bounty hunter to save our client's son who had been kidnapped by a crack cocaine ring and because he's like a bulldog that never lets go when representing a client—and I will not let you go down on this bullshit indictment. And when we win, we'll decide whether we want to go after the hospital and Deutsch. Ok?"

Margaret broke out crying again, clearly audible over the phone. John felt very frustrated that he couldn't magically make her problem go away, and from having read *Men Are from Mars, Women Are from Venus,* he knew that what she needed was a big hug and a shoulder to cry on rather than his male problem-solving. But he was 544 miles away and couldn't offer her his shoulder to cry on at this moment. So he just muttered vague words of comfort. Poor as they may have been, they seemed to help because Margaret stopped crying and again thanked John and told him to hang up and make his calls.

"Ok, but you must call me at any time, day or night, if you need me or even if you just want to vent. Ok?"

"Yes. Goodnight."

John almost blurted out, "Love you, goodnight," but caught himself in time and simply said, "Hang in there. I'll be in touch. Goodnight." He had bit his tongue and not said the "love you" part because he didn't want to give her some false hope of a relationship in her fragile emotional state that both of them might regret after her case was over. After the case, they could see where, if anywhere, their relationship was going to go.

After he had hung up the phone with Margaret, he called Dog Dvorak, who was more than enthused to be local counsel in a HIPAA case going up against the U.S. Attorney. Sure, it would be easy and fun for Dog. He wasn't falling for the client.

40

Bangkok Pavilion
Windmill Village, Overland Park, Kansas

Pam was already seated in what was certainly one of the
Kansas City area's best Thai restaurants when Margaret walked in.
She hadn't really wanted to drive from her apartment on the Plaza
all the way out to Overland Park, but when Pam had said that she
was going to treat her to a great Thai meal, she didn't know how to
refuse. And Pam had certainly been supportive ever since she had
had to leave her job and face federal criminal charges.

"Hi, Pam. Thanks for inviting me," Margaret smiled as she
walked up to the booth where Pam sat. Pam was wearing a white
blouse with what appeared to be a gorgeous Thai silk skirt. As
befitting her new leisure status, Margaret, on the other hand, was
dressed more casually in blue jeans, a polo shirt, and running
shoes. The restaurant was almost empty. Only one Asian couple sat
at a booth on the other side of the room. Pam had told her that, if
they got there before six-thirty, they would almost have the
restaurant to themselves and could talk freely. After that time, the
popular restaurant would get crowded.

"Sawatdee Kaa," Pam returned the greeting in Thai—
appropriate for a Thai restaurant.

"I hope that you mean 'hello' in what I suppose is Thai—and
not you're going to jail, girl!" Margaret laughed.

"I'm glad that you are able to laugh about your situation.
You're looking good."

"Yeah, right."

"No, seriously. Maybe it's all the pressure that you've been under, but you no longer look like some wet-behind-the-ears kid. You now have a certain gravitas."

"What's that? Is gravity dragging my butt down?" Margaret laughed.

"Maturity. Dignity." Pam may not have had a master's degree, but she had been well educated at KU, and she was even better read.

"Thanks, I guess," Margaret said as she sat down. The waitress bustled up and performed a little bow that Pam informed Margaret was a "wai" in Thai. After they had ordered the house blend hot tea and Thai spring rolls for an appetizer, Margaret asked, "Are you trying to teach me how to speak Thai in case I have to flee the country?"

"No. Just trying to be polite before grilling you on what's happened. Give, girl. I thought that you'd be all depressed after having to surrender yourself."

"Well, it sucked, but it could have been so much worse that I can't feel too bad about it."

"Well, tell me quick, before the restaurant fills up."

"Well, I decided to call John, and just as I was getting my cell phone out of my purse when I got home that last day that I was at the hospital, he called me. Telling him what happened was the best thing that I've done lately, way smarter than agreeing to be interviewed by the FBI." Margaret's eyes teared up as she continued, "John's taking my case. He also refused to take any money for my defense other than to pay local counsel—someone here who could handle what he called 'status calls,' so he wouldn't have to fly to Kansas City for a five-minute hearing. And John was right that the local lawyer that he hired, Mr. Dvorak, would take care of me. He picked me up at my apartment. He had previously briefed me on exactly what would happen. He told me that it was all greased and that I wouldn't be put in pretrial detention—what they call jail before trial. But he suggested that I not wear any expensive jewelry and to take my cash and credit cards out of my wallet just in case. As if I had any expensive jewelry! Apparently, such items could magically disappear if I were put in detention. He also told me to wear a business suit so that I looked like a professional.

"Then, we went to the FBI Field Office, where I was to surrender. If the skids hadn't been greased and I were going through the normal arrest procedure, they would have strip-searched me before turning me over to the U.S. Marshals to take me to the detention facility. As it was, they just wanded me and rummaged around in my purse to make certain that I wasn't carrying a weapon."

"Sounds way better than a strip search!"

"Yes. Then, they booked me—asked my name, age, address, and so forth and entered it into the computer and fingerprinted me. I had expected them to pull out the old roller and ink and ink up my fingers and press them on a fingerprint card as you see on television, but it's all digital now. So I didn't even get my fingertips dirty. And Mr. Dvorak, whom John calls Dog Dvorak, after Dog the Bounty Hunter, because he had once gone with some real bounty hunters to extract one of his client's sons who was AWOL from the Army from crack cocaine dealers who were blackmailing the client to keep her son alive—"

"Come on, girl. I don't need to hear the legal history of this Dvorak person. Get on with your story."

"Ok. Well, anyway, he's about six foot five and a former Marine drill instructor, and he kept himself right next to me, glowering at the agents."

"Was it the same agents who questioned you?"

"Yes, and they were really nice. They seemed as if they wanted no part of the matter. So anyway, after the booking was over, the agents and Mr. Dvorak and I rode to the federal courthouse together and went to the Pretrial Services Office where a Pretrial Services Officer asked me a bunch of questions. He said that normally these questions would be used to determine whether a defendant would be released on her own recognizance, like I was going to be, what, if any, conditions on release were necessary, whether the court would grant bail and how much would it be, or whether pretrial detention was required. He said that, because the U.S. Attorney had called him and specified that I could be released on my own recognizance, the decision had already been made, but he still had to get the information from me to complete the formalities. He added that I appeared eligible for pretrial diversion, which means that I would basically admit guilt but if I completed the diversion program successfully, I wouldn't have a federal conviction on my record. Finally, he gave me a document specifying the charge and stating that I was released on my own recognizance without any conditions other than showing up for every court appearance, that, if I failed to show up for an appearance, the judge would issue a bench warrant for my arrest, and that I could end up in pretrial detention. Finally, the document specified the date for my initial appearance."

"What's that? And when is it?"

"In two weeks. According to John and Dog, it's a time for the judge to make sure that you know what you are charged with and what your rights are. You can enter a plea at that point."

"Are you going to try for the diversion?"

"I don't think so, unless the hospital comes up with some damning evidence that I can't imagine and John tells me to. Diversion is for people who are willing to admit guilt. I'm not. I'm not admitting that I contributed to Gibbons's crime because I didn't.

"So having Dog Dvorak with me the entire time, avoiding the strip search, avoiding riding to the courthouse in handcuffs—doing the perp walk—and avoiding pretrial detention is way better than it could have been."

"Sounds way better. What have you been doing with yourself now that you are a woman of leisure?"

"I couldn't just sit around my apartment, go jogging for several hours a day, or shop till I dropped, so I'm doing some volunteer work at a long-term care facility. Reading to the residents, just talking to them, that kind of stuff. Oh, and I'm studying for my RHIA. I don't know whether I'll ever be able to work in health information management again, but trying to get the higher level credential can't hurt, and it helps pass the time and keep my mind off my troubles."

"Have you talked to John much?"

"Yes, he calls every evening to see how I'm doing and to update me on the case. Just short, business-like calls, but I'm sure glad to get them."

"How are things with your mother?"

"Well, I screwed up. I was afraid to face her, and she found out about it in the *Kansas City Star*. She reads the paper voraciously to see what dirt has been dredged up on local celebrities. But she certainly didn't want to see any dirt on her daughter. She called me up and berated me for embarrassing her. When she asked me how she could face her friends, I told her that my lawyer had instructed me not to talk about the matter with anyone, said goodbye, and hung up. I haven't heard from her since. But enough about me. How are you doing? How are things at the hospital?"

"I'm doing pretty well. I'm not sure that I'm cut out to be the Acting Director. I don't know how you did it, just out of school. Not like the doctors would listen to any medical records type anyway, but they, at least the male ones, view me as some sort of demure China doll—even though I'm Thai, not Chinese—and just ogle me rather than listening to what I'm saying. Other than a few decent ones, like Doctor Hass, they really make my job tough. They won't authenticate their charts on time, they keep trying to sign them with a "dictated but not read" stamp, and they lose the paper charts all the time."

"Yeah, at the HIPAA seminar where I met John, he said that such a stamp gave no legal protection whatsoever and was an invitation to malpractice liability. I wish that the old fossil doctors realized how important correct, complete, and available charts were not only to good patient care but also to avoiding malpractice liability."

"I couldn't agree more. Get this. Doctor Benvenista actually asked me to delete an entry in the EHR after he had authenticated it, saying that it made it look as if he had committed malpractice."

"What did you do?"

"Well, I knew that it was futile to argue with him, so I told him that he had locked down the computer by affixing his digital signature so that all he could do was to add an addendum. He didn't like it one bit, but just stomped out of the department in a huff."

"You lucked out there! He can be a real shit. Any gossip going on about my case?"

"Yes, everyone thinks you're getting screwed. Albright actually had the nerve to send out an email "reminding" us that we didn't have to answer your defense attorney's questions if he tried to interview us. He didn't go so far as to order us not to, but I got the drift."

"That asshole. He pretended to be sympathetic by paying me while on administrative leave and paying my legal fees. I suspect that he sold me out to protect himself and the board members, but John can deal with him."

"Oh, I almost forgot. Those two FBI agents came back and were interviewing anyone and everyone—trying to get some dirt on you. But I can guarantee you that they went away empty-handed. No one, except maybe Albright and Deutsch, told them anything except that you were the HIPAA lady who tried her level best to keep the hospital HIPAA compliant. No one can understand why they don't just drop the case or why the fuck they brought it in the first place."

Margaret was shocked to hear Pam use the f word. She had never used it before in Margaret's presence. But Margaret took it as more proof that Pam cared about her and what happened to her.

"So let's talk about more pleasant matters," Margaret had had enough talk about her case. "How's your family in Thailand?"

"Oh, they're fine. But I've got something that I want to run by you and make sure that you're okay with it. I'm dating Doctor Hass."

Margaret smiled broadly, "Oh, that's wonderful news! Of course, it's fine with me. I think he's great fun to banter with, but I was never really interested in a relationship with him. So go for it, my dear friend. Is it serious?"

"I don't know, but I think that it could be. He brings me flowers when we go out, and he takes me to pricey restaurants. And he always calls, and we have nice long talks on nights that we don't go out."

"Sounds great. You must keep me posted."

"Are you ladies rcady to order?" the waitress had approached and stood there patiently while they were talking.

"Let me order," Pam said. "I won't get anything too spicy since you're such a wimp. We'll have pad Thai and red curry chicken with white rice. And we'd better have two Singhas. Can't have hot tea with spicy food."

"What is it? Some kind of Thai wine?"

"No, Thai beer."

"I don't know whether I should."

"Come on girlfriend, lighten up. Try it, if you don't like it, I'll finish it off."

"Ok. But when I get busted on the way home for DUI and they revoke my release on my own recognizance, you're going to have to face John!"

"All right, be a party-pooper. You only have to drink half of it, and I'll drink the rest. After all, I'm not a federal felon!"

41

Windmill Village Office Park, Overland Park, Kansas

Margaret didn't know it, but Dog Dvorak was only about the
length of a football field away from her and talking about her with
John as she ate dinner with Pam at the Bangkok Pavilion. The
restaurant was in the Windmill Village Office Park, which had,
besides several stores and a daycare center, a number of office
condos, one of which housed Dick Dvorak's law offices.

John, who had been working late at his office in the
Monadnock Building in Chicago, immediately picked up the phone
when the display read "Dvorak Law Firm."

"Dog, thanks for calling and for your email informing me
about Margaret's surrender. I'm so glad that it went smoothly,
thanks to you." John and Dick had always called each other by
nicknames, with the longest running being Kemo from the Lone
Ranger's name for his trusty scout sidekick, "Kemosabe,"
allegedly from the Potawatomi language. When they had done a
court-martial defense together in Japan, Kemosabe had morphed
into Kemo San, which they called each other until Dick had
performed his bounty hunter trick of extracting one of John's
friend's sons from the clutches of crack cocaine dealers outside
Fort Benning, Georgia, which had earned Dick the honorific of
"Dog" after Dog the Bounty Hunter of TV fame. The
circumstances of that "full-service law firm" work would have
made a TV episode worthy of Dog the Bounty Hunter.

"I didn't do much, except glower at the FBI agents, who were,
by the way, pretty cool. They didn't seem much into hassling our

client. In fact, one of them, Agent Millar, slipped me his card and said to call him if we needed anything. He said that if he could legally help out, he would."

"That's good to know."

"Are you covering the arraignment, or am I? Or both of us?"

"Both of us. I want to really show the flag, that we are not going to roll over and play dead on this one, even with the might and majesty of the U.S. government arrayed against us. I'm going to hit them with some motions to dismiss that may or may not work this early in the process but that will cause whatever AUSA will handle the case to respond to our motions rather than working on improving the government's case."

"What motions, O Mighty Motion Master? Like our tactics in that court-martial in Japan?"

Dog was referring to a court-martial defense that John had brought him aboard (literally) on in Yokosuka, Japan, in which they defended a very senior Navy Master Chief Petty Officer on a number of computer pornography charges for which he faced 65 years in Portsmouth Naval Prison and a Dishonorable Discharge— hardly the way to end 30 years' service. While there for the military version of a grand jury hearing—the accused and his counsel may be present, unlike in the civilian system—the Article 32b investigation, John and Dog had learned that the command was almost out of funds to try courts-martial and had a big case coming up involving the rape of a Japanese national on Okinawa— a crime that, if not resolved to the satisfaction of the victim and her family, had implications as to whether the United States could continue to base forces on that strategic island. And the command was going to have to bring in witnesses from all over the Pacific for both cases and, for John and Dog's case, from the continental United States, as well. They also learned that the trial counsel (military term for prosecutor) was on leave on his way back to Florida to get married and go on his honeymoon.

So when the military judge and the chief trial counsel had called John to set a trial date, John had said, "Day after tomorrow—that's the quickest that my cocounsel and I can get to Japan."

Well, the chief trial counsel had expected that civilian counsel would want at least a month's delay and maybe more, but had dutifully responded to the military judge with the stock answer, "The government is ready for trial, Your Honor," even though it wasn't. So the government was stuck. The chief trial counsel called the trial counsel off his leave—he got to complete the marriage ceremony, but then had to leave before the reception to fly back to Japan. In the meantime, the chief trial counsel got last-minute passports for the two American witnesses, got them aboard a flight from the East Coast of the United States to Tokyo, and rounded up the other witnesses from various parts of the Pacific where they were stationed.

So when John and not-yet Dog—still Kemosabe—arrived at the Yokosuka Naval Base, they found a pretty pissed-off prosecutor who had little interest in trying the case. His mind was elsewhere—on the honeymoon that he could have been enjoying. So Dog-to-be invited him over to his room in the BOQ to commiserate over some single malt scotch whiskey while John— not without some scotch libations of his own—cranked out more than a dozen motions, several of which were going to delay the trial for weeks, such as the motion to fund a Tanner staging expert for the defense at government expense. The government had a Tanner staging expert—a medical doctor who could opine as to the age of a child based on physical development, a key issue in the case—so the defense needed one, too, if only to advise whether the government expert witness had a clue. The military judge was going to grant the defense a continuance to get such an expert, which meant that the government would have to turn all of the witnesses around, send them back to wherever they had been summoned from, and pay to have them fly back on another date, for which the command had no funds. So the trial counsel begged John and Dick for a plea bargain to avoid this situation, and they entered into a pretrial agreement that, in return for a guilty plea to one of the charges, the convening authority—the admiral who was responsible for all general courts-martial in the command—would disapprove those portions of any sentence that reduced the client more than one grade, imprisoned him for more than two months, or gave him a dishonorable or bad-conduct discharge. But in the military, the plea bargain is merely the worst that you can get. If the court-martial sentences you to a lesser sentence than the plea bargain, you get the lesser sentence. So John and Dick put on the sentencing case from hell, which resulted in the military judge sentencing their client to a reprimand. Their grateful client got them each caps with gold "scrambled eggs" around the visor, with "USS John S. McCain (DDG-56)" embroidered across the front and with "Motion Master" embroidered on the back for John and "Pimp Master" embroidered on the back for Dick—for his success in pimping the prosecutor while John was cranking out the motions. The grateful client presented them the caps as they were being piped aboard that destroyer for the VIP tour.

"Well, we're not going to get the U.S. Attorney's office to where they can't afford to try the case by the shenanigans that we pulled off in Yokosuka," Dog continued. "So what motions are you going to confound them with in this case?"

"Just three so far, other than the standard discovery motions and so forth. First, we'll file a motion to dismiss the indictment. Then, we'll file another motion to dismiss the indictment. The argument in the first motion is that the indictment fails to allege the offense of corporate criminal liability, and the argument in the second motion is that, because the law does not apply to our client, she cannot have violated it."

"The first one I can see. But how does HIPAA not apply to her?"

"Well, I know that you know HIPAA pretty well by reason of having covered some HIPAA seminars for me when I had a last-minute court conflict. Whom does HIPAA apply to?"

"Covered entities."

"Right. Can a person be a health plan? Nooooo. Can a person be a clearinghouse? Nooooo. So the only person who can be a covered entity is a provider who transmits one or more of the standard transactions in electronic format."

"Right."

"Is Margaret a provider? Is the Acting Director of Health Information Management a provider?"

"Well, she's not a clinician, so I guess not. But she's an employee of a provider."

"But the HIPAA statute does not say that the criminal statute applies to employees of providers. And although the Department of Justice has ignored it, it issued a memorandum in early June of this year for all U.S. Attorneys basically saying that they could prosecute only covered entities and that, unless the alleged perpetrators had aided and abetted a covered entity, had conspired with a covered entity, or had been an accessory after the fact, they don't fall under the HIPAA criminal statute. And Margaret's indictment doesn't allege that she's an aider and abetter, a coconspirator, or an accessory after the fact. I think that it's a potential winner. How is the Justice Department going to get around its own memo?"

"You've got me, but like you, I trust federal judges about as far as I can throw the whole courthouse."

"Well, I want to set up the motion by the first one—to show the judge how flaky the government's theory of corporate criminal responsibility is. He probably won't grant it, saying that it is a matter to decide after all of the evidence is in. But that motion will make it easier for him to dismiss the case because the law, quite simply, does not apply to our client."

"That's why they call you Motion Master. What's the third motion?"

"Well, you know that I requested all of the hospital's HIPAA compliance files in my initial discovery request. Well, they provided their discovery response, and several documents were missing."

"How do you know that they were missing?"

"Margaret's principal assistant, Pam something—some long Thai name that I can't pronounce—downloaded the entire HIPAA compliance folder onto a memory stick and gave it to Margaret, who FedExed it to me. And two documents were missing in the discovery that the AUSA had provided. One was a letter of commendation back in 2003 from the hospital administrator—Albright—commending Margaret for her good work in getting the hospital HIPAA complaint, and the other was Margaret's email thread to Albright stating that it was not sufficient for him to refuse to sanction the board member who had improperly used the report to the Cancer Registry for his commercial advantage and, further, to not inform her of exactly what, if anything, was done about the matter so that she could complete and maintain the required HIPAA security incident report."

"The letter of commendation and the emails would tend to blow their corporate criminal liability case against Margaret out of the water. They're hanging her out to dry to protect Albright, the governing board, and outside counsel," Dog surmised.

John smiled, but there was no warmth in the smile. "No shit, Sherlock. But I'm going to cram this spoliation of evidence down their throats."

As John had explained earlier to Margaret, spoliation of evidence—not "spoil" but "spol" iation of evidence—is the unauthorized, illegal concealment, alteration, or destruction of potential evidence, which is exactly what the hospital had done. So a letter of commendation to Margaret or her email exchange saying that stronger sanctions were needed was critical evidence that would show that she had done all that she could to get the hospital HIPAA complaint and that, if anyone was liable, it was the higher ups, the ones that had hung her out to dry.

"Sounds good. Again, that's why you're the Motion Master. Anything else you need from me right now?"

"Not now. Thanks again for taking good care of Margaret."

"No problem. Semper Fi, Kemosabe."

42

U.S. Attorney's Office
Federal Courthouse
Kansas City, Missouri

AUSA Katie DiGeorgia walked into the office of her boss, the
U.S. Attorney for the Western District of Missouri. Katie's
somewhat sweet girl-next-door first name didn't match her
appearance. Black hair pulled back in a tight bun. Wire rimmed
glasses. A severe, mannish, gray pin-stripe suit, and a close, but
slightly feminine approximation of a bow tie. "Thank you for
giving me a few moments, Ma'am. We need to talk about the
Nicks case."

"Ok. Shoot." Ms. Thorp seldom wasted time on pleasantries,
such as the weather, whether one had a smiley face day, or the like.
She valued only ruthless efficiency, which Katie had demonstrated,
at least up to this point.

"I don't think that we can get a conviction."

"I don't want to hear it, counselor. I need a conviction," she
replied, as she thought to herself, and I need Stanley Deutsch's
firm's contribution to my campaign fund, which I won't get unless
we get a conviction. "Her defense counsel can't be that swift. I've
never heard of him."

"I never did either, but I googled him and sent out an email to
all the U.S. Attorney's offices. And I may be missing something,
but he's never lost a case against the federal government."

"You've got to be shitting me."

"No, Ma'am."

"What is he winning? Low-level traffic cases in Magistrate Court on some federal enclave, like speeding in the Pentagon parking lot?"

"No, Ma'am."

"What then?"

"Admittedly a lot of them were courts-martial. More than half. But they were all big defense wins. I found a number of news stories about his cases on Google, so I talked to the JAG attorneys involved. It's gotten to where the military brings in their best hired gun trial counsel whenever he makes an appearance. But it doesn't matter. He got the serious charges dismissed in a general court-martial in Korea for the government's failure to follow the waiver provisions of the Korean Status of Forces Agreement in a case with concurrent jurisdiction, for God's sake. He recently got his client off with a reprimand in a case in Japan in which his client was facing 65 years imprisonment and a dishonorable discharge for internet child pornography."

Ms. Thorp's reply was dripping with sarcasm, "Ok, but that's some dipshit military lawyer he's up against, not the U.S. Attorney's Office."

"Well, I've worked with some military prosecutors, and they are seldom dipshit. I haven't found any history of federal criminal defense on his part, but he settled two med mal cases for big bucks against the Civil Division—one here and the other out of Southern California. In the California case, he got a $3.4 million settlement for his client for failure to diagnose and report child abuse. Pretty ballsy when you think that it was his child abuser client who had caused the brain damage, not the radiologist or the emergency department physician."

"Whoop-de the f____ do." Marsha could swear like a trooper when she was pissed, but didn't normally do so in front of her AUSAs. "Still doesn't sound like Johnny Cochran to me."

"Have you read his motions?"

"I skimmed them. You can get around them."

"Well, in light of our own memo, I don't think that we can prosecute an employee of a covered entity. But I'll argue the hell out of it. My theory is that, although the first part of our memo seems to exclude non-covered entities, the second part of the memo stating that, in an appropriate case, management may be criminally liable indicates in those cases that the defendant does not have to be a covered entity because management will seldom, if ever, be actual providers."

"I couldn't have said it better myself." Marsha actually smiled, although it had about as much warmth as a shark opening its jaw before striking.

"But the real problem is that, even if we survive his motion to dismiss, I don't have much evidence. Gibbons is pretty weak and can certainly be impeached—he's trying to shift the blame to Ms. Nicks to lessen his sentence. Deutsch and Albright are ok, but Thomas can impeach them too. They certainly have some self-interest in hanging Ms. Nicks out to dry. Actually, if any member of management is guilty under a corporate criminal liability theory, it's probably both Deutsch and Albright. And the FBI agents came up with nothing when they went back to the hospital to interview more of the staff. In fact, one wonders whether they were trying to develop exculpatory evidence.

"And he's got a pretty good spoliation of evidence motion. The hospital concealed or destroyed HIPAA compliance documents showing that the defendant had done a good job getting the hospital compliant and had objected to their failure to take sanctions against the board member who had committed a serious breach. That email to the hospital administrator shows that, if there is management liability, it's on the part of the hospital administrator and maybe outside legal counsel, not Ms. Nicks."

The U.S. Attorney was far from happy at seeing her large campaign contribution from Stanley Deustch's law firm go down the tubes. But she was a shark and never gave up. "Katie, I'm very surprised to hear this defeatist attitude from you. I have a lot of faith in you." Yeah right, Marsha thought, as she continued, "And I know that you can pull this conviction out of the fire. As you know, a Senior Assistant U.S. Attorney position will open up shortly when Joe Hoyt leaves to go to work for Stinson, Morrison,

Hecker. You are my first choice for the promotion. But you've got to win this case. I'll jack up the FBI to go back and try again. And I'll call Gibbons's counsel and see whether we can improve his testimony. In the meantime, you go back and figure out how to defeat this Thomas asshole's motions. Got it?"

"Yes, Ma'am. Thanks for your help and your confidence in me."

"That will be all."

As Katie left, she thought, thanks a hell of a lot for nothing.

Marsha immediately called the FBI Field Office, reamed out Bill Millar, and ordered him back to the hospital to develop some fucking evidence. Then, she called Mr. Mogridge and, when he didn't answer, left a message that she needed better cooperation from his client and that, if it was forthcoming, the Zone C sentence under the Federal Sentencing Guidelines of between 12 and 14 months could magically turn into probation with no jail time. She also strongly hinted that, if Mogridge was interested in the upcoming vacancy for a U.S. Magistrate Judge position, she could help make it happen. She didn't expressly condition it on Gibbons's becoming a lot more helpful, but the implication was there for anyone with half a brain—and Mogridge had a brain and a half.

After the calls, Marsha leaned back in her expensive leather chair, buzzed her secretary for a cup of tea, and smiled. She had done all that she could do to ensure that she got the first management conviction for a HIPAA violation notwithstanding that asshole defense counsel's motions.

What she didn't realize was that not only did Mogridge have a brain and a half, but also he had the highest legal ethics and not only didn't bite on Marsha's not-so-subtle bribe, but also actually called John and forwarded her voicemail message to him. They had served together in the U.S. Army JACG Corps and had professional loyalty to each other. John was appropriately grateful and said that, if the case went to trial, he'd make something out of the information. But he really hoped that his motions succeeded and that it would never go to trial. He didn't want Margaret to go

through a trial. Because one never knew what would happen—
what the jury might do. No, his motions had to work.

43

Health Information Management Department
Kansas City Memorial Hospital

Pam was all alone in the HIM Department. It was Friday, December 23, 2005, the last weekday before Christmas, and she had let her staff go home early to finish their last-minute Christmas shopping. All of a sudden, the door to the department flew off its hinges and crashed down onto the floor. Three large men burst in yelling, "Search warrant! Search warrant!" The agents were huge. They were dressed all in black, coveralls, boots, body armor, gauntlets, with FBI emblazoned across their chests in white. Pam, who at less than half their size, was totally panicked, but briefly thought, why did they break down the door? It wasn't locked. But then reality set in, and she threw up her hands, almost peed down her legs, and said, "I'm not a Columbian drug lord. I'm only a medical records type." Pam had been a young girl when the Thai Army had burst into her parents' home looking for a rebel, and she still had moments of panic, irrational or not, at the thought of law enforcement bursting in waving automatic weapons. So she had such a moment of panic when the FBI reprised the Royal Thai Army break-in of her parents' house. But she was made of stronger stuff than Gibbons and did not show her fear.

An agent shoved a warrant at her. It authorized them to seize all evidence relating to HIPAA compliance or lack thereof. Pam asked whether they could wait until she got hospital counsel to review the warrant. They didn't even answer. They just started pulling files out of file cabinets and unplugging the hard drives of the computers at the work stations.

Pam somewhat recovered from her fear of the armed agents at the thought that the hospital would be missing charts that were necessary to ensure continuity of care and to avoid medical errors. So she felt that Uzis in the agents' hands or not, she had to do something. "You can't take those charts. We need that data! We need it to take care of our patients!"

The biggest of the three agents swung his Uzi or whatever automatic weapon it was around to where it was too close to pointing at Pam and replied, "Ma'am, have you ever heard of obstruction of justice? Well, unless you give us access now, we are going to charge you with obstruction of justice."

So Pam, who was a typical Thai—brave notwithstanding her moment of initial panic but aware that when one was outgunned three to nothing by law enforcement it was time to shut up and get out of the way—did exactly that. So she watched, helpless, as the FBI agents trashed the HIM Department and walked off with paper records, hard drives, and media, including CDs, memory sticks, and the like.

But Pam, even though she was mortified at being so scared that she had not done a better job of standing up to the agents, took some comfort from the thought that she had backed up the HIPAA compliance files and given that backup to Margaret. But she was also scared for her former boss and current friend. If the FBI were going to these lengths to get evidence to convict Margaret, what chance did her friend have? And was Pam next on the list?

So after the agents had left, Pam picked up her cell phone, called Margaret, and left a message telling her about the search. Then, she used her camera phone to take pictures of the carnage, emailed the photos to both her office and her home email addresses, and saved the photos to her computer. Then, she emailed the photos to Mr. Mahan, the IT Director, and the Chief of the Medical Staff along with an account of the FBI's search and seizure of hospital records and that she had no way to estimate which ones the agents had actually taken because they had trashed the department. Then, she called security and asked for someone to come down to guard the door so that no one could take any more records or destroy the evidence of what the agents had done. After the security guard had arrived and finished gasping, she walked out the doorway, now with no door to lock, and went home, wondering why on earth she wanted to work for Kansas City Memorial as the Acting Director of Health Information Management.

44

Judge Maddox's Courtroom
Federal Courthouse
Kansas City, Missouri

"All rise," the bailiff announced. Everyone rose as Judge
Maddox entered the courtroom from the door leading to his
chambers and sat down on the high-backed leather chair behind the
bench. Judge Maddox looked like a judge. Tall, slim, white-haired
with a regal bearing. "Thank you. Please be seated," he said, with
the severity of his tone mitigated by a small smile.

Everyone sat. Margaret was glad to sit down because, even in
the brief moment that she had had to stand when the judge entered,
her knees felt weak, and she was afraid that she would lose her
balance and fall or commit some other embarrassing act that would
convince the judge that she was actually as guilty as sin. She was
so grateful to be between John and Mr. Dvorak. She had the
feeling that nothing really bad could happen to her with them to
support her, not only in the event that her knees locked and she fell
over in a dead faint but also in every aspect of this legal hassle.

John had told her that this court session was just an
arraignment, that the judge would handle some preliminary
matters, and that nothing bad could happen today. He had even put
two pieces of paper in front of her with the words "Yes, Your
Honor" written on one and "No, Your Honor" written on the other,
telling her that he would point to the one that she should say if the
judge asked her a question. She had been slightly insulted by this
plan when John told her about it, but now realized the wisdom of

it. She might spazz and screw up out of nerves at being in federal court as a criminal defendant, even if she was innocent.

"Number CR-05-51-BLG-JMB, United States v. Margaret Nicks," the clerk announced.

"Your Honor, AUSA Katie DiGeorgia for the United States." Katie was dressed as severely as she had been in her boss's office, but it was not inappropriate for Judge Maddox's courtroom. He was not the most sympathetic to women counsel in the Western District Judiciary, so a female lawyer had to look as professional as possible.

"Good morning, Ms. DiGeorgia. Nice to see you again."

"Thank you, Your Honor."

"And you, Sirs. I take it that you are representing the defendant?" The judge had read the two defense lawyers' entries of appearance, but had to go through this drill on the record. The court reporter's fingers danced over the keys to her stenography machine as the parties talked.

"Yes, Your Honor. John Thomas. I haven't previously appeared before Your Honor but am admitted to this court, as well as the U.S. District Courts for the Northern District of Illinois—trial bar—and the District of Kansas. My cocounsel, Mr. Dvorak," said John, gesturing to Dog, "is also admitted to those courts and to this court."

"You appear well qualified, Sir. Welcome to the Western District of Missouri."

Margaret didn't know what to make of this exchange of pleasantries. The U.S. Attorney wanted to put her in jail, but all of them were acting so, well, civilized.

"Ms. Nicks?"

"Yes, Your Honor." Margaret felt a little satisfaction that John had not had to point at a "yes" or "no" card.

"Are you Margaret Nicks?"

"Yes, Your Honor."

"Are you under the influence of alcohol or drugs or have you been within the last 24 hours?"

"No, Your Honor."

"Do you understand why you are here today?"

"Yes, Sir."

"And Mr. Thomas and Mr. Dvorak represent you?"

"Yes, Your Honor."

"Are you satisfied with their representation?"

"Very much so, Your Honor."

As the judge went through his stock questions of a criminal defendant appearing before the court for the first time for a preliminary hearing, he thought that she certainly didn't look like the typical criminal defendant who appeared before him. Margaret looked good in the same business suit that she had worn for her surrender except that it was livened up with a nice, but hardly ostentatious, string of pearls. She looked like the girl-next-door young professional and anything but a criminal defendant. But he had been involved in enough criminal trials to know that appearances could be deceiving.

So he continued, "Have you been given a copy of the charges in this case?"

"Yes, Your Honor."

Looking at Mr. Thomas, the judge asked, "Does your client waive reading of the charges?"

"Yes, Your Honor."

"Ms. Nicks, do you understand what you are charged with and the possible penalties?"

For the first time, Margaret hesitated. Yes, she knew what she was charged with and the possible penalties, but she still had no idea why she found herself in this nightmare. But John pointed at the card that read, "Yes, Your Honor," so she gave that answer.

"How do you plead?"

John had told Margaret that he would answer that question, so she remained silent while he entered a not guilty plea for her.

"As I understand it, there is no issue as to bail today because the government has agreed to release on the defendant's own recognizance with no conditions other than making all court appearances. Am I correct?"

"Yes, Your Honor," both sides intoned.

"Now Ms. Nicks, I'm sure that you understand all of this information, but the law requires me to go over it with you. I have to advise you of the penalties if you don't show up for a court appearance. If you don't appear, an arrest warrant can be issued for you, and you can be detained pending your trial. Further, you could be prosecuted for contempt of court, which could result in imprisonment or a fine. If you commit a criminal offense while released on your own recognizance, you can be sentenced to an additional term of imprisonment, to be served consecutive to any other sentence that you might receive. Also, there are additional penalties for intimidating or attempting to intimidate a witness, juror, officer of the court, or obstructing a criminal investigation or tampering with a witness or retaliating against a witness, victim, or informant.

"If you fail to appear for court at any time, or if you fail to report to begin service of a sentence that might be imposed, you could be prosecuted for failure to appear, and receive a consecutive sentence for that offense. Do you have any questions about anything that I have said?"

"No, Your Honor."

"Now, today's hearing is only to advise you of your rights, the charges against you, and, if there was an issue as to whether you should be released from pretrial detention, to resolve it. You've already indicated that you understand the charges and you have been released on your own recognizance, so the only issue remaining is to make sure that you understand your rights. Correct?"

In a classroom or a friendly discussion, Margaret would have understood every nuance. But it was all coming so fast, and she was so scared that she felt a surge of gratitude when John pointed at the "Yes, Your Honor," card, which she dutifully parroted.

"You have the right to remain silent. In other words, you don't have to say anything. And anything you say can be used against you. You have a right to a trial by a jury of your peers. You have a right to confront and I mean to see, hear, and cross-examine witnesses against you." Margaret somewhat tuned this out. John had told her all this stuff, which seemed almost irrelevant somehow. The whole process seemed more and more like some kind of sick chess game in which she was the prize. But she knew that she had to play the game to avoid being checkmated. So she listened well enough to respond, "Yes, Your Honor," when the judge asked whether she understood her rights, even before John pointed to the correct card.

"Very well, are there any other matters that we need to take up at this time?" the judge asked counsel.

"None from the government," Katie responded.

"Yes, Your Honor. The defense has two motions that we believe the Court should take up at this time. And one more, a spoliation of evidence motion that may need to be deferred until the close of discovery. The government has failed to allege the offense of corporate criminal responsibility, and even if they had, the HIPAA criminal statute applies only to covered entities, and my client is not a covered entity. You have our motions and our memoranda in support of our motions before you, and our position is that you should dismiss these baseless charges against my client so that she does not have to undergo any more of the stress of being an innocent federal defendant."

The judge did not look happy at having to deal with these issues. But he knew that he had to. "Counsel, I'll admit that the government's pleadings are not a model of alleging corporate criminal liability and that your client is a fairly low-level member of management so that it may be a stretch to convict upon the theory that her malfeasance somehow contributed to the employee's crime. But I think that the issue is one to decide once the evidence is in, so I'm going to deny that motion at this time. You may bring it up again at the conclusion of the evidence. And I'm going to table the motion for appropriate relief for spoliation of evidence until the close of discovery. I will, however, order the government to preserve all potential evidence and make a diligent search for the documents that the defense contends were hidden or destroyed. And if they are not found and provided to the defense, I'll entertain a motion to allow the defense to bring a forensic computer expert to see what he can recover from the hospital's system. But I will hear argument on the issue of whether an employee of a covered entity can be criminally liable, especially in light of the Department of Justice Memorandum that the defense has cited and provided to the court. Counsel?"

"Thank you, Your Honor," John rose to his feet. "As we noted in our motion, the issue is simple. HIPAA applies to covered entities. The original covered entities were health plans, health care clearinghouses, and health care providers who transmitted one or more of the so-called standard transactions in electronic format. They consist of billing transactions. Subsequently, HIPAA was modified to add Medicare prescription drug sponsors to the list of covered entities. A person cannot be a health plan, a clearinghouse, or a Medicare prescription drug sponsor. The only person who can be a covered entity is a provider. And I'll admit that the HIPAA definition of provider is very broad, including chiropractors; physical, occupational, and other therapists; the whole mental and behavioral health range—licensed clinical social workers, substance abuse counselors, and the like—and providers of durable medical equipment. But a medical records type—an acting director of health information management—is nowhere near the HIPAA or any other definition of provider. She may be an employee of a covered entity, but she's not a covered entity herself.

"And the DOJ memo that we attached to our motion proves our point. It basically says that DOJ cannot prosecute non-covered entity individuals unless they are coconspirators, aiders and abettors, or accessories after the fact, and nothing in the charge here alleges that my client functioned in any of those capacities. So, Your Honor, the government is hoist with its own petard, and no jurisdiction exists in this case to try my client. Thank you, Your Honor."

"Government?"

"Thank you, Your Honor," Katie began. "I'll admit that an unsophisticated reading of the DOJ memo might lead one to the conclusion that Mr. Thomas argues. But read as a whole, the memo clearly recognizes that a member of management may be criminally liable under general principles of corporate criminal liability regardless of whether the member of management qualifies as a covered entity provider herself or not. Yes, one can read the memo to exclude non-covered entities from direct criminal liability. But then it goes on to say that management may be criminally liable, again, under general principles of corporate criminal liability, a statement that indicates that management does not have to constitute a covered entity itself. To decide otherwise would be to rule out management liability, something that Congress clearly did not contemplate. Indeed, HIPAA requires compliance not just by employees but also by, quote, 'officers and employees.' Thank you."

"Anything further, Mr. Thomas?"

"Just briefly, your honor. If Congress had wanted to subject non-covered entity management to criminal liability, it could have written the statute to do so. Remember the legal doctrine *contra proferentum*—construe the document against the drafter. I've got to give Ms. DiGeorgia credit for a creative argument. But it flies in the face of due process—a law must inform people of what they cannot do without incurring criminal liability. And this one doesn't unless one is a covered entity. Yes, the DOJ has ignored its own memo and convicted employees of covered entities. But no one has previously raised this issue. But I have now, Your Honor. Although it's an issue of first impression, we need to determine that not just anyone can be prosecuted for violation of a criminal law that does not, on its face, apply to them. Thank you."

The judge sat there for a long, pregnant moment before announcing, "I'll take the issue of whether the HIPAA statute applies to the defendant under advisement. My clerk will inform you of the next court date. Adjourned."

All rose as the judge left the courtroom. Margaret turned to John, "How did we do?"

"I think that we did all that we could do up to now. It went ok. I didn't expect the judge to magically dismiss the charges today. It's better that he took our main motion under advisement. That result today means that he wants to think about it, so we have a chance. And it sounds as if he may grant us some relief on the spoliation issue. So let's get out of here. We can talk outside."

As they left, Katie grabbed John's suit coat sleeve, pulled him away from his client, and in a low voice so that Margaret could not overhear, said, "It's not too late to deal this away for no confinement."

"Counsel, you know that I cannot ethically plead an innocent client guilty. Put another way, tell your boss to stuff it. Have a nice day."

"But aren't you ethically bound to pass on the offer to your client?"

"Ok. I'll pass it on. But I can tell you now what she'll say."

John returned to Margaret's side and motioned for her to enter one of the rooms outside the courtroom that were reserved for attorneys conferring with other counsel or with their clients or witnesses. He didn't suggest that Margaret take a seat at one of the chairs around the small conference table. He didn't think that the meeting would take that long.

"The Assistant U.S. Attorney told me that it wasn't too late to enter into a plea bargain under which you would not get any jail time."

Margaret responded, about as heatedly as John had ever seen from her, "What? You mean plead *guilty?* I'm not pleading guilty. I didn't do anything wrong. They can put me under the jail before I'll admit to having done anything wrong."

"That's what I thought you'd say. But ethically, I had to pass the offer on to you."

"Do you think I should take the deal?"

"No. Not for a minute. In fact, I think that the offer is a good sign. Ms. DiGeorgia doesn't think that she has much of a case, so she's trying to salvage a conviction by offering a sweetheart deal."

"Well, that's decided then."

As John and Margaret walked back past the open courtroom door, John caught the AUSA's eye, shrugged his shoulders, held his hands out palm up as if to say, "What could I do?" and shook his head no.

As they left the courthouse, Margaret saw John and Dog high-five each other. Maybe it had gone better than she had thought. But her too often pessimistic nature intruded. Maybe it hadn't gone so well. Grateful as she was for John's and Dog's help, she couldn't help but wonder when, if ever, this nightmare would end.

45

EMR Legal
Monadnock Building, Downtown Chicago

John was once again back in his office after a lunch of Kung Pao chicken at his favorite Chinese fast food place a few doors east down Jackson Boulevard toward Grant Park and Lake Michigan. He began scrolling down through his email inbox, not really focused because most of his email wasn't all that important. Junk mail that his spam filter had missed. Advertisements for continuing legal education courses that had no relevance to his interests and the like. But an email from the U.S. District Court for the Western District of Missouri suddenly got his total undivided attention.

From: ecf.notification@mow.uscourts.gov. Sent 2/17/06
To: john@emrconsultants.com
CC:
Subject: Activity in case CR-96-51-BLG-JMB, United States v. Margaret Nicks

---

*** NOTE TO PUBLIC ACCESS USERS ***
You may view the filed documents once without charge. To avoid later charges, download a copy of each document during this first viewing.

U.S. District Court
Western District of Missouri

Notice of Electronic Filing

The following transaction was received from Maddox, J. entered on 2/17/2006 at 3:13 PM CST and filed on 2/17/2006.

Case Name: United States v. Nicks
Case Number: CR-05-51-BLG-JMB
Filer:
Document Number 12

Docket text:

ORDER granting Defendant's motion to dismiss. The charges are dismissed without prejudice. Defendant is discharged from any and all own recognizance restrictions and is free to go. Signed by Judge Maddox on 2/17/2006 (Marsh, Carol)

The following documents are associated with this transaction:
Main document.
Original filename: N/A
Electronic Stamp: [STAMP MOWS-ID=857559776[Date=2/17/2006][Filenumber=1451737-0][e43rtux99nxc11e0vwa99klc39fjsojnco3xxjkeiccp30j]

Notice will be provided to

Katie DiGeorgia kdigeorgia@usdoj.gov/electronic casefiling@usdoj.gov.

John Thomas john@emrconsultants.com

John was famous for not showing any emotion. But if anyone had been in his office, he would have blown his reputation, because he literally screamed in elation, raising a clenched fist in the air and pumping it furiously back and forth. But then he quickly sobered up. The judge had dismissed the charge without prejudice, meaning that the government could refile the charge after having amended it, and another federal district judge might not dismiss it. So he immediately called AUSA DiGeorgia, who congratulated him and told him that she had told the U.S. Attorney that they had no case. She also told John that the case was closed and that the U.S. Attorney's Office would not be refiling. She added that she believed that the hospital or its outside counsel, Deutsch, had destroyed evidence and, thus, committed spoliation. She said that, if John wanted to make an ethics complaint, she would support it. John thanked her, complimented her on her professionalism, and told her that, if she ever had a HIPAA issue come up that she needed help with, she should feel free to contact him. After he had hung up the phone, he reprised his scream of elation and fist pumping. Now, it was a done deal—a total defense win.

Then, he called and left a message about the win for Dog, who, because he was not in his office to take the call, was probably at his farm slopping pigs or mucking the horse stalls or shearing the sheep or whatever else it was that he did with the menagerie of farm animals that he kept just across the Johnson County line in Miami County, Kansas, south of Kansas City. Even though John was fairly bored with the practice of law—that's why he had turned to consulting—except when he pulled off a big win like this one, he couldn't understand how anyone could prefer shoveling horse manure to practicing law. But Dog did. John concluded the message by asking Dog not to tell Margaret in case John had trouble tracking her down. He wanted to tell her the good news himself.

He had started to dial her cell phone but then paused, stared into space, and hung up. He had to tell her in person. He wanted to see her face when she learned that the matter was over and done with. Instead of calling her, he dialed American Express Platinum Travel Services and told them to get him on the next available plane—yes, he knew that it was the Friday evening of a three-day holiday weekend. He said that he would go first class or tourist, he didn't care, out of Midway or O'Hare, and asked to have a rental car waiting for him when he arrived in Kansas City and to get him a room at a good hotel on the Plaza, close to Margaret's apartment.

The Platinum Card Concierge took only about ten minutes to call back. All that he could get John on was a 7:00 P.M. United flight out of O'Hare, and the only available seat was first class, which sounded just fine to John. And a rental car and a suite at the Raphael Hotel just across Brush Creek from the Plaza were reserved for him in his name.

John printed out a copy of the email from the court's ECF system for Margaret, powered off his computer, grabbed his brief case and running bag, and hurried to his apartment to pack a carry-on before taking the El to O'Hare. The Blue Line was much faster than driving, especially during rush hour.

At the airport, John checked in, got his boarding pass, went through security, and headed to the United Red Carpet Club to relax until they called his flight. Between his first class ticket, his Mileage Plus frequent flier status, and his American Express Platinum Card, he qualified to enter the lounge three different ways. As he sipped a Diet Coke—he wanted to have a drink in first class on the plane and didn't want to get pulled over for DUI on his way to Margaret's apartment—he ignored the lounge's amenities that he normally would have availed himself of—Fox News on the TV, the *Wall Street Journal*, and almost every magazine known to man. Instead, he just pulled out the email and read it over and over again, smiling, until they called his flight. And reading the email over and over and thinking how happy it would make Margaret was about all that he could do on the flight other than sipping the one Chivas on the rocks that he allowed himself. He thought to himself that he may have had greater wins, in the sense of getting an obviously guilty client off by a legal miracle, but this one was the most satisfying. Getting an innocent client off—one that he really cared about—was way more satisfying than any other win that he had ever pulled out of his hat. Way more satisfying indeed.

46

Margaret's apartment, just off the Plaza, Kansas City

John—this was getting to be quite a habit—again raised a clenched fist and pumped it back and forth when he saw the light on in Margaret's apartment. She was home! As he had been driving down I-29 toward downtown from KCI (Kansas City Inconvenient, as he'd heard the locals call it), he had wondered whether he was a little bit nuts flying to Kansas City first class for big bucks when, for all he knew, Margaret was out of town visiting some relative for the long weekend or, worse, out on a date with some guy, like Doctor Hass. But she wasn't. She was home.

Fortunately, another tenant entered just as John walked up to the door, which would have otherwise required him to buzz Margaret for admittance, thereby ruining the surprise. But apparently his appearance, dressed in gray slacks, a polo shirt, and a Brooks Brothers blazer caused the other tenant to believe that he lived in the upscale Plaza area apartment or that he was well dressed and couth enough looking to be let in. He noted that the tenant, an attractive, well-dressed older woman looked at his wrist to evaluate the watch that he was wearing. His antique Omega watch with a leather band, à la James Bond, rather than some ostentatious metal band apparently satisfied her that he was a gentleman. She even held the door open until he was able to walk through it. As a criminal defense attorney, John knew that that kind of thinking could lead to horrific crimes against those who thought that they were safe in their supposedly secure environments, but he would take advantage of the tenant's kindness this once to surprise Margaret.

As he found himself before her door, however, he wondered whether he was going to scare the snot out of her by appearing out of the blue. Would she conclude that he was there because they were going to put her in pretrial detention or because some other horrible result awaited her? So he pulled out his cell and called her.

After jumping out of the shower that she was taking to answer the phone and pulling her nightgown on, Margaret answered the phone. "Hello?"

"Margaret, it's John."

"Hello, John. Nice to hear from you. What's up?"

"Well, don't worry, but I've got to talk to you. Nothing to worry about, but it couldn't wait. I'm in the hall outside your apartment."

Margaret didn't answer. Apparently, she just dropped the phone because she flung the door open just a second or two after John's last words even though she was dressed in her flannel granny nightgown with her hair dripping wet from the shower and a towel slung over her shoulder and looked like anything but a femme fatale.

"What's wrong? Why are you here?" Margaret looked pale and worried, exactly what John had wanted to avoid.

"I told you that it was nothing to worry about. I've got some pretty good news and a little bad news that I wanted to tell you in person. Which do you want to hear first—the very good news or the arguably bad news?" As soon as he had said it, John regretted it. Margaret didn't seem in the mood to play good news, bad news about her case even though John felt that she had taken it all with a great sense of humor up to this point. But it was out there now.

"The bad news."

"Ok. I don't have an excuse anymore to keep from dating you. You are no longer my client."

John so wished that he had had a video camera with him to capture the range of emotions that played across Margaret's face in just a few seconds. Confusion, hope, joy, and an ineffable emotion that he could not begin to describe.

"Does this mean—? Am I off the hook? Is it over?"

"Yes, Dear. The judge granted our motion to dismiss. And I called the AUSA. They are not going to refile. It's over. You've been discharged. It's over. The judge said that you are free to go. Here's the email from the court."

"Oh thank God," Margaret almost sobbed. "And thank you," as she threw herself at John ending up in a tight embrace with her wet head buried in his shoulder, sobbing.

John, who, as a typical male, had no clue what to do with a sobbing female who had just received great news and whose wet hair was dripping water all over his expensive blazer, thought about quipping, "Well, you could decide that in this case God and I were the one and the same," but thought that, knowing that Margaret was way more religious than he was, she might not see the humor in the comment. So he merely said, while awkwardly patting her on the back much as one would a crying baby, "Hey, this is good news. You're not supposed to cry about it."

"I know. I'm just so happy. I'm just so relieved. I'm just so grateful to you and Dog. Particularly you." Margaret was almost babbling, but John didn't care. He found it strangely endearing. But ever the cold, calculating litigator, he thought that they should perhaps get out of the hall into some place private to discuss her case. "Come on, aren't you going to invite me in?"

Margaret unceremoniously wiped her eyes with her bath towel, took a deep breath, and said, "Oh, yes. Come in. Please come in." She took him by the arm and practically dragged him into her apartment.

After Margaret had closed the door behind them, she excused herself so that she could change from her nightgown and nothing else, into a more attractive outfit and do something about her sopping wet hair. "Have a seat. Help yourself to a drink. I won't be long."

In what was probably record time for a woman to make herself presentable, she was ready to face John, who was sipping the scotch on the rocks that he had denied himself at the Admiral's Club so that he wouldn't be driving DUI and thus possibly be in jail instead of at Margaret's apartment giving her the good news.

Wow, John thought as he stood up when she returned. What a stunner. But he maintained his composure long enough to hand her the copy of the email dismissing her case. She read it twice and then handed it back to John with a big smile. She gave him a quick, but thorough hug. But then to her chagrin, he gently pushed her away, turned all business-like, and started talking lawyer to her. "We've got to make a couple of decisions. First, the U.S. Attorney isn't going to publicize that she lost this case. Do we want to let the media know that you have been exonerated? Second, we have to decide what to do about the hospital now that you have been exonerated. Do you want to go back to work there, or do you want me to negotiate a severance package? I think that I can force them into a generous severance by noting that, under Missouri law, if one wins even one dollar in a sexual discrimination lawsuit, the plaintiff's attorney gets legal fees. And I can, even at a lower hourly rate than I get in Chicago, easily bill six figures in your employment discrimination case against the hospital. After all, they hung the low-level management female out to dry to protect the male hospital administrator and destroyed evidence showing that you weren't guilty."

"John."

John was somewhat taken aback at how sternly Margaret said his name as if she were going to brook no nonsense. Even though she was dressed in a very feminine skirt and low-cut blouse, she looked pretty determined to him.

"Yes?"

"I'll tell you what I don't want. I don't want to discuss the case any more tonight. Save it for later. Now, I don't know exactly what you meant by the bad news being that, because I'm no longer your client, we can date, although your questions about what we do next kind of makes me sound as if I'm still your client. But I do know that, although I was brought up that the woman never makes the first move, I'm going to cut to the chase because I'm afraid that you won't and that I'll miss the best opportunity for a relationship that I've ever had. If I'm more than a client to you, let me know. You are certainly more than a lawyer or a consultant to me."

John hesitated for only a moment, looking Margaret in the eyes, which were still a little moist. Her tears did not make her look less attractive. "All right, Margaret. I'll cut to the chase, too. I love you. I have loved you since the first time that I saw you at the Cross Country seminar. It just took me a while to admit it, and then I used my legal ethics fear of getting involved with a client to hide it. But even though we have a little mopping up to do with your case, I'll take that risk because I'd rather lose my law license than lose you." John held out his arms, and Margaret fell into them.

After what they both felt was the best kiss and embrace of their lives, Margaret asked, "Where's your luggage? Where are you staying?"

"Luggage is in my rental car outside. Hotel reservation for tonight is at the Rafael."

Margaret knew the Rafael Hotel was a romantic little hotel just south of the Plaza because she had gone to dinner at its fine restaurant, Chaz, once. "Ok, Mr. Defense Counsel, you have two choices. Go get your luggage and stay here with me. Or I pack a little bag, and we spend the night together at the Raphael."

"Which do you prefer?"

"Well, I've always wanted to have a romantic assignation at the Raphael and a romantic dinner at Chaz."

"Done."

After they had finished dining on a sumptuous dinner of lamb chops—lamb was a signature dish at Chaz—John asked Margaret whether they should order dessert. She had the perfect answer, "No, I'm your dessert tonight.

325 Ward Parkway, Kansas City, MO 64112
For reservations call 800-821-5343
http://www.raphaelkc.com/html/kansas-city-missouri-hotel.asp

Folio

THOMAS. JOHN		Room	218
555 West Madison St.		Arrival Date	2/17/2006
Tower 4		Departure Date	2/20/2006
Chicago, IL 60661		Adult/Child	2/0

DATE	REFERENCE	DESCRIPTION	AMOUNT
2/17/2006	513267	Chaz Restaurant	$219.59
2/17/2006	513370	Guest Room	$169.00
2/17/2006	513370	Room Taxes	$ 24.67
2/17/2006	513382	Dom Perignon Champagne—room service	$149.99
2/18/2006	513899	Guest Room	$169.00
2/18/2006	513899	Room Taxes	$ 24.67
2/18/2006	514011	Room Service—brunch	$ 78.58
2/18/2006	514034	Room Service—dinner	$178.15
2/18/2006	514039	Dom Perignon Champagne—room service	$149.99
2/19/2006	514091	Guest Room	$169.00
2/19/2006	514091	Room Taxes	$ 24.67
2/19/2006	514111	Room Service—breakfast	$ 39.87
2/19/2006	514127	Room Service—lunch	$ 67.88
2/19/2006	514144	Room Service—dinner	$195.49
2/20/2006	514203	Room Service—brunch	$ 81.05
2/20/2006	514209	AX * 6001	($1467.53)
2/20/2006	514336	**BALANCE**	$0.00

ACCOUNT NO	DATE OF CHARGE
AX * 6001	2/20/2006
CARD MEMBERS NAME	AUTHORIZATION
THOMAS, JOHN	1193451

CARDMEMBER'S SIGNATURE

X_____

47

Corner Office, Badami, Lower, Huffman, & Deutsch
Crown Center Office Building, 2301 McGee, Kansas City

As an equity partner in name only as a result of the Kansas
City Memorial Hospital HIPAA debacle, Stanley wondered how
much longer he would have his large corner office or even whether
his name would be dropped off the firm name. He took a hefty belt
of single malt scotch as he obsessed over his downfall. It was bad
enough that the idiotic federal judge had granted Thomas's motion
to dismiss the charges against that bitch Margaret whatever-her-
name-was. But for Thomas's sidekick, Dvorak, to send the hospital
a demand letter with a draft of an employment discrimination
lawsuit alleging that he had conspired with the hospital to violate
Margaret's civil rights by falsely implicating her as being
criminally liable under principles of corporate criminal liability
was too much. And it was really Thomas who was behind the
letter. He just didn't send it himself because doing so could be
construed as a conflict of interest because he had been a consultant
for the hospital. And that asshole Albright wouldn't hire his firm to
defend the case but hired a small insurance defense firm
recommended by their errors and omissions policy carrier. And
that defense firm recommended that the hospital settle on the b.s.
theory that, if Margaret won even a dollar of damages, the hospital
would have to pay Dvorak's (really Thomas's) entire legal fees
because, under Missouri civil rights laws, any plaintiff verdict for
even only one dollar entitled the plaintiff to recover attorney's
fees. And many of the judges on the Jackson County Circuit Court

were more than willing to award large fees in such cases. Dvorak's demand letter estimated the legal fees for a trial at more than $200,000. Dvorak brashly asserted that he would win some, if not all, of the discrimination actions pled in the lawsuit. And the final straw was that Albright got the board to fire Deutsch's firm, saying that his machinations had caused the hospital to have to pay six figures to Margaret—the amount of their deductible. And their insurance carrier was not happy about having to pay an amount over the deductible and was making noises about raising the hospital's premium.

So Stanley was not overly popular at his firm for having lost seven figures of legal business and not all of it his. Losing the hospital's business meant that the Medicare fraud and abuse transactional lawyers no longer got to review physician contracts to ensure that they didn't violate the anti-kickback laws. The firm's employment law division no longer got to advise on employment contracts for the staff or to defend wrongful termination cases. And the list went on and on.

Deutsch took another pull at the strong malt whiskey. He was drinking too much, but he didn't care. The humiliation really got to him. The other partners barely spoke to him, and the associates avoided him like the plague. The managing partner had refused to send him to a conference that he had attended every year for the past decade, citing the bad economy. But Stanley knew that it was really because he had lost the large book of business. And when his secretary retired, they didn't replace her. They said that, for the time being, he had to use the secretarial pool—a fate normally reserved for new associates and non-producing of counsel attorneys—never for named partners.

And to top it all off, Albright had managed to scrape through unscathed. When the *Kansas City Star* newspaper asked him for a quote for the article reporting that the charges against Margaret had been dismissed, he said that he had believed in Ms. Nicks's innocence from the start and that the hospital had therefore put her on paid administrative leave and had paid her legal expenses. He added that they welcomed her back if she were willing to come back. And everyone fell for this transparent b.s., and Deutsch and his firm were the only ones thrown under the bus.

To add insult to injury, the headline of the latest edition of the *Star,* which was lying on his desk, read, "U.S. Attorney Thorp earns Democratic nomination for the U.S. House of Representatives, 4th District." How could she have so thoroughly blown the case and still win the nomination for the house seat? And in a Democratic district that she would almost certainly win in the general election in a few months.

So Stanley was pissed. Another drink, and he began to focus on revenge. He wasn't that mad at Margaret. She was just a pawn. But Thomas? He had embarrassed him at the HIPAA training session for physicians. He had stolen his chance for the hospital's HIPAA business. And he had really disrespected Stanley at the board meeting to determine whether to keep Thomas on board. And he had thwarted Stanley's brilliant plan to hang Margaret out to dry to discredit Thomas.

He toyed with reporting Thomas to the Missouri Supreme Court for committing the unauthorized practice of law, but vaguely remembered that Thomas was licensed in Illinois, Missouri, Kansas, and Oklahoma. And even if it weren't true that Thomas was licensed to practice in Missouri, the Missouri Supreme Court would want to know why he hadn't reported it when the hospital first hired Thomas as its HIPAA consultant. The Court could view Stanley as unethical for not having reported an ethics violation when he had first known that it had occurred. Even when more than a little drunk, Stanley had a strong survival sense. He didn't want an investigation into his actions, and Thomas would undoubtedly counterattack if he made an ethics complaint against him.

No, he would just bide his time, attend all the hospital's fundraisers, and see whether he could inveigle his way back into Albright's good graces and get some business back. Maybe he'd even donate to candidate Thorp's opponent's campaign, even if, God forbid, that meant donating to a Republican. And sooner or later, he would get something on Thomas that he could use to get his revenge. Yes, sooner or later.

48

Pam's apartment, just off the Plaza, near Margaret's apartment
Kansas City

Pam entered her apartment, weighed down by two sacks of groceries, her purse, her briefcase, and the mail she that had scooped out of her mailbox. After she had put the groceries away, she turned to the copy of the *Kansas City Star* that she had bought at the grocery store when she saw the article on the first page with the headline, "Former Kansas City Memorial Employee Sentenced for HIPAA Violation." She quickly read the story, which said that, pursuant to a plea bargain for a Zone C sentence of between 10 and 16 months, the judge had sentenced Gibbons to 14 months followed by two years' supervised probation. He also had to make restitution to the victim and pay a fine.

Pam had thought that an appropriate sentence would have been to put Gibbons under the jail after what he, and admittedly others, had tried to do to Margaret. But she could live with envisioning him in Leavenworth for 14 months. He didn't seem like the type to adapt to prison life very easily.

Then, Pam turned her attention to the stack of mail. Aside from the never-ending junk mail, two envelopes caught her eye. The first one was from EMR Legal, John's consulting firm. She ripped it open. In it was an engraved announcement:

> John Thomas, President, EMR Legal, Inc.
> is proud to announce that
> Margaret Nicks, B.S., M.A. in Health Information Management
> and Registered Health Information Administrator,
> has joined EMR Legal, Inc., as the Vice President
> and Director of Health Information Management Services.

Way to go, girl, Pam thought. You fell into a pile of shit and came up smelling like roses. And wow! You got your RHIA already! Working for John and consulting all over the country have to be way better than working for those assholes at the hospital. I wonder whether they would hire me, she thought. Then, she turned to the next envelope. Its return address was Margaret's. When Pam opened it, she found two envelopes. One was marked, "Open this envelope first." The other was marked, "Open this envelope second." Pam followed the instructions, opening the first, smaller, envelope first. She removed an engraved card that read:

> Lieutenant Colonel (Retired) John Thomas
> and
> Ms. Margaret Nicks
> are pleased to announce their wedding at the Grand Hyatt, Erawan
> 494 Rajdampi Road, Bangkok, Thailand, 10330
> Telephone + 66 2 254 1234
> On Saturday, June 17, 2006, at 1:00 P.M.
> Reception to follow.

Pam broke into tears. Yes, Margaret had done well indeed. John's consulting firm's vice president and now this! She quickly turned to the second envelope that she wasn't supposed to open until after she had opened the first envelope containing what had turned out to be the wedding announcement.

The second envelope contained two first class round-trip airplane tickets in Pam's name. One on United from Kansas City to Los Angeles and return and the second on Royal Thai Airlines from Los Angles to Bangkok and return. The return dates were left open. There was a handwritten note from Margaret clipped to the tickets:

"Dear Pam, John and I want you there for the wedding. I want you to be my maid of honor. John has some high-ranking Thai military officers that he was friends with from his Army days who will perform a saber arch for us to walk under after the ceremony. It will be so romantic. We are going to a resort on Phuket on the Andaman Sea for the honeymoon, then on to Singapore, and then Hawaii on the way home. *Please come.* Your support during my HIPAA hassle meant so much to me. And you can see your family in Thailand before and after the ceremony. John got me so much money in the severance package that he got from the hospital that we can easily afford to fly you there and put you up in the Grand Hyatt, especially with his frequent flier miles covering most of the cost. And if you want to bring Doctor Hass, feel free. Let me know, and we'll get you tickets for him. You'll note that the wedding is scheduled a couple of weeks after this year's Hospital Hill Run, which I know you and Doctor Hass will be running. I won't take no for an answer. I can't wait to see you there! Love, Margaret"

Pam and Doctor Hass attended the wedding, as did Ken Mahan and his wife, whom Margaret had also invited after he had retired in large part because of the way that the hospital had treated Margaret. When Pam's Thai friends asked Pam how the wedding was, she answered, "Suai," which is beautiful in Thai.

Epilogue

HITECH ACT SEC. 13409. CLARIFICATION OF APPLICATION OF WRONGFUL DISCLOSURES CRIMINAL PENALTIES.

Section 1177(a) of the Social Security Act (42 U.S.C. 1320d-6(a)) is amended by adding at the end the following new sentence: "For purposes of the previous sentence, a person (including an employee or other individual) shall be considered to have obtained or disclosed individually identifiable health information in violation of this part if the information is maintained by a covered entity (as defined in the HIPAA privacy regulation described in section 1180(b)(3)) and the individual obtained or disclosed such information without authorization."

HITECH ACT SEC. 13404. APPLICATION OF PRIVACY PROVISIONS AND PENALTIES TO BUSINESS ASSOCIATES OF COVERED ENTITIES.

(c) Application of Civil and Criminal Penalties.—In the case of a business associate that violates any provision of subsection (a) or (b), the provisions of sections 1176 and 1177 of the Social Security Act (42 U.S.C. 1320d–5, 1320d–6) shall apply to the business associate with respect to such violation in the same manner as such provisions apply to a person who violates a provision of part C of title XI of such Act.

EFFECTIVE DATE: February 17, 2009.

About the Author

Jonathan P. Tomes is a health care attorney practicing in the greater Kansas City area in the law firm of TOMES & DVORAK, CHARTERED. He is a nationally recognized authority on the legal requirements for health information, having written the following books: *The Compliance Guide to HIPAA and the HHS Regulations* (now in its 4th edition) and *Electronic Health Records: A Practical Compliance Guide* (now in its 2d edition), both for Veterans press, *Healthcare Records: A Practical Legal Guide* for Healthcare Financial Management Association ("HFMA"), *Healthcare Records Manual* for Warren Gorham & Lamont, *Healthcare Records Management, Disclosure & Retention* for Probus Publishing and HFMA (now provided through McGraw-Hill Healthcare Education Group), *Compliance Guide to Electronic Health Records* and *Compliance Guide to Electronic Health Payments,* both for Faulkner & Gray, and *Healthcare Privacy and Confidentiality* for Probus Publishing. His other health law books include *Responding to AIDS; Regulation of the Health Care Industry; Informed Consent; Fraud, Waste, and Abuse and Safe Harbors; Healthcare Environmental Law;* and *Medical Staff Privileges.* His articles have appeared in *Journal of AHIMA, Health Data Management, Medical Claims Management, Credit Card Management, Journal of the Healthcare Financial Management Association, Journal of Health Care Finance, Journal of Health Care Compliance,* and *ACCA Docket,* among others.

Jon is a skilled attorney, having litigated hundreds of cases, including medical malpractice, Public Health Service disciplinary actions, Merit Systems Protection Board cases, physician discipline, and criminal cases. He has consulted in various hospital cases and has provided legal opinions on telemedicine issues. He has also represented physicians in disciplinary actions.

He has presented programs for Faulkner & Gray, American Health Information Management Association ("AHIMA"), HFMA, American Bar Association, American Society of Association

Executives, Business Network, Lorman Business Centers, and Heritage Professional Education, now Cross Country Education. He is a member of the editorial board of the *Journal of Health Care Finance,* the board of advisors for the University of Kansas Medical Schools' Mini-Medical School, a member of HFMA, and an associate member of AHIMA. He is a member of the Illinois, Oklahoma, Kansas, and Missouri bars and the federal district courts for the Northern District of Illinois (Trial Bar), the District of Kansas, and the Western District of Missouri, U.S. Court of Appeals for the 5th, 7th, 8th, 10th, and Federal Circuits, and the U.S. Supreme Court.

Jon is also President of EMR Legal, Inc., which provides HIPAA consulting nationwide, and of Veterans Press, which publishes HIPAA compliance materials, including books, training videos, and the *HIPAA Documents Resource Center CD* (now in its 4th edition).

His law firm, TOMES & DVORAK, CHARTERED, provides health law services, among others, including health information law, medical malpractice, representation before peer review and credentialing committees, fraud and abuse evaluation and defense, legal review of managed care entities and operations, and analysis of records retention programs for legal sufficiency.

Jon is also a retired U.S. Army JAG Corps officer. Before he was a JAGC-Off, however, he was an Infantry platoon leader in Vietnam and then a Military Intelligence officer in West Germany. He received the Silver Star, the Combat Infantry Badge, and the Legion of Merit, among other awards. He was also a military judge.

Email him at jon@tomesdvorak.com or call him at 913-385-7990, ext. 306.